ALLURE
PART ONE

ALLURE
PART ONE

KNOTTY BY NATURE

T.S. SNOW
COLETTE RHODES

WHAT IS OMEGAVERSE?

"OMEGAVERSE" IS BASED ON THE IDEA OF A
DOMINANCE HIERARCHY AMONG HUMANS
— DOMINANT ALPHAS, NEUTRAL BETAS,
AND SUBMISSIVE OMEGAS. HOW A PERSON
"PRESENTS" (AKA WHETHER THEY'RE AN ALPHA,
BETA, OR OMEGA) IMPACTS THEIR PLACE IN
SOCIETY, AS WELL AS THEIR ROMANTIC AND
SEXUAL RELATIONSHIPS.

WHILE THERE IS NO SHIFTING INVOLVED,
OMEGAVERSE DOES TYPICALLY INCLUDE
KNOTTING, HEATS, SCENT MARKING, AND OTHER
ANIMALISTIC BEHAVIORS.

THIS BOOK IS DEDICATED TO RACHEL, WHO
FORCED TWO ANTISOCIAL AUTHORS TO
INTERACT WITH EACH OTHER. THIS DUET
WOULDN'T HAVE HAPPENED IF YOU HADN'T
ARRANGED OUR FIRST PLAY DATE, AND
WE'RE FOREVER GRATEFUL TO YOU FOR IT.

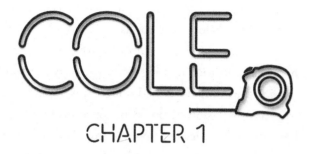

CHAPTER 1

"Merrrrrrry Christmas, bitches!"

I spared a glance at the drunken beta hanging out the passenger window as the car drove past. She was probably on her way home from a boozy holiday dinner with her happy little family, where they did happy family things like wear stupid light-up necklaces, listen to cheesy Christmas carols, and argue about politics.

Basically, the opposite of what I was doing, which was dragging my feet along the sidewalk to delay catching up with the rest of my pack. The three of them were not-so-patiently waiting outside the black lacquered door that led to a nondescript single-story brick building. The only thing that stood out was the glowing neon-pink sign overhead that spelled out *Allure*.

The name was apt, advertising the alluring omegas within, dancing for tragic, lonely alphas who'd sell a kidney for just a whiff of an unmated omega's scent. We'd had some pretty sad pack Christmases over the years, but Christmas at a strip club was a new low, even for us.

"Hurry up," Kaito grumbled, arms crossed over his chest and foot tapping impatiently as he stood outside the door. His dark, hooded eyes flashed with irritation as I slowed down on purpose, the neon light overhead highlighting his angular features in a way that made him look a bit demonic, especially with his black stubble, slicked-back black hair, and all-black outfit. "I want to be inside as soon as the buffet opens."

"Hangry?" his twin, Arata, teased. Kaito wasn't hangry; that was just his usual sparkling personality shining through—although he was marginally less of an asshole when he was eating.

Kaito and Arata were identical twins—they even smelled similar—but there was absolutely no mistaking them. Kaito's face was almost permanently set in a scowl, whereas Arata's was smiling and open. Plus, Arata was fond of old band t-shirts, and finger combing his hair was his version of getting dressed up. Kaito wore button-up shirts even on the job site, and his hair was always unnaturally neat.

"I don't want to miss the good food by being late," Kaito huffed. "Besides, it's a buffet. I don't want stuff everyone else has breathed all over."

"This sucks," I muttered. Kaito's crappy mood

was only making mine worse. I wished we'd stayed home, watched a Christmas movie about a dog finding its forever family, and eaten frozenw turkey meals. "Who comes to a strip club on Christmas?" I asked as I finally caught up to them.

"It's not just *a* strip club," Arata reminded me impatiently. We'd already had this argument more times than I could remember, and I'd been outvoted every single time. "It's *the* strip club. You know we've been on the list for-fucking-ever to get into this place, and now we've finally got a membership. At Christmas! Do you have any idea how many alphas would kill to be here right now? Think of it as a Christmas present!"

"More like a Christmas curse," I grumbled. *Can't believe I went through my full hair routine for this.* "All I want for Christmas is an omega, and now I'm going to sit there and watch a bunch of them through a glass wall and be reminded of what I don't have. This is a Christmas torture. You are Christmas torturing me."

"Don't be so dramatic," Kaito said with an eye roll, pulling open the heavy black door.

Our fourth packmate, Zach, was leaning against the club's brick wall, silently observing. He'd dressed up in a cotton navy dress shirt and gray slacks, his dark, slightly too-long hair combed and his short beard trimmed since tonight was a *special occasion* and all. His dark hair and outfit made his pale skin stand out even more, making him a perfect target for vampire jokes while we were stuck in this god-forsaken hellhole. He'd pretend to be annoyed, but secretly, he liked my teasing. After all, out of the four of us, I was the only one with a sense of humor.

Well, not tonight. But most of the time.

"Are you seriously okay with this?" I mumbled to Zach, following the twins into the small lobby where Kaito was already talking to the beta hostess, exchanging the printed paperwork we'd been emailed this afternoon for a shiny new membership card.

Everything about this place was dark shadows and neon lights, which I'd usually find kind of cool, but I was in a bad mood and didn't want to be here, so I refused to appreciate it. It felt like the neon sign behind the hostess stand that said *Knot Your Average Club* in glowing turquoise letters was a personal insult.

"We all filled out the application form together," Zach pointed out mildly, taking in the architectural details of the small foyer. We renovated properties together, and Zach did all the design stuff even though he didn't particularly enjoy it. "I didn't expect you to be so upset about actually coming here."

"It's *Christmas*, Zach. Christmas *night*. We should be drinking peppermint Schnapps by the fire right now."

Zach wrinkled his nose. "I'm sure we can order

you peppermint Schnapps at the bar."

"That is so far from the point it's not even funny," I groused, pulling out my ID at the hostess' request for her to verify while Zach did the same.

Betas were often tongue-tied in our presence— our pheromones could be a little overwhelming— but this woman was cool, calm, and professional. I guessed she was stuck sniffing alpha pheromones in an enclosed space all the time. *Horny* alpha pheromones, which were even worse. I hoped they paid her extra for putting up with the odor.

"Thank you, gentlemen," the beta said with her best customer service smile, handing the ID cards back. "Head right on through these doors and down the stairs. The Christmas dinner is being laid out now, and the show will begin in an hour or so. Since it's a special occasion, they're going to start with a holiday-themed group number, followed by individual performances."

Great, multiple performances. I was going to have a knot-ache that I'd probably be working out with my fist until New Year's Eve.

"Just to remind you of all the rules you agreed to on membership—you will need to leave your phones in one of those lockers which can only be opened by your membership card," she explained, tipping her chin towards sleek black lockers in the shadows by another set of doors that I assumed led to the club.

"There are no phones allowed inside, and absolutely no photography. Violence will not be tolerated and will result in an immediate lifelong ban from this club and all Pack Kennedy-owned properties. The omegas remain behind the glass at all times; tips for individual dancers are done electronically using the tablet on your table—just swipe your membership card, and it'll be charged automatically. You can order drinks via tablet, our friendly servers, or at the bar. Any questions?"

I wanted to ask how many other sad alphas were here on Christmas, but Zach gave me a warning look like he knew what I was thinking, so I reluctantly kept my mouth shut.

"I think we're good to go," Arata replied with a charming smile, smooth as always, already moving towards the lockers. We all took our turns pulling our phones out of our pockets under the hostess' watchful eye and depositing them in the lockbox.

Kaito impatiently drummed his fingers against his forearm as we got ourselves organized, glaring at the double doors like he'd be able to see through them if he stared hard enough. I was surprised he'd even agreed to this. Kaito was the greediest of all of us in many ways—looking at something he couldn't have should be his personal hell.

Maybe he was just that desperate for the barest hint of omega company. It didn't bode well for a pack of alphas approaching thirty years old who actually *wanted* to be mated to be without an omega. We really needed to up our game. Travel less. Find fancier jobs. Wear ties. Something.

"All right," the hostess said, reaching under the desk. "Enjoy yourselves. Welcome to Allure."

The double doors swung open, revealing a dark staircase illuminated by more pink neon lights on each stair, leading down to the basement club.

Kaito strode ahead, unafraid of anything, while the rest of us fell into line behind him, following the sound of sexy Christmas carols and the smell of cooked meat and gravy.

Neither of which particularly got me in the mood, but maybe roast turkey and sexied-up Santa songs did it for some people.

A server stood at the bottom of the steps, a tray of clear drinks with candy canes sticking out the top in his hand and a beaming smile on his face.

"Good evening, alphas. Could I interest you in tonight's signature drink? It's a Christmas Martini made with mint, lime, vanilla vodka, and peppermint Schnapps."

"He'll take one," Zach said, leaning around me to swipe a martini off the tray and shoving it into my hand. "There you go. Peppermint Schnapps: check. Maybe there are some candles around here you can sit next to for that Christmassy fire you apparently need."

I scowled at his triumphant grin as I swirled the candy cane around my drink and followed my pack to the table at the back, where an admittedly impressive Christmas buffet had been laid out.

From here, it was difficult to make out the dark stage on the other side of the room, past the sea of tiered circular booths that made up the seating area. I could see that it was framed by more neon lights, but other than that, it just looked like a large, eerily still glass box. Like an aquarium for half-naked dancers.

Soon it would be filled with beautiful, untouchable omegas. The elusive missing piece to our pack puzzle that we'd never been able to secure.

Too rough around the edges. Too working class. Too much of all the things that omegas would never settle for.

I pulled the candy cane out of my glass and downed the entire sickly sweet martini in one gulp.

CHAPTER 2

Christmas.

A time when the world became all twinkly lights and bright colors. Where packs spent the day at home to celebrate, share a meal, and spoil their omegas.

Well, at least for the packs who had one.

The rest of the alphas?

They were either out drinking, feeling sorry for themselves, or they were here at Allure.

The club provided a hint of what they wanted the most. Us omegas. Even a small hint of our pheromones would be enough to appease them or to bring them to their knees. It all depended on how desperate they were.

I felt bad for the alphas out there, really, but I was kind of glad I had something to do today other than be alone, too. Being alone on Christmas *sucked*. And if I could give these alphas a moment of happiness, well then, was that such a bad thing?

After all, it was Christmas, and our dancing was going to be pure *magic*.

"Amy, are you ready?" Sean asked from beside me, and I startled a little. Placing a hand over my rapidly beating heart, I stared at the beta stage manager who coordinated everything behind the scenes and just nodded.

I was *so* ready for the group number. We'd been practicing for what felt like *ages*.

Even though I'd only started working at Allure six months ago and was still pretty new to this life, Roxy, one of the club's owners and the head dancer, had been giving me private lessons over the past month. As well as the group rehearsal we'd started two months ago to ensure it would all be perfect. Roxy's private tutelage, though, showed me she really did expect great things from me. I was honored and determined to make sure I knocked some alpha's socks off with my sexy elf routine.

After all, I really, *really* wanted to keep my job. Of all the omega-approved careers, dancing was the one that appealed to me the most. It wasn't my dream job by any stretch, but it gave me the most freedom. Plus, dancing was fun. It was in my blood; I *was* Brazilian, after all. And dancing had always made me feel great. Granted, I was still learning to dance while playing sexy, but it wasn't all that hard. I just had to follow the steps and move my body.

Basically, it was a piece of yummy, champagne-flavored cake.

"Ready," I answered brightly, giving myself a final glance in the mirror to make sure my little red-and-green-striped elf hat was properly placed on my head. My long, curly brown hair cascaded down my back, with enough hairspray on it to make sure by the time I was done, it wouldn't be a crazy frizzy party.

Even though the Santa's little helper hat also helped keep things hidden, I still had to ensure it wouldn't fall off during the number. That would be a double disaster.

I'd placed enough bobby pins in my hair to make sure the hat would stay in place, that was for damn sure. Everything had to be perfect tonight, and it started with our looks.

My skimpy naughty elf outfit was similar to all the other omegas' who would be dancing today—at least the ones dressed as elves—but since I wasn't very ... blessed in the curves department, I'd had to put tape on my breasts to make them look bigger and fill the bikini-like top out.

Looking down, I made sure the tape wasn't showing anywhere, fluffed my red-and-green-striped skirt, and prepared to follow the other dancers on stage. I closed my eyes and ran through the routine in my mind one more time like one would a movie with no sound. The music didn't matter, really, just the steps.

Feeling confident and all but bubbling with excitement, I opened my eyes. Backstage, it was all a messy flurry of movement, with betas going back and forth to cater to us omegas. They did the bulk of the work at the club, from costume designing to bartending, to making sure we had everything we needed, and helping keep any persistent alphas away from us. Due to the temptation of an omega's pheromones, no alpha could be allowed backstage. Even the ones who worked security had to either be placed at the doors and exits or be mated alphas. It was just another way Roxy ensured our safety.

Betas, though, didn't usually have a hard time resisting us, which was why we relied so heavily on them. They had none of the constraints of being an omega. They were free to go wherever they wanted, whenever they wanted, without having to worry about hiding their scents or attracting unwanted attention. Sometimes I wished I was a beta rather than an omega. I'd be able to work with what I loved, do what I loved, and not rely on others. But then I got home to my nest, surrounded by soft pillows and blankets, and I was reminded that I liked being spoiled.

I supposed each side had its perks and downsides, just like anything else in life. That was fine, too.

Shaking off the weird mood, I smiled brightly

at Sean and headed straight into chaos.

I walked to the line of omegas, who were all waiting for our moment to shine. Some were doing a last-minute adjustment to their outfits, while others chatted with whoever was in front or behind them in line.

Exciting energy was like a cloud in the area all around us, the sense of expectation that made me all but vibrate as I headed to the end of the line.

If I remembered the schedule correctly, the big Christmas feast for the alphas would've ended about half an hour ago. Even as I reached my spot and gave one final glance down to check my boobs, I knew the alphas would have all found their seats, eagerly waiting for the main event.

Us.

And we were about to knock their socks off with our group performance. Usually, only a handful of omegas danced on the opening number, and then each omega would have their own solo, with the stage all to themselves. Tonight, though, for the first time since I'd started working here, we'd *all* be taking the stage together for the first routine.

Each omega would have a pole spread around the stage, with Roxy's—Nicole's, since that was her real name—at the center. After all, while we were all amazing, Roxy was, without a doubt, the main event.

Well, her and Henry.

As such, the two of them were the only ones not wearing the elf outfit. Instead, they were in the traditional Santa red and white.

The lights on the stage dimmed, and I smiled, feeling giddy. I triple-checked my boobs—seriously, there was absolutely no way the tape could fall off, I may be acting paranoid, but I had good reason to. The damn thing had fallen off twice during our last rehearsal, and I promised Roxy it wouldn't happen tonight.

I really, *really* did not want the alphas to find out about my little breast-ception. Plus, bigger curves meant bigger tips, and I had my heart set on some new, extra-soft throw pillows for my nest.

Henry—that was his stage name; I had no idea what his real name was—the lead male omega dancer passed by me on his way to his position, wearing nothing but some red suspenders and boxers and with Santa's face over his ... erh ... Christmas present. He saw me staring and gave me a cheeky grin. The omega was almost six feet of pure deliciousness. He wasn't super bulky, but he had a swimmer's body, with broad shoulders, defined muscles, and a smile that immediately put you at ease.

If he were an alpha, I'd probably have begged him to rut me during my heat, but as it stood, we were friendly-ish. It was just that—while his smile was great, and *he* was great—he could get a bit ... competitive. And since he had been working here longer than I had—like almost every omega at the club—he felt territorial. It'd take a while before they accepted me and stopped feeling threatened by me.

The fact I looked more like a beta than an omega probably helped put some of the others at ease. I was a tall, lanky abomination by omega standards, but I liked my five-foot-ten stature and the muscle tone I'd worked hard for. Even if it meant I had to tape my boobs and wear padding in my shorts to give me some extra booty.

I gave Henry a little wave right before he turned his back to me and disappeared among the other omegas, and then I waited.

Over the speakers, we could all hear the announcer calling the alphas to attention, and then we were walking in line, gently swaying our hips and moving to the beat of the music. Each dancer would walk on stage, get close to the glass, do a little something to show off, and then take their place at their respective poles.

Anticipation had my stomach tied up in knots and a smile taking over my whole face.

This was it. The moment we had all been waiting for.

Sean, who had been making sure we all entered at the appropriate time, giving each omega enough time to take their position, sent me a look.

"*Bubbles, go,*" he mouthed, all but pushing me

through the door.

Yup. My stripper name was Bubbles. I'd picked it myself, and I was pretty damn proud of how unique it was. I didn't care what the other omegas thought about it.

The song changed, a sultry version of *Santa Baby* started, and I amped up my smile, following the other omegas on stage.

A single beam of light shone on me as I walked, heading straight to the edge of the glass that would keep us from the alphas. It was there both for our security and to ensure we wouldn't be overwhelmed by the scents. However, to keep our customers happy, there was a whole complex venting system that allowed a whiff of our perfume to go out to the club. Just enough to tease them. To tempt them. Just enough to leave them wanting more. Wanting us.

As I did a slow, sexy walk, I glimpsed the eight omega dancers who were already in position, slowly gyrating to the song, their bodies cast in light, with tiny neon beams at the bottom providing the only illumination on them right now. Once we were all in position, things would change. But until then ... well.

Once I was at the front of the stage, I started to twirl and sway, remembering my hours of training with Roxy. I got even closer to the edge of the sheer glass, leaned forward to give the alphas a glimpse of my taped-up goodies, and blew them a kiss.

Then, when the tempo was just right, I crouched down on my heels, legs closed, waited a second, and then opened them before slamming them shut again. I quickly stood up, did a sassy little hair flip, turned my back to the audience, making sure to put on a show, and sashayed to one of the poles at the edge of the stage.

As the final omega walked onstage, I grabbed my pole and spun around it with everything I had, following the fancy footwork routine exactly like I'd practiced so many times.

The minute the last omega took her place, the actual party would start.

I didn't really have the muscles needed to do the entire dance on the pole, but I'd learned enough that I'd be able to do the steps for this routine, at least. My solo, however, would be mainly on the ground.

Trusting my muscle memory, I focused all my attention on my dancing. In the dark like this, without the spotlight on me, it felt so ... intimate. Like I was moving for myself and myself only. Like there was no one watching. Except, there was. I was here to make some alphas very, *very* happy, and as the final omega took her position and the music changed once more, I smiled.

This Christmas miracle was about to start.

CHAPTER 3

This woman was, hands down, the worst dancer I had ever seen in my life.

I couldn't look away.

Every move, delivered with unfailing enthusiasm, was half a beat late. Her long tanned limbs all seemed to move out of sync with each other like there was a different person in charge of each one.

Either no one had told this beautiful, bright, grinning woman that she was a terrible dancer, or she just didn't care, because she was beaming. She was having so much fun that I found myself smiling along, even though I was spending Christmas at the most exclusive strip club in the city, watching a dancer who couldn't dance.

It truly was a Christmas miracle.

"You think that one is really an omega?" my twin, Arata, asked. He sounded as awestruck as I felt.

"They said all the dancers are omegas," I pointed out, even though I understood his confusion.

She wasn't particularly omega-looking. Where most omegas were soft and curvaceous, she was tall, lean, and athletic. The sexy elf costume most of the dancers wore—a red-and-green-striped bikini top with a matching swishy skirt, designed to show off that omega hourglass figure—looked loose on our dancer. She had to constantly readjust the elf hat, seemingly forgetting she was wearing it whenever she flicked her long curly brown hair and nearly sent the thing flying.

Frankly, the black heels were a health-and-safety hazard.

"Why the fuck are there so many scents?" I growled, frustrated I couldn't tell which omega scent belonged to who when they all filtered out of that godforsaken vent at the same time. I had a strong desire to know what this *specific* omega smelled like.

"Don't get any ideas," Zach warned, his pale skin turning a distinct shade of plum under the pink neon lights. One glance at my packmates told me that we were all fixated on the same person, which was slightly surprising, given how many omegas were on stage. "The omegas here *want* to be here. They're not looking for packs."

"Not necessarily," Cole argued, eyes transfixed on the clumsiest woman to ever call herself a dancer. He'd been a mopey bastard the whole way here, but now he was looking at the stage with heart-eyes and a slack jaw, his pheromones clogging up my airspace. "I mean, they want to be here. But that doesn't mean they don't want a pack someday."

I rolled my eyes, watching Cole fall in love in real-time. He was a romantic. He talked about "happily ever after" like it was a real, guaranteed thing, rather than a marketing gimmick set up by corporations who wanted to sell fairy-tale love stories between delicate omegas and their knots-in-shining-armor to jealous betas and lonely alphas.

I knew better. There were five alphas for every omega, which was why we formed packs. Well, that and one omega could easily wear out multiple alphas during their heat. But the disparity meant omegas had their pick of packs, and the wealthiest ones with the most luxurious nests were always picked first.

We did okay. We wouldn't be here if we didn't—the membership fees were exorbitant—but we would never be any omega's first pick. Or at least we hadn't been before. Not when some far wealthier pack had always swept in at the last minute and swept the omega we'd been interested in off her feet.

All four of us tensed, half-standing from our seats as the beautiful omega stumbled on shaky legs, grabbing the pole behind her to right herself and shooting a beaming smile at the dancer next to her, who shook her head slightly.

Why had they hired this woman? She looked

like a baby deer learning to walk up there.

"She's so beautiful," Cole whispered reverently.

Well, I couldn't argue with that.

I supposed that was why they'd hired her. Because she was beautiful and cheerful, a ray of sunshine in a room of mostly jaded alphas.

Despite not having Cole's idiotic romantic inclinations, I still caught myself hoping that she'd look at us, and feeling disappointed when she didn't. There were lights shining directly in her face, so I knew it wasn't possible, but the lack of eye contact bothered me more than I expected it to.

It was stupid. The room was packed with alphas, and she was having a hard enough time keeping upright while concentrating on the steps. It was a good thing that she didn't let the crowd distract her.

Still, I wanted her eyes on mine.

"You're growling," Arata noted smugly.

"I am *not* growling," I shot back, cutting the stupid sound off. "I'm just hungry."

"Oh please," he scoffed. "You ate half the Christmas buffet yourself."

I couldn't even deny that. It had been excellent too. It was a pity they didn't have a buffet every night—frankly, for the cost, they should.

One of the reasons, I amended in my head as the beautiful omega in front of me leaned back against the pole, swaying her hips off-beat. Her eyes were closed, head thrown back, making the elf hat wobble precariously, but there was nothing forced or fake about how much she was enjoying herself.

I noticed that I was tapping my foot along to the beat and quickly forced myself to stay still, hoping my brother hadn't noticed.

He grinned obnoxiously at me, the asshole.

A beta server approached to see if we needed more drinks, and Cole wasted no time in flagging him down, eager as a new pup for information about the omega.

"Can I help you, sir?"

"Huh? Oh yeah, four more of the same," Cole replied absently, gesturing at our beers. "And could you tell me the name of that dancer?"

The server's eyes followed Cole's back to the glass-covered stage, widening a fraction when he saw who Cole was indicating.

"The brunette?" he confirmed dubiously. "The one whose hat is falling off?"

"Yeah," Cole sighed dreamily. Zach and I exchanged wary looks. We were the killjoys of the pack, constantly reining in Cole's romantic impulsiveness and Arata's inability to take anything seriously. Zach did it because he was sensible and logical—if not a little anxious—and looked for rational explanations for everything he did.

I did because I was an asshole. Someone had to be.

The beta looked so stunned that we were asking after her, I almost started growling again. She was a beautiful omega, even if she didn't look like other omegas and couldn't dance for shit. Surely, other alphas had taken notice of her?

"She performs under the name Bubbles," the beta said apologetically. Of course they couldn't give us her real name. I was glad they didn't; it would be tremendously unsafe for the omegas here if the club was giving out their information, even after all the screening they'd done on us.

Still, I wished I knew it. I had a hard time calling her *Bubbles,* even in my head.

"Bubbles?" Arata repeated with a laugh. "Cute."

"She chose it because she likes champagne," the beta muttered, face flushing red. "She's a very ... bubbly person."

That, I believed.

Further proof that *she was totally unsuitable for us,* regardless of whatever ridiculous notions Cole was harboring. That we were all harboring. *If* we ever found an omega, which seemed unlikely at this point, they would have to be the hardy, practical sort. One that didn't mind her pack coming home after a long day on-site with calloused hands and clothes covered in sawdust. This beautiful *bubbly* omega with absolutely zero rhythm, who probably didn't even *want* a pack based on her decision to work here, would never fit with us.

It was an impossible dream. That was probably what the owners intended this place to be. Impossible dreams for sad, desperate alphas.

But then a spotlight shone over the crowd, illuminating us for just a moment, and that was all it took. Bubbles looked right at me like she could see all the negative thoughts in my head and wanted to beam them away with the force of her dazzling smile alone.

Arata chuckled. Zach groaned. Cole *purred*.

My knot inflated like a goddamn balloon.

I'd thought I'd wanted her to look at us, and now she had, I realized just how dangerous that desire had been. We were so incredibly fucked.

CHAPTER 4

The Christmas special had been amazing.

There had been so many alphas there, watching us, and when our group number was done, we'd received a standing ovation from them.

For a moment, right before the routine ended, I even thought I'd made eye contact with an alpha. It had probably been a trick of the light, or wishful thinking, really, but it had been enough to almost make me lose my balance.

Then the crowd had broken into applause, and the moment was lost.

I hadn't even known applause was a thing at strip clubs—I'd certainly never seen it happening here at Allure—but apparently, our dance had been that good. Even though most of the dancers had been slightly out of sync.

I was so happy that I hadn't been able to stop smiling.

This. This was exactly the kind of thing I'd

wanted when I became a stripper. It hadn't been about the money. I just wanted to make people happy. Dancing was so much *fun*, and knowing I was bringing others joy while I enjoyed myself really did it for me.

Was there even a better way to spend the rest of my life? It was thrilling, fulfilling, and I didn't need to rely on anyone other than myself. That way, even if I never found a pack who'd accept me, I'd still be able to live my best life without burdening my aunt. She'd done enough for me already, taking me in after my parents died in a plane crash.

Aunt Raquel had flown in to stay with me while my parents took a trip together right before my mother's heat, but my parents had never made it to their destination.

I'd only been eleven then. An eleven-year-old omega who was suddenly adrift and deep in mourning.

Aunt Raquel had given me a home in Recife, a place to heal, and even though suddenly being saddled with a pre-teen was far from what she'd planned for her life, she'd never made me feel unwelcome. She and Aunt Lu—the beta Aunt Raquel had taken as a mate—had both welcomed me and given me everything I might need. They'd even supported my decision to move here to the US, to the city I'd been born in, and to find a job, even if they'd have preferred I stay in Brazil with them.

I loved them wholeheartedly, but I knew that if I'd stayed, it would've been all too easy to constantly give in and keep relying on them until I grew old and gray. I wanted more from life, though. I wanted to have adventures and see places and *do* things. Working at Allure allowed me all of that.

Thinking about my aunts, I made a mental note to call them later to check up on them. After I got some sleep, at least. The time difference would ensure I could still call early enough that Aunt Raquel wouldn't have a chance to use the "you never call us anymore, we're just an afterthought now" speech.

The fact we'd spoken on the phone only yesterday when I wished them a Merry Christmas would be a pointless argument to try to make.

All but bouncing on the heels of my feet, I let myself into my condo building, giving the beta doorman a quick smile and heading straight to the elevators that would lead me to my unit.

Once I reached my floor, I stepped out of the elevator and headed to the first door on the right.

Another perk of working for Allure was that the club owned a building near it that had been designed for single omegas. Each floor had four units and was no bigger than a studio, but each one had been prepared with omegas in mind. Even though there were lots of windows, they all came equipped with blackout curtains that kept all the light at bay. The rooms came furnished, and the bedroom had a bed big enough to fit four adults ... or an army of pillows, making it the ultimate nest.

I let myself into my unit using an electronic keypad and my fingerprint, taking off my shoes at the door before I entered. It was easier than having to clean after myself every day.

To my right, there was an open-concept kitchen with just a white marble counter separating it from the living room. The kitchen was small, but it had all the appliances an omega might need to cook solo meals. And the living room ... well, I liked the shade of green the walls had been painted, and I had an assortment of throw pillows on the couch that made it comfy. However, to me, the highlight of the place, and my favorite spot in the entire condo, was the window seat. It was on the far left of the living room, right after the couch and tv, and it was in the middle of the white, floor-to-ceiling bookshelves that I'd filled mostly with knick-knacks. The seat was as soft as a cloud, all but hidden by my throw pillows. A multitude of them in all colors, shapes, and sizes.

It was my little safe haven, even more than my nest. I just loved to sit there sipping tea and looking out of the window to people-watch.

I absolutely loved people-watching. It was like, one of my favorite hobbies. Right up there with dancing. Although, now I danced for a living, so I supposed it was no longer a hobby.

And last, I liked playing Nest Fest. It was a game I'd downloaded on my phone ages ago, and it allowed the players to build not only nests but full houses. Decorating them as we saw fit. The coolest part was that they had real furniture from actual stores, which made the whole thing seem even more legit. Playing the game, building multiple nest options, and trying different placements for things to create the ultimate nest helped soothe some of my omega instincts. One day, I'd have my own home with a nest I designed myself, but until then, I'd make do with playing Nest Fest.

But unfortunately, for now, I rented this unit, and there were only so many changes I could make to my current nest.

My stomach growled in protest, and I went straight to the kitchen. I'd hoped to wash off the sweat, glitter, and boob tape before eating, but my belly had other priorities.

Food. Lots and lots of food.

And about a gallon of water. Then shower, then bed for the foreseeable future.

Since we'd worked through on Christmas, Roxy had decided to throw a little Christmas party at the building today, on Boxing Day, but I was going to have to bow out on that. I had big, luxurious plans that involved my bed, the Nest Fest app, and lots of sugar.

I'd make it up to her by attending the club's New Year's Eve party. Though I'd be working that night, so I'd have to attend it regardless.

When I saw the time on the microwave, I winced. Three in the morning the day after Christmas, and I was just now getting home from work.

I hadn't even eaten anything since the little Christmas buffet Roxy had set up for the Allure staff *before* the club opened. So that had been, what, almost ten hours ago? No wonder I was starving.

Good thing I'd had the foresight of filling a to-go bag with some leftovers from the club. Classy? Not really, but yummy as hell. I grabbed some bread from the cupboard, wincing when I noticed I was getting low on supplies. I seriously needed to take the time to go to the grocery store soon.

Tomorrow, I promised myself.

I'd wake up early and go during the omega-only hours. I loved that most places now had specific hours when unmated omegas could go about their business and do things without worrying about being overwhelmed by scents and crowds. Supermarkets, stores, and even some tourist attractions had omega-only hours, and it really made a difference for those who, like me, hadn't found a pack. Usually, only betas or bound alphas worked during these hours—though mostly betas, since even a bound alpha could still have an overwhelming scent that betas simply didn't, making it easier for us to interact with them without worrying too much. It was awesome.

I finished making my sandwich and was just about to take a bite when my phone started buzzing in my pocket. Frowning, I put my food down and picked up my phone to see who was calling, immediately smiling at the name on the caller ID.

"Hey," I answered, putting the phone on speaker and taking a bite out of my sandwich.

Might as well eat while we talked. Not like my aunt was going to be disgusted by my manners. Aunt Raquel simply didn't care about that kind of thing.

"Good Morning, Lia!" My aunt's bright voice came through the phone, way too cheerful for the early hour.

I swallowed. "'Morning, Aunt Raquel"—was it even morning if the sun hadn't risen yet?—"you're up early," I commented, mentally going over the time difference once again, wondering if I'd made a mistake before.

But nope. It was a four-hour difference, which meant it was seven in the morning for her.

Aunt Raquel *never* got out of bed before eight if she could help it.

My aunt snorted. "You're telling me. Lu joined a functional training group by the beach, and they think it's perfectly acceptable to get up at six every weekend to do so." Even though my aunt's tone was filled with disdain, there was no actual bitterness to it. She loved Aunt Lu with all her heart, despite Aunt Lu's crazy healthy habits. "The other day, it was raining, and she went anyway. I don't understand why she can't just go to the gym and work out where there's air conditioning, like a normal person."

It was my turn to snort. Aunt Luciana used to be a professional beach volleyball player when she was about my age, and she'd even won a couple of gold medals in Beta cups. Now, even though she was older, she was still insanely active and did all sorts of things. The fact she'd fallen for Aunt Raquel, whose idea of physical exercise was to go from the bed to the couch, was hilarious.

When I'd lived with them, Aunt Lu had fully encouraged me to pursue any and every type of sport or physical activity my little heart might desire, and when I'd found dancing, something had clicked for me. Although dancing was the one thing Aunt Lu was terrible at—two left feet was what she claimed to have—she'd always taken me to every class.

"They didn't take time off for the holidays?" I asked before taking another bite of my sandwich.

"You'd think, right? But no. In fact, they doubled the workout. Every day this week, Lia. I honestly don't mind her going. I mean, if she wants to be fit and flexible, good for her, and for me." *Gross.* "But I can't go back to sleep after she's gone, and I hate mornings."

"So you decided to call me up at three am because misery loves company?" I teased. She didn't need to know I hadn't even made it to bed yet.

Aunt Raquel cursed. "Lia, I'm so sorry! Did I wake you up? I forgot about the time difference. I'm sorry! I'm hanging up now!"

I laughed. "Don't worry, Aunt Raquel. You didn't wake me up. I haven't gone to bed yet," I admitted.

There was a pregnant pause. "My, my, Amélia da Silva Cavalcanti, did I catch you doing the walk of shame?" She sounded way happier about it than any parental figure should be.

But then, again, Aunt Raquel hardly ever did what anyone would.

It was one of the things I loved most about her.

"No, Auntie." I shook my head even though she couldn't see it. I wasn't entirely sure if I'd rather have been doing the walk of shame or not, but either way, if I didn't correct her soon, she'd start planning bonding ceremonies and demanding to meet them. "Nothing like that. I just got home from work. Sorry to disappoint."

Aunt Raquel sighed. "You know I'm not against you working, right? And that I admire the fact that you're going after what you want and fighting to be financially independent even though you're an omega and everyone expects you to be taken care of and looked after. The fact you do it when you could simply be living off your inheritance only makes me even prouder of you."

"But?"

"But I worry about you, Lia. I really wish you'd reconsider living there, so far from us. Come back to Brazil. Even if you decide you don't want to find a pack of your own, even if you want to work at a club here or not work at all, since it's not like you need it. I don't like having you so far away. You know how much Aunt Lu misses you."

Yeah, right. Just Aunt Lu. Not her. *Could've fooled me.*

I grinned, walking around the kitchen to grab some water now that the food was gone. The only reason Aunt Raquel was even saying all that was because her mate wasn't home with her.

Unbothered by my silence, Aunt Raquel continued. "Besides, if you do decide on a pack, what will we do about our grandbabies? Your Aunt Lu would just about die if she can't be near to spoil them."

I almost choked on my drink. That was definitely a new spin on the come back home speech.

"*Grandbabies*?" I asked, in between coughs, my voice choked and my eyes watering.

There was putting the cart in front of the horse,

and then there was putting the cart in front of the whole damn road that hadn't even been built yet.

"Of course, grandbabies! You're not getting any younger, Lia, dear. Even if you don't bond with a pack, you could at least consider that having partners for your heat can result in children. If you were here, we could help you. Give you all the support. Then you would truly be independent." There was a little pause. "And, of course, that's all stuff your Aunt Lu says. I'm just repeating her speech. You know how I feel about all this. I couldn't care less about children. Not you, dear, of course. But someone else's kids."

I forced myself to swallow past the lump in my throat. "Auntie..."

She didn't even let me finish the thought. "I know. I know. You're only twenty-four. I did tell her you still have your whole life ahead of you. We miss you, sweetie. Why don't you come for a visit? I can buy your ticket, and you could spend New Year's with us. We'll have a feast at night, watch the fireworks at the beach, and then you and Lu could keep the tradition and jump over the seven waves! Drink champagne, toss coins into the sea, the whole thing. It'd be such a great surprise for Lu."

It was so, so tempting to just go there, see them. I could admit, at least to myself, that spending Christmas alone hadn't been all that great. Oh, the dance number had been fun, and being able to provide some happiness to all those lonely alphas had been amazing, but I'd still spent Christmas Eve on my own, and it had been ... less than great.

Still, there was a reason I hadn't gone down before the holidays, and this call had served to remind me of that.

I only had a few weeks until my heat—it should hit right around Valentine's Day—and I had to find a pack to see me through it ... preferably one that wasn't a twelve-hour flight away.

"I'm sorry, Auntie. I already made plans for New Year's Eve. I promise, next year I'll be there, yeah? We can drink coconut water in the shade while we watch Aunt Lu and her crew working out like psychos."

"Fine. But I swear, Amélia, if you haven't booked a ticket by July, you'll have to contend with both Lu and me staying for a whole month. I don't care if this cramps your style."

They would, too, and knowing Aunt Raquel, she'd find every single unbound pack and throw a party. Speed dating on steroids.

"I promise. If I don't have my ticket by July, you can storm my apartment and take me hostage. I won't even complain."

I'd book a flight regardless once my heat was over. I seriously missed my aunts.

"It's a deal. Now go to sleep, Lia. I'll tell Aunt

Lu not to call you until later so you can get some rest."

"Thanks, Auntie. Have a great day. I love you."

"Aww. I love you too, kiddo."

We hung up, and I just stood there, tears running down my face, my heart feeling incredibly tight.

Yeah, I'd definitely be spending the next holidays with them.

CHAPTER 5

"They're *closing*, Cole," I sighed impatiently, grabbing his collar as he attempted to sneak up to the glass window in front of the stage again. "She's probably gone home."

"What if we found like a cleaning closet or something I could hide out in, I'll spill some bleach to cover my scent—"

"The fact that I can't tell whether you're joking or not is unsettling," I told him, dragging him towards the stairs before the security guards came to kick us out on our first night of being members here. Then we'd really never see the beautiful Bubbles the Omega again, and that would be a travesty.

She'd made me *purr*.

The spotlight had shone down, and for a moment, it seemed like she was smiling right at us. My purr had rumbled out of my chest without conscious thought, rusty and clumsy though it was.

I'd never purred for anyone. We'd courted

omegas before with absolutely zero success, but I'd never purred for them.

I wasn't an alpha who acted on instinct. I was an alpha who overanalyzed every single thing I did before I did it. A purr should have required three changes of mind before committing, at the very least.

"We're coming back tonight," Cole muttered, shaking off my grip and stomping up the stairs. Kaito was ahead of us, the unspoken leader of our pack, his shoulders stiffer than usual. Probably because Cole had already descended into The Sulk, Arata was humming some kind of love ballad under his breath, and even I was feeling a little less *sensible* than usual.

Embarrassing, really. We'd seen the omega dance on stage—terribly, I might add—and that had been it. We couldn't tell her scent apart from the other omegas. We didn't even know her actual name, just her stage one. And yet, even though she'd left the stage hours ago, my cock was only now starting to soften.

It had been a while. Unlike the rest of my pack, I didn't have many romantic entanglements with betas. Not that I wasn't interested or that I didn't *want* to; I was just terrible at flirting. Cole was a charmer who looked like he belonged in a boyband, and Arata was a smooth talker who could put anyone at ease. Kaito was a tactless a-hole most of the time, but apparently, some women liked that.

Meanwhile, there was little on this earth I

found more distressing than making small talk with strangers. The last time I'd tried to flirt with a woman at a bar, I'd ended up helping her find a better insurance plan for her vehicle than the overpriced one she was on.

"Guys! We are coming back tonight, *right*?" Cole pressed as we emerged in the foyer, waiting for the pack ahead of us to grab their things from the lockers. Cole ran his hands through his chin-length brown hair again like he'd been doing all night, messing it up even more. A total giveaway that he was full of energy and had no idea what to do with it.

"I don't think they're open tonight, but we are definitely coming back every other night," Arata assured him, all dopey smiles, before resuming humming the song from the last number we'd watched.

I nodded at the hostess as we collected our things from the locker in the foyer and made our way out into the crisp morning air. The sky had lightened a little, but there were no rays of sun yet to take the edge off the icy chill. I couldn't remember the last time we'd had a winter with this much snowfall.

"We'll see about that," Kaito grumbled, pulling his jacket collar up against the cold. "We do have *jobs*, don't forget."

"Ooh, you must like her," Arata teased. "We're getting a supercharged dose of Asshole Kaito this morning."

"I haven't slept," Kaito replied curtly, absolutely more assholish than usual, as he stomped ahead of us.

"Come on," I sighed, pulling the keys out of my pocket with numb fingers. "We're all exhausted. Let's just get home, warm up, and get some rest. We can discuss the plans for tonight later."

"There's nothing to discuss," Cole countered as we climbed into our silver SUV. Our other vehicles were all trucks or vans, meant for transporting tools and supplies around the city, but this was Kaito's fancy ride. He handled the business side of our construction company and had to make a good impression. "Do you think she saw us? She looked right at us."

"She definitely saw us," Arata replied, both of them slumping tiredly in the backseat after they fastened their seatbelts.

"She sees a bunch of alphas every week sitting in the audience," Kaito pointed out quietly from the passenger seat, killing the conversation as he had a tendency to do.

It was a short drive on quiet streets back to our two-story craftsman in a historic neighborhood near the locks. It had boomed into a hip, trendy area full of fusion restaurants and craft breweries in the decade we'd lived there. As always, Kaito had been ahead of the curve when he'd insisted we buy this place for our pack home.

It had been a renovation nightmare, the basement still looked like a good setting for a horror film, and the attic—which would eventually be the nest—was unfinished. However, it was still my favorite project we'd ever worked on because it was ours. Or it *would* be my favorite project, once it was finished. We just needed a long enough break between jobs to get our own home in order.

"Home, sweet home," Arata said happily as I pulled into the alley behind the house and parked.

"Do you think she'll like it here?" Cole asked, perking up like it wasn't five in the morning. "We need to finish the nest. Zach! Arata! Design the nest!"

"You are so far ahead of yourself, you've entered a completely alternate reality," I sighed, stifling a yawn while Arata laughed and Kaito glared at nothing. Arata was right—Kaito really must like her. Why else would he be looking like that if not because of the Big Feelings he was struggling to process?

We were a tired, sorry-looking group of alphas as we traipsed through the path that cut through the backyard and up the stairs to the covered porch we'd converted into a mudroom. Sans coats and shoes, we made our way into the kitchen, where Kaito immediately beelined for the coffee machine.

"Absolutely not," Arata laughed tiredly, throwing his arm around his twin's shoulders and guiding him to the base of the stairs. "You are not going to burn yourself out trying not to think about the curious little omega. Tonight, we'll go back to the club and try to find her, but right now, we're all going to get some sleep. I don't know about you guys, but I've got some bubbly dreams ahead of me."

———————————

The four of us sat around the table in the breakfast nook, nursing our rapidly cooling coffees at five o'clock in the evening, searching for the internal motivation to get ready to go back to Allure for the sixth time since we'd first seen Bubbles dance.

She'd disappeared.

We'd been every night it was open, stayed as late as we could before one of us started dozing in our seats. Spent a small *fortune* on overpriced drinks.

And still no Bubbles.

"Maybe she's, like, super exclusive or something," Cole suggested, twisting his half-full coffee cup between his hands. Even with the reduced hours we were doing on the few projects we had over the holidays, we were still burning the candle at both ends by spending almost every night at Allure. "She was in the big Christmas show, maybe only the best of the best get to do that, and she only comes out for special occasions."

Kaito hit him with a withering look across the table, appearing a lot more put together than the rest of us in his button-down and dark trousers. "First of all, she was a terrible dancer."

"Hey—" Arata protested weakly.

"She was, don't even try to deny it," Kaito countered. I wasn't going to argue with him, though I personally found her dire lack of rhythm to be quite awe-inspiring. Maybe because I never attempted anything unless I was one hundred percent certain I wouldn't screw it up and humiliate myself. "Besides, we've seen other performers from the Christmas show on stage this week, so your argument sucks regardless."

"I'm frustrated too, but you don't see me being an insufferable prick about it," Cole grumbled, glaring at Kaito even though Cole had definitely been the more insufferable out of the two. He'd spent the past five days vacillating between moping and hyperactive excitement. I'd caught him trying to smuggle some extra materials from the yard onto the truck so he could finish the attic nest on the down-low, as though none of us would *hear* the construction work.

"Don't I?" Kaito shot back, arching an eyebrow at him. "Really? You're absolutely sure about that?"

"We're all very invested, no need for name calling," I sighed, pushing my cup away from me and running a hand through my hair, finding it filled with dust from spending the day sanding. Gross. I definitely needed a shower before we headed out tonight. "*Bubbles* is the only omega that has truly appealed to all four of us, but as exciting as that is, we do need to think with our brains rather than our knots. On the off-chance she's performing in the New Year's Eve performance tonight, we should all probably temper our expectations."

"Exactly," Kaito agreed, which was never a good sign for me—if Kaito liked the idea, it was probably miserable. "We've probably built her up in our heads anyway. Maybe she quit working there. Maybe she was fired for being a shit dancer—"

"You're such an asshole," Cole mumbled, rolling his eyes.

"—whatever the case, we should probably just all accept that she's unlikely to ever be *our* omega, no matter how much she appeals to all of us."

Absolute silence met Kaito's grim declaration. He was probably right. Who knew if Bubbles was even interested in a pack, given the fact that she worked at Allure. While the club was very discreet, it was rumored that the omegas who worked there were well-compensated and were provided with their own apartment in an undisclosed building.

Could we really compete with the life she already had?

I wanted to hyperventilate a little just thinking about it. What if she *did* want a pack, and it was our chance to impress her, and we totally screwed it up?

What if she'd seen us that night, realized the big tip was from us, and was waiting for us to make the first move, and we *hadn't*? None of us had ever been with an omega before. What if we couldn't satisfy her? What if—

"You have your overthinking face on," Arata teased, kicking my ankle under the table and snapping me out of my panic spiral.

"Let's try again tonight, *please*," Cole begged, breaking out the ridiculous puppy-dog eyes. "If she's not on the New Year's Eve lineup, then I promise I'll stop dragging you all to the club every day of the week."

"But *you* won't stop going?" Arata asked, a smile playing around his mouth. Not that anything would stop Arata either, he was just as much of a dreamer as Cole, but in a slightly less hysterical way.

I wasn't sure I had their confidence. My brain tended to present every new opportunity in life as a potential disaster—or a potential *series* of disasters, if I was feeling super creative. In theory, I was very on-board with the idea of pursuing an omega. In practice, I was pretty confident I'd panic, humiliate myself in front of said omega, and screw it up for the whole pack.

"I'm not giving up," Cole said stubbornly. "I know she's the one for us; I can feel it in my bones. Bubbles is *our* omega."

The club was *packed*. We had to wait in line just to deposit our belongings, and there was extra security upstairs checking membership cards.

"Are they even going to let us in?" Arata asked quietly, snagging a neon pink flier from the wall and passing it to me to read.

ALLURE EXCLUSIVE NYE PARTY
Join the Allure family for a night of celebration!
We reserve the right to refuse entry to anyone.

"What does that mean?" I replied instantly, nightmare visions of us being loudly turned away in front of the crowd of alphas in the lobby running through my head.

Arata snorted. "Look at all the rich-as-fuck alphas around us, Z. It probably means 'ballers only,' and we are not ballers."

There *were* a lot of expensive-looking suits and obnoxious watches in the lobby tonight. We were wearing suits too, but they weren't tailored. Only Kaito had a watch, and I was pretty sure he'd gotten it at an estate sale.

We did well enough to afford an Allure membership, but we weren't what anyone would consider a wealthy pack. If a couple of projects in a row went direly wrong or over budget, we'd be in trouble.

Cole was practically bouncing on his heels in front of us, his barely-used dress shoes squeaking on the floor, eager as a goddamn kid in a candy store, and a slither of unease ran down my spine. It was all very well us liking Bubbles and agreeing as a pack to pursue her, but what did we have to offer compared to these packs?

An almost finished fixer-upper?

A workaholic pack leader?

We didn't even have a nest. At best, we had a *quarter* of a nest. It didn't even have drywall yet.

"Back again, Pack Knight?" the hostess asked with a knowing smile as we approached the front of the line. Kaito grunted in acknowledgment, arms crossed over his chest as he scowled at every alpha who got too close to his precious personal bubble.

"We're happy to welcome you back! Tonight's event will be a little different. The show will only start after midnight, however, while you wait, drinks will be on the house. You'll be restricted to the regular audience area, but the performance tonight is so great, I promise you won't be missing out," she assured us, waving us through.

The regular audience area? As opposed to what?

The answer became clear the moment we entered the main club area. The balcony above the entryway that was usually barely visible was illuminated tonight and *packed* with posturing alphas and beautiful omegas.

And right at the edge, surrounded by alphas in suits that probably cost more than our house, was Bubbles.

CHAPTER 6

"Bubbles! There you are!" Roxy called out, her throaty voice sounding far away. I turned around, trying to see where she was, but I couldn't find her. There were just *so many* people. So many scents. The other omegas, the betas, the *alphas*. So, so many alphas, and they were *all* on hyper-drive. It felt like the single alphas were all releasing as many pheromones in the air as they could in an attempt to catch our attention. It was, after all, the first step towards seducing us omegas.

The result, however, was one overpowering wave of confusion that made me lightheaded.

Even though one of my goals tonight was to take advantage of the party and meet some potential alphas who might help me through my heat, I hadn't expected things to be this overwhelming. After all, this wasn't a dating event; it was just a closed-door party organized by Allure, a prelude for the show we'd put on right after midnight to start the new year well.

The one thing I hadn't anticipated was that being in the presence of so many single alphas would rouse my heat. Not the main event, really, just those first, smaller waves that were a warning to the big one.

My hormones didn't care that even though there were lots of scents, most of them were just *wrong*. It didn't care that some of the alphas were clearly trying to court other omegas. My impulses were *screaming* at me to get closer, to rub myself all over them until I was drowning in their scents. My whole body *demanded* I climb on the first available alpha's lap and *begged* for his knot and bite.

Just thinking about it made me rub my legs together in search of friction. The alphas closest to me all turned in unison. Their nostrils flared, their gazes heated, and their scents grew even *more potent*.

I forced the whimper to die down in my throat before it could get out.

I shouldn't have come tonight.

As soon as the thought formed in my head, I shook it off. It was, after all, a lie. Just because I hadn't expected to be this crazy horny didn't mean I couldn't use it to my advantage. My goal tonight was still the same, and if my pre-heat scent attracted more alphas who would be willing to help me take the edge off? That would make my life so much easier.

I just had to play my cards right to avoid causing a scene. After all, this was still a work event. One catering to friends and *family*. They did not need to see me climbing over the first alpha who smiled at me and dry humping his knot until I came.

I *could* and I *would* find a pack willing to help me through my heat without making things awkward for everyone around me. I was not a slave to my instincts.

I wasn't.

"I've been looking *everywhere* for you, Bubbles, dear!" Roxy's voice came again, this time from closer, and I watched with both relief and dread as the crowd *parted* to let the sultry omega through. Her bonded pack formed a semi-circle around her, covering her and guarding her, as was their job, both as her bodyguards—it was, after all, how they met—and her pack.

Roxy was, hands down, the most beautiful omega I'd ever seen. She glided forward with the confidence of someone who *knew* people would make space for her. Her long, red hair fell in perfectly styled waves down her back. Her pale skin had just the right number of freckles covering her nose, giving her an air of innocence. Roxy was wearing a white dress with details in gold that did a fantastic job of highlighting all her best attributes. It was snug against her ample breasts, then tight around her tiny waist, and molded to her hips before falling to the ground. Even the way the metallic details shimmered drew everyone's attention to every single one of her curves. Roxy could've been a movie star worth millions. Instead, she'd chosen to open a strip club, a place where other omegas could shine and be independent. She took us in, gave us a haven, and always tried her best to look out for us.

Every omega working at Allure worshipped the very ground she walked on. Every alpha who had a membership was beyond grateful for her, and all the betas who worked at the club had nothing but great things to say about her. She was one hell of a woman.

She walked to the corner where I'd been trying to avoid the crowds until she stood in front of me, with enough distance to respect my personal space. Her alphas stood even farther apart, and it felt like we were suddenly in our own little bubble.

I looked down at her—because our height difference was really that big—thankful she didn't comment on the fact my perfume was acting up nor on my blatant attempt to hide out for a while.

Just because I was on the hunt didn't mean I'd have an easy time of it. I was very aware of the differences between myself and the other omegas, and that was fine. I'd just hoped prospective packs would approach *me* rather than having to go to *them*. It was another courting rule, and I quite liked that one.

"Hey Ni ... Roxy! You look amazing!" I

complimented, plastering a smile on my face and hoping she'd forgive me for the slip. I'd almost used her actual name instead of her stripper name, and that was taboo around here. Our stripper names were meant to keep us safe, just in case any alphas had... scary ideas. It shouldn't be a problem, not with the amount of screening they did with the clientele, but one could never be too careful. And Roxy and her pack really did do everything in their power to care for us. They were just that nice.

"Thank you, Bubbles, hun," she replied breezily, her throaty voice clear in spite of the noise in the room. "You look great too. I'm glad you went with the dress I suggested; the red does amazing things to your skin tone!"

I looked down at my clothes. Compared to most omegas here tonight, I'd dressed quite conservatively. I was wearing a long-sleeved cocktail dress that reached midway down my thighs. It *did* have quite the neckline, though. It was one clear cut that went almost to my belly button. However, since I didn't have that much up above, there was no side boob showing—not that that would be a problem, really. I looked good. Hot, even.

But it felt weird to wear red for a New Year's party. I'd been raised by my Brazilian side of the family, and it was a *big* thing to always wear white when the clock struck midnight on New Year's Eve.

Even if it wasn't the entire outfit—and usually people picked different colored underwear for the secret wishes for the upcoming year—most of it *should* be.

I'd never *not* worn white before. Until now.

Wearing white during the passing of the year was supposed to be a way to wish that the coming year was peaceful and, I guess, a way to bring good vibes. I wasn't entirely sure where the tradition had started or why, but it was a well-known rule.

On the other hand, red was supposed to represent love or, well, *sex*.

Although I *did* want to find a pack and have lots of sex with them, I'd initially just planned on making sure my panties would be red, not the whole outfit. But when Roxy had seen the cute white pantsuit I'd planned on wearing, she'd talked me into changing my mind and pushed this one on me.

There was no denying a request from Roxy, so here I was. In a red dress ... and white underwear.

Had to keep the tradition, somehow.

"Yeah, I—" I trailed off, unsure what to say.

I shouldn't have worried. Roxy wasn't paying attention to me anymore. Or rather, she was, just not what I was saying.

"Hmm, I wish I'd thought to lend you one of my pearl necklaces. It would've looked great with the dress." She paused, her finger tapping against her lipstick, showing off her well-manicured nails.

"Well, no matter. Let's go. There's a pack I'd like you to meet!" Then she grabbed my arm and not-so-gently pulled me through the crowd. Actually, she was pulling me along with her as her pack parted the crowd for her. We never actually touched anyone else or even got close.

It was quite the handy trick.

It made me wish for a pack of my own to make transitioning around crowds that much easier. Except, no pack had ever chosen me, and even if I finally found one, I had no idea if they'd be okay with me continuing to work.

Most alphas wouldn't be okay with letting their omegas work, let alone being strippers. Roxy's alphas were one in a million. Pack Kennedy not only didn't mind their omega working, but they also went above and beyond to ensure the club they owned together was one of the best.

I didn't bother protesting. I just let Roxy pull me, thankful for the distraction.

Besides, I was curious.

Roxy wanted to introduce me to a pack! Did I dare hope? Had she found some hot alphas who'd be willing to see me through my heat?

No, wait. That couldn't be, could it? I had never really explained my situation to her or told her why I wanted the job. Although …. Roxy *had* been in the business for quite some time, and she was an *omega*, after all. Maybe I didn't have to say anything? Maybe she just *knew*?

Brimming with curiosity, I let Roxy lead me until we reached the furthest corner from where I'd been, straight to the balcony where they'd get the best view of tonight's performance. Well, tomorrow morning's, or whatever the proper term was for right after midnight.

Standing side by side with their backs to the stage were three tall, cute alphas. They stood in a little bubble of their own, with all the other room's occupants giving them a wide berth while whispering about them.

Either they were famous, or trouble.

Still, as we approached, all three didn't spare anyone else in the room a single look. Their whole focus was on us.

Well, on *me*.

The handsome alphas had their eyes locked on *me*, and I was omega enough to admit that being the sole focus of their attention had my hormones going a little crazy.

Well, *crazier*.

Their eyes widened, pupils dilating when a big wave of my scent hit them, and I totally used the moment to my advantage to drink them in.

The pack looked incredibly good in their tailored suits that probably cost more than I could make in a few months of tips. The shortest of the three was a blond who was a little taller than me. His well-trimmed beard was almost red, which made for a pretty cool effect and made him seem like the friendliest of the three. Or maybe it was the clear blue eyes.

I frowned. He kind of looked familiar, but I couldn't quite place why.

Then there were the other two alphas, who stood shoulder-to-shoulder at practically the same height. The one closest to the blond had dark skin and filled out his suit with such confidence, it was like he'd been born for it. His hair was cut super low, his face shaved to perfection, and his eyes ... well, they actually looked black right now from how dilated his pupils were.

The final alpha had a tan to die for. The kind I could spend hours under the sun trying to achieve, and only accomplish after a few days of sunbathing like a rotisserie chicken. If Aunt Lu were here, she'd immediately bombard him with questions about what kind of outdoorsy exercise he did and how often, while giving me not-so-subtle stares that I should do some of them too.

Wouldn't work, though, because while I loved the beach, any exercise taking place on it would undoubtedly result in sand getting in places sand should never be, and I'd learned my lesson the hard way long ago. I was an indoorsy exercising type of girl.

This pack looked older than me, probably somewhere in their thirties, and they held themselves with the confidence of alphas who *knew* their power and worth. I should feel intimidated by them; I mean, it was clear others felt that way by the space left between this pack and the others, and the way people kept looking at them while pretending *not* to look.

I loved that big, strong alpha energy they had going for them. The one that promised an omega she'd be taken care of.

The closer we got, the more it seemed like they were practically eating me up with their eyes. It was a powerful, heady feeling that made me even *wetter*.

It was embarrassing.

Or, it would be. Except, I was a fucking omega, which meant getting horny in the presence of unmated alphas was almost a given, *and* the alphas loved it when we reacted to them.

Roxy wrinkled her nose slightly, the move barely perceptible, and that was the only indicator my perfume going crazy was bothering her. Still, she smiled, gently pushing me so I'd stand right in front of the three hot alphas.

"Bubbles, I'd like to introduce you to my brother's pack, Pack Carmichael."

That was why he looked familiar! Blondie was a younger, taller, more rugged version of Roxy!

Her *brother*.

Roxy continued, unaware of the direction my thoughts had gone to. "Gentlemen, this is Bubbles, the omega I was telling you about."

CHAPTER 7

I leaned back against the bar, taking a swig of my beer and observing my pack losing their freaking minds with a shit-eating grin on my face.

It wasn't that I *wanted* them to be enduring the clear crisis they were currently going through—I loved my pack brothers—but this was a *sign*. They were invested, and we were all on the same page. They were going crazy because the beautiful Bubbles—in a red dress so sinful that, frankly, it should be illegal—was talking to some other alphas. Specifically, rich-as-fuck looking *fancy* alphas, ones who were allowed up on the balcony where the omegas were mingling.

Despite how expensive membership at Allure was, we were very much in the cheap seats down here in the main heart of the club, making uncomfortable small talk with other alphas in front of the empty stage.

I took a moment to assess my own responses, to see if I was feeling as unhinged as my packmates clearly were. As much as I was *jealous* of any other alpha getting a sliver of Bubbles' attention, I couldn't deny it ignited a satisfying sense of *challenge* within me too. *Bring it on, fancy alphas. We're a pack worth considering too.*

"We may as well leave now," Kaito grumbled, glaring up at the three alphas like he could shoot laser beams out of his eyes and vaporize them. "Look at those fucking guys. I'm pretty sure I've seen them on the cover of Alpha Entrepreneurs magazine."

"Since when is the great Kaito Knight afraid of a little competition?" I teased, barely suppressing a laugh at the fact he'd *read* Alpha Entrepreneurs magazine. Kaito needed a hobby.

My twin shot me a filthy look in response that I was confident had never appeared on my face. We may have been identical, but for the most part, we were incredibly easy to tell apart. Kaito had collected all the grumpy genes while we were in the womb like they were rare Pokémon cards. He'd been a frowny bastard from the day we were born.

"It isn't just a little competition," Zach pointed out quietly, twisting his beer bottle between his hands—a sign that he was nervous at best, panicking at worst. "We've been down this road before. Every omega we've ever expressed an interest in has ended up mating a pack with more money and a fancier job title."

Cole's eyes flashed with hurt as he stared at Bubbles. Okay, maybe Cole was a little *too* invested.

I knew he was almost desperate to find an omega, and that Bubbles had been the first to actually have *all* of us interested, unanimously trying to see more of her. No matter what Kaito attempted to claim, even he was eager to catch a glimpse of her whenever we could. Cole wanted the same thing his parents had, and even though, like his family, we'd formed our pack in high school, we hadn't found our omega there. For his parents, it had been love at first scent. They'd been together since they were teenagers, and they were still the most sickeningly happy pack I'd ever encountered. Cole's siblings had been lucky in love too, and it bothered him more each year that he hadn't gotten his happily ever after yet.

"They're just talking," I soothed, trying to keep everyone in check. "Look at the way the red-haired omega gestured between them—she's clearly introducing them. I don't care how many boring business magazine covers they've been on. We're not going to give up before we've even *met* Bubbles."

Not that I knew exactly *how* we were going to meet her, but there had to be a way. Maybe she'd get bored hobnobbing with the alphas up there and come downstairs for a while? It couldn't hurt to hope.

"Who said anything about giving up?" Kaito snapped, shoving a hand through his styled hair until it looked more like the unkempt way I wore it.

"You did," I laughed, bumping his shoulder with my own like an alpha with a death wish. He couldn't stay mad at me, we'd shared a placenta. Them's the rules of twinhood.

Kaito huffed, conveniently ignoring the fact that he'd absolutely suggested we just leave now.

"We just need to find a way to get up on that balcony," I mused, looking around the room. Obviously, we weren't the first alphas to have that idea. There were bouncers stationed at the bottom of the staircase for that reason, turning eager packs away.

I leaned back against the bar, staring up at the ceiling. The club looked smaller from this angle, facing away from the glittering stage. Was it too much to hope that Bubbles would spot us among the crowd and descend the stairs as if in a trance, drawn to us by fate and sexual chemistry the way it happened in the movies?

A fat drop of cold water splashed onto my cheek, and I started wiping the moisture.

"Are you *crying*?" Kaito asked in disbelief.

"What? No, of course not," I scoffed, squinting up at the ceiling. "Something dripped on me."

Zach made a sound of discontent next to me, wiping at his own face. "Yeah, something is definitely leaking. Shit, that's... not ideal."

To say the least. No good came from leaking ceilings. The neon light above the bar rotated, casting a wave of pink in its wake.

It was hard to tell, since the ceiling was painted black, but it definitely *looked* like it was bulging slightly. I glanced at Kaito to see if he'd seen it, finding him frowning as he stared at the same spot I'd been looking at.

"You'd think for the amount of money we pay to be members here that the building would at least be watertight," he grumbled.

I sighed. Kaito *thought* he got all the brains of the two of us, but I was totally the smart one.

"How fortunate, then, for the club owners that they have the best goddamn contractors in the city among their member ranks," I said slowly. "The owners, who are probably standing on that balcony *right now*, possibly oblivious to this very serious problem."

"Oh," Kaito murmured as the ceiling lit up again, dollar signs practically flashing behind his eyes. "Ohhh."

"My guess is that it's from the heavy snow. Maybe even an ice dam," Cole breathed with so much reverence you'd think he'd discovered the holy grail rather than a legitimate structural—and probably electrical—hazard. "That really seems like the kind of thing the owners should be *urgently* informed of," Cole added with a smug grin, flicking his curls out of his hazel eyes. Even Zach looked cautiously optimistic.

"Alright, let's go," Kaito announced, striding confidently toward the bouncers in front of the stairs, never one to stop and make a group game plan.

"Invitations," the bouncer clipped, arms crossed over his chest, looking down at us with absolute confidence we didn't have whatever special VIP invite got us up those stairs. He could probably tell I'd gotten my suit off a clearance rack, even though it had been an awesome deal and I looked pretty damn suave, if I said so myself.

"We need to speak to management," Kaito replied, all cool professionalism and zero people skills. "It will only take a moment, then we'll come back downstairs."

The bouncer was *maybe* the biggest alpha I'd ever seen, with skull and dagger tattoos poking out the bottom of his black button down, covering his hands. A muscle in his jaw ticced in irritation as he stared down my brother.

"It'll have to wait until—"

Kaito growled in irritation, and I tensed automatically, worried that he was about to pick a fight with an alpha twice his size out of sheer stubbornness.

"The ceiling is leaking. Do you know the risks water damage in light fittings can present? An electric shock to whichever unfortunate soul happens to turn the light on, a fire, maybe even a ceiling collapse. I assure you that the owners would much rather have a five-minute conversation with us than their delightful New Year's Eve party end in carnage." Kaito gestured absently at the damaged section of the ceiling, and the bouncer squinted to see it in the dark. This was why Kaito was our de facto pack leader—he wasn't afraid to stand his ground. "However, I can't make you change your mind. I'll just hope, for your sake, that no one dies because of your negligence. Here's my business card if you'd like to pass it on to your—"

"Wait, wait," the bouncer said, holding up his hands placatingly, a nervous bead of sweat forming on his forehead as he looked between the ceiling and the bright white business card Kaito was holding out. "That does sound like the kind of thing they'd want to know about."

He blew out a breath, glancing at the balcony, the worry at leaving his post written all over his face.

"We'll be quick," I assured him. "No funny business."

"Just one of you. I can't allow a whole uninvited pack up there. Security on the balcony will be keeping watch, and I need to photograph your membership card—do *anything* stupid, and I'll have you all banned."

"Fine," Kaito agreed, procuring the card from

his inner suit pocket and holding it out for the guy to snap a picture. The bouncer nodded curtly when it was done, and Kaito immediately stepped past him, heading up the stairs without giving us an opportunity to discuss it first, the fucker.

Cole groaned loudly, and I was right there with him. Kaito didn't have a romantic bone in his body; he was going to scare Bubbles off for good before we even got a chance to meet her.

CHAPTER 8

"Hi!" I squeaked, immediately blushing in embarrassment.

But hey, at least I had managed to catch myself before I did the weird finger-waving thing to go along with my squeaky hello, so that was something, at least.

All three alphas smiled at me, but it was the blond who stepped up first, offering me his hand for a shake.

Americans and their weird habit of shaking hands upon meeting. Aunt Raquel would have a blast watching the interactions here. It was so impersonal when compared to how I grew up. Half-hugging and air kisses were the way to go. Though even back home, there was a second of awkwardness depending on where you were from because some did one kiss, others two, and it was always a toss-up as to which one you should be doing. We never actually touched strangers, though, to avoid scent markings. Here?

There was absolutely no way to avoid it.

As I got close enough to touch Blondie's hand, I almost drowned in the smell of chocolate orange.

The fact I never liked the taste was a bit unfortunate, but the smell was ... pleasant enough. Rich with a citric note to it that wasn't too overpowering.

"Hi, Bubbles. It's nice to meet you. I'm Caleb Carmichael," Roxy's brother said, smiling brightly at me.

"Hey, Caleb, it's nice to meet you too!" I exclaimed, smiling at him and doing my best to ignore the way my perfume was growing stronger at the small physical contact. The heat of an *alpha's* hand on mine. The slight brush of fingers, the strength behind the hands that were smoother than even my own.

My body didn't give a shit whether I liked the taste of chocolate orange or not; it wanted one thing, and one thing only.

I knew part of it was a punishment for having spent all my previous heats alone. It also probably explained why my pre-heat was starting way sooner than it should. My body was growing desperate for a knot, and the longer I denied it, the worse it would be. It was why I'd decided to find a pack to help me with it this time.

His hand tightened around mine, his pupils blowing wide in response to my scent growing stronger, but he got brownie points for not reacting to it in any other way. Instead, with admirable control, he stepped back slightly, releasing my hand as he did so, and introduced me to his pack.

"These are my packmates, Asher Carmichael," he nodded in the surly alphas' direction, "and Connor Carmichael."

The scent of lime and coconut tickled my nose as Connor approached, offering me his hand. Still smiling, I shook his hand, amused at how his hand engulfed mine.

I was tall for an omega, but damn, this guy's fingers were extremely long, and there were calluses on his palm that hadn't been on Caleb's.

Hmmm, someone who had done at least some manual labor. Just the way I liked them. I wondered if he knew his way around a sledgehammer because I definitely had some fantasies that involved a strong, shirtless guy swinging one around, all sexy and sweaty. His muscles would strain with the weight of it, and I would just—

Get a grip, Amy. This is neither the time nor the place. You're here to work, I reminded myself, trying to break the little fantasy before it got out of hand.

Besides, I was all too familiar with how things like these went. Sure, they'd agreed to meet me, and they'd probably heard about me from Roxy. They might even consider courting me for a bit as a change of pace from the usual omegas they'd probably tried to court. But at the end of the day, they'd pick another over me. Someone smaller, curvier, *softer*. Someone more like Roxy, who fit the ideal image of what an omega should be to a T.

I'd done this dance before, and I'd learned my lesson.

I'd also learned to be okay with it. One of the reasons I'd gotten a job and looked for independence was so I wouldn't build expectations only to see them crumble into dust.

It was alright, though. I mean, there was still the possibility they'd be interested enough to help me through my heat, no strings attached, and then we could go our separate ways. That wasn't so bad, right? Lots of omegas did that, all the time.

And if they weren't interested at all, well, there was still time. I could find another pack, or maybe even a few betas who wouldn't mind helping an omega through her heat. It wouldn't be the same, not by a long shot, but there were toys and stuff they could put on that could make it seem like I was being knotted ... sort of.

I knew I sounded pathetic even to my own ears, but desperate times called for desperate measures.

"It's nice to meet you, Connor," I offered when the silence between us stretched a little longer than I knew what to do with.

His lips curled up, dark eyes meeting mine and holding my gaze hostage. "The *pleasure* is all mine, *Bubbles*." There was a slight purr when he said the word "pleasure" that was ruined by the clear amusement over my stage name.

I wanted to roll my eyes. What was it with people always hating on my stage name? Bubbles was an *awesome* stripper name. Better than Candi or Brandy or whatever else the other omegas had picked. It was also a lot more original and unique, which meant people only had to hear it once to remember.

Plus, bubbles were light and shiny and made everyone happy, and that was the vibe I wanted to have. The vibe I *did* have.

Connor let go of my hand and stepped back, and I turned to the final alpha with expectant eyes.

Asher.

He smelled like lemon and lavender.

I not-so-subtly gave him another sniff, enjoying his scent more than chocolate-orange.

Though, even without knowing him, I was already pretty damn sure he wouldn't like knowing he smelled kind of floral. A guy like him? He probably expected to smell like sandalwood or leather or something—a more rugged, manly scent.

Asher didn't offer me his hand like his packmates had. No, instead, he pulled something from the pocket of his suit and offered it to me.

My breath caught in my throat when I saw the black jewelry box.

There was no questioning what this was, and I didn't really know how to react.

I'd considered that this was why Roxy had introduced me to Pack Carmichael, but I hadn't expected them to be quite so forward in our very first meeting.

Courting gifts were standard behavior for alphas who wanted to woo an omega, regardless of the reason, but a courting gift at the very first meeting? Definitely not traditional. In fact, some omegas might even find it disrespectful.

Not me, though. I had zero complaints. It had been a long, long time since I'd received a gift from an alpha I wasn't related to, and the fact they had taken the leap ... did I dare hope?

"We know it's a little unconventional," Caleb said, smiling at me from beside Asher, "but my sister has spoken so much about you, we feel like we already know you. Consider it a late Christmas present from us." Then he shrugged like it was no big deal.

I glanced from him to Connor, then to Asher, the only one who hadn't said a word to me yet.

"Thank you." I didn't bother adding that they didn't have to, or that they shouldn't have, or any of the polite things to be said because I could tell by

Asher's gaze that they'd just ignore it anyway.

They knew the gesture was over the top, and they were probably banking on it.

Definitely something they'd done knowing it would make a statement.

Slowly, carefully, I opened the black box and just ... stared.

Inside, nestled on the dark velvet, was a beautiful diamond necklace that probably cost more than I'd ever make working at Allure, and the alphas here tipped *generously*. It was the most delicate, beautiful thing I'd ever seen. The diamonds were small pendants that shone under the light at the center of tiny flowers all along the golden chain. The gift was feminine, tasteful, and so incredibly thoughtful.

"OH!" Roxy clapped beside me, and it was such an unexpected noise that it almost made me drop the box. "How *marvelous*! Just what you needed, Bubbles! It'll go perfectly with your dress! Oh, you *must* try it on!"

Speechless, I just looked at her, taking in the big, knowing smile.

It crossed my mind that Roxy had known about the gift, but it wasn't like I was protesting. It was just ... a diamond necklace.

"Allow me," Asher said, and then he lifted the chain from the box, raising it to put on me.

It took me a second, but I finally caught myself. Turning around, I twisted my hair up to let him put the necklace on me.

I realized what I'd done a little too late to change course. Showing an alpha my bare, unmarked neck made me insanely vulnerable. I'd just basically offered myself up on a silver platter to him and his pack.

Asher growled a little, quickly catching himself and stopping, but the damage was done. Pack Carmichael knew what I'd just done, and they also knew what it meant. Or, at least, what it could mean.

I had to wet my lips twice before I was able to speak over my suddenly dry throat.

"Thank you." The words were barely a whisper, but I knew he heard me despite the noise in the room.

Under Roxy's approving gaze, Asher secured the clasp, his fingers brushing against my neck and making my heart race at the contact. I could feel the heat of his body on my back, smell his overpowering scent of lemon and lavender, and hear his breaths near my ear.

A whine left my lips before I could stop it. Need filled my stomach and made me so fucking wet, I wondered if my underwear would survive this. Even the industrial, pre-heat pads I'd put on them might not be enough to make it through the night.

Asher answered my whine with a soothing purr of his own, and I had to close my eyes and try to think unsexy thoughts to get myself together.

I needed to get out of here. I needed to find an unoccupied room and a toy—specifically, a vibrator with the biggest knot I could handle—to take the edge off before I did something very, very reckless.

Or even more reckless, considering I'd already bared my freaking neck to an alpha I'd just met.

Suddenly, it was too much.

The crowd, the noise, the scents. Everything was too much for me. My body felt hot, sweaty even, like I'd just done three consecutive routines on the pole under the hot summer sun.

I needed to get out of here. *Now.*

I just had to turn around, thank them for the gift, and then I'd talk to Roxy to let her know I needed to leave. Then I could flee to the safety of my home and break down all my vibrators until I was under control again.

Feeling resolved, I raked my nails against my palms, using pain to help me focus.

Five minutes, and then I could leave.

I turned around, forcing a smile on my face, wishing it was genuine. The Carmichaels had done nothing but be nice to me, I had to repay them in kind. It wasn't their fault my hormones were going haywire; it was just bad timing.

I just hoped I didn't come off as rude for this.

"Thank you," I said, doing my best to sound

cheerful. "This is gorgeous. I ... I have no words."

"It looks great on you," Connor supplied, his voice strained as he struggled to suppress a growl of his own.

None of them were smiling anymore. Oh no, in fact, they all looked seconds away from jumping me right here, right now.

And I wouldn't say no.

But...this wasn't how I wanted things. I was not going to jump a pack I'd only just met simply because they smelled kind of nice and had good taste in jewelry.

"I... ah," I cleared my throat to buy myself some time. "I really am grateful. And I hope you don't find me rude for this, but..." I trailed off, not knowing a polite way to phrase this.

How did one say "I'm two seconds away from presenting my ass and begging for your knots in a room full of people even though you're strangers, and I'd probably be willing to take just about any knot, and it might cause a bigger commotion than I'd be able to live with afterward" in a polite way?

Roxy saved me from having to say anything, though. "They understand. Go home, Bubbles. I'll have Sean drive you there. I'll call you tomorrow." Her words came out soft, and her face was open, but there was a glint in her eyes, and there was no hiding the steel in the command.

I was too damn horny to care.

"Thank you," I told her before turning to the Carmichaels. "It was nice meeting you," I added to them before I turned tail and let a couple members of Roxy's pack escort me out through a side door, the now empty jewelry box tight in my grip.

I needed a few hours with my toys, and then I'd be good as new. Then I could ask Roxy for Pack Carmichael's contact info and message them a proper apology.

KAITO

CHAPTER 9

Arata's eyes burned into my back as I took the stairs two at a time, but the alpha bouncers were eventually able to shoo my pack away from the stairs. I had no doubt they'd resume their staring post near the bar, hoping to catch a glimpse of how this interaction went.

A sense of unease snaked through my gut at the thought. I had no doubt I'd be able to pitch the ceiling fix, I was good at what I did. But fixing the ceiling had been at the forefront of my mind when I'd made a mad dash for the stairs, and now I remembered just *why* my pack had wanted to gain access to the balcony in the first place.

Bubbles.

When it came to wooing omegas, I wasn't so confident.

Not confident at all, actually.

Omegas were creatures of contrast. They liked hard cocks and soft blankets in their nests, and they wanted that balance in their alphas too. I was all hard edges, and omegas *noticed* that shit. Arata must have absorbed my soft side in the womb, and really he should have been the one to come up here and introduce himself to Bubbles, except then we wouldn't have a chance of getting the ceiling repair job.

It was a conundrum.

I turned sharply at the top of the stairs, intending to follow the glass balustrade to the far edge of the balcony where I'd seen the club owners, but was immediately hit with a wave of gingerbread. *Literally* hit. My hands snapped out immediately, grabbing the upper arms of the delicious-smelling omega who'd crashed into me, probably trying to get to the stairs.

I sucked in a breath, maintaining my grip until I was confident she was steady on her feet, and taking a small step back. Glossy brown hair, big dark eyes with pupils blown wide, lips parted as she inhaled just as deeply as I was.

Bubbles.

Her perfume was so thick, I almost choked on it, and the speed at which all the blood in my body seemed to drain to my cock made my head spin. We'd never been able to tell Bubbles' scent apart from the others, and now that I could, it only made me want her more.

Pre-heat. There was a syrupy sweet extra layer

to her already delectable gingerbread scent that signaled her heat was approaching, and I was torn between a growl of approval and telling her off for leaving the house. Especially to spend the night mingling in a room full of alphas that were probably making her hormones go crazy.

Though maybe that was exactly the reason she'd come out tonight. Maybe she was pack shopping for alphas to help her through her heat.

The idea filled me with a bitter kind of jealousy, and I hated myself for it. Of course, Bubbles was perfectly entitled to spend her heat with whoever she deemed worthy of entering her nest. We may have spent the past week pining for her, but the truth was that Bubbles probably didn't even know we existed. So why shouldn't she have gone out to find a pack?

It was logical. My emotional response was *illogical.*

All that before I even took in the dress that she was wearing. It was cut down the middle almost to her navel, showcasing the smooth, slight swell of her breasts and golden tan skin. Fuck me, Bubbles smelled like heaven and looked like sin. If she was my omega, I'd buy her a whole closet of slinky red dresses.

"I'm sorry," she gasped, not moving out of my light hold, her pupils so dilated that I could barely make out the rich brown of her irises.

"No need to apologize," I rasped, fighting down a growl as two alphas moved in closer to Bubbles like they were going to take her away from me. "Are you hurt?"

I scanned her face for injuries, my gaze moving down and settling on the golden strand at her neck, dotted with diamonds. Had she been wearing that earlier? I didn't think so. Surely I would have noticed—my eyes had been automatically drawn to her unmarked neck.

There was the faintest hint of alpha scent lingering, like they'd put the necklace on her, scent marking her with light touches, and I forced myself to release her before I said or did something regrettable.

Obviously, Arata had been wrong in his assumption that tonight was just an introduction between Bubbles and those alphas, unless they were *really* overconfident. No one gave courting gifts at the first meeting.

There was a pause, and I couldn't help but notice her tongue darting out briefly to slide across her lower lip. Was she breathing a little more deeply? Was it too much to hope she found my scent as enticing as I found hers?

"No, I'm ... I'm not hurt." Bubbles gave me a tremulous smile; her fingers lightly drifted over the necklace, seeing where my gaze had gone. The gesture probably meant something, but I'd never gotten fluent in the language of omega courtship.

There were two alphas with her, hovering close like they were ready to intercede the moment I overstepped, but they smelled mated. More security guards, perhaps?

"I'm glad," I replied gruffly, sidestepping her. I knew she was too good to be true. I knew my pack shouldn't have gotten so enamored with her. Omegas like her didn't want packs like ours. We'd never be able to afford to buy her gifts like that. I wasn't sure we would even if we *could* afford it—spending that much money on jewelry seemed so wasteful. A stance that the omegas we'd attempted to court found ... off-putting, to say the least.

"Excuse me," I rasped, breathing shallowly so I didn't take on any more of Bubbles' intoxicating scent. *Focus*. Business, I could do. Construction, I knew. Omegas were unfamiliar territory.

I didn't let myself look back as I wound my way through the crush of posturing alphas, all trying to make themselves seem as large and impressive as possible while they flirted with glamorous omegas. I could just make out Roxy with two of her alphas, still talking to the suits, and from what I could tell in the time we'd spent here, her pack ran Allure. I needed to talk to the decision-makers to pitch this job.

That was what I was going to focus on. Not the fading scent of gingerbread as it drifted away, though the remnants would cling to my clothes until I washed them. I grimaced, already bracing myself for the moment I got back downstairs, knowing I'd be trying to have a serious conversation with my pack while they bombarded me with questions the entire time, wondering why I smelled so good.

I pushed past one last pack to get to the end of the balcony, and the necklace-gifting alphas spotted me first. The Ken doll-looking one sniffed, frowning as he picked up Bubbles' scent on my shirt.

Good. Fuck that guy.

The thought died the minute I got closer and smelled the lingering scent of Bubbles' arousal clinging to the tall blonde with the reddish beard. Idly, I wondered if they were younger than they looked. We were in our late twenties—old to not have found an omega yet—and they definitely looked older than my pack.

I wanted to growl at him, at all three of them, but held it back, barely. I was clearly the fool here, really, not them. The only reason I smelled like her was that she'd crashed into me by accident. The scent on them? That was probably on purpose.

I resented them for it.

An alpha with dark skin and slicked-back hair that curled at the ends stepped in front of me, pale green eyes flashing with irritation. His scent told me he was mated, though I could have guessed it from the protective way he'd slid in front of Roxy. Now that I had a decent whiff of Roxy's scent, I realized that the alphas who'd been escorting Bubbles were Roxy's alphas too.

"Can I help you?" the alpha asked. "You don't look like one of our VIP members."

Maybe he could tell by my untailored suit. Then again, for all I knew, all these rich fuckers knew one another by name.

"I'm not, and I apologize for barging in like this and interrupting your night. Don't fire your bouncers—they let me through because I spotted a concerning safety hazard that I wanted to bring to your attention. You're the managers, right?"

The guy glanced around, looking uncomfortable. "Let's discuss this somewhere more ... quiet."

Right. He probably wouldn't want to draw attention to a glaring hazard around all of his patrons. He tipped his chin back toward the stairs, and I fell into step behind him, hearing Roxy, her other alpha, and the three unmated alphas following behind, talking amongst each other. The two packs must be close if they were coming along for a private conversation.

Great.

Instead of heading down the stairs that I'd come up earlier, the alpha kept going, discreetly waving a key fob over a panel in what seemed like a smooth black wall and pushing it open. It led to a concrete stairwell that was probably meant to serve as a fire escape—not that it was properly signposted—but they were clearly used as an omega thoroughfare, judging by the mixture of scents that lingered in the space. The door closed quietly behind the rest of the group, the loud music of the club growing muffled as we descended a flight of stairs.

There was a faint trace of Bubbles' gingerbread scent in the air, and I swallowed thickly, forcing myself to take shallow breaths, so I didn't entirely lose my cool.

"Our office is just down here," the alpha volunteered. "My pack owns Allure. I'm Lorne Kennedy. That's my packmate, Curtis, and our omega, who performs as 'Roxy.' And you are?"

"Kaito Knight."

Lorne grunted, unlocking another door just off a landing and pulling it open, indicating for the rest of us to file in first. I stood politely off to the side while Roxy, her alpha, Curtis, and the other pack took their seats in a small sitting area in the corner. The rest of the space was dominated by an enormous square table, with workstations haphazardly set up on each side, laptops and paperwork, and old coffee mugs littering the space.

Lorne pulled two rolling chairs away from the

table, sliding one toward me and gesturing for me to sit. "Pack Knight. You're new members."

I nodded curtly. New members who were either about to make a very good or very bad first impression.

"Well, you can speak to me about any supposed safety hazards, though I can assure you the club has strict health and safety protocols in place to protect our patrons and employees."

Curtis—a tall, somewhat gangly blonde alpha with thick-rimmed glasses—handed us each a tumbler of amber liquid, and I nodded in thanks, taking a sip and relishing the burn of the whisky as it slid down my throat.

I was experiencing emotional whiplash from encountering Bubbles up close, smelling her delicious pre-heat scent, then realizing she was somehow at courting gift-level with another pack already, which usually didn't happen until two or three dates in, even though it had looked like they'd just met. But this was business. *This* I could do. I'd put the omega from my mind and focus on the task at hand. I wouldn't go back to my pack empty-handed. If there was one thing I'd always been able to deliver Pack Knight, it was steady employment and financial stability.

Besides, even if she was already close to settling on the other pack, I still didn't want Bubbles to be injured by a collapsing ceiling. I didn't want *anyone* to be injured, but the idea of omegas hurting created a visceral reaction in me that I knew my packmates would share, even though we had other jobs we'd need to balance.

"I'm sure you have strict health and safety rules in place, but water damage doesn't care about protocols. You have a leak, right above the bar. My packmates and I are licensed contractors, and while we can't know without properly inspecting it, it's been a cold winter, and there have been more ice dams on roofs than usual."

Lorne grimaced, and I guessed this wasn't news to him. Roxy moved closer to listen in, her scent giving off distress signals, and he immediately pulled her into his lap, stroking the bare skin of her arms to soothe her.

Nope, not jealous at all, I told myself.

Though I could admit to myself, even if I *had* an omega, I'd be useless at that sort of thing. Soothing. *Purring.* Comforting. I wouldn't even know where to begin.

"We've been meaning to replace the old shingle roof since we bought the place," Lorne admitted. "It was just never a good time."

"It's still not a good time!" Roxy hissed. Lorne purred quietly for her, even as he frowned to himself. Fucking bonded alphas. Stupid, lucky bastards. "Would we need to close the club for repairs?" she added in a despairing voice.

"You shouldn't be open now," I told her flatly. "Who knows how much standing water is in the attic right now that it's dripping through the plasterboard? Or what kind of state your electrical is in? Your ceiling could collapse. Plus, mold can develop within twenty-four hours—"

"This is a disaster!" Roxy wailed. "No, we can't close. Can't you just pretend you didn't see it? We've got all these themed nights coming up and—"

"Sis," the blond alphahole from the other pack said in a low voice. Ah, they were related. I'd assumed they were friendly, given the fact that they were allowed to sit in on this conversation, but the omega's *brother*? Just our luck. Surely that was some kind of conflict of interest? "I get that closing is not ideal, but do you really want to risk the club catching fire, or the roof falling on everyone, over something you could've prevented? Over a risk you were made aware of and chose to ignore? That would be so much worse. Water damage isn't the sort of thing you want to mess around with. It's the kind of thing that only gets worse."

One of the blond's packmates—the one with thick dark hair and an admittedly enviable jawline—shot Lorne a disapproving look. "If you knew the roof needed replacing, you should have done it before winter. What were you thinking?" he clipped, disapproving.

I didn't want to agree with them, and it annoyed me that I did. It was incredibly irresponsible that they knew about this issue and had chosen to ignore it because it was inconvenient. There were *omegas* here—dozens of them. They were in danger because of Pack Kennedy's choices.

"We were thinking it wasn't that urgent," Lorne sighed. "And we weren't expecting so much snow. We've been so busy with the holiday season stuff that we kind of put it out of our minds."

Lorne's packmate-in-law looked ready to rip into him, and I decided to interject to get this discussion back on track.

"Considering how much we like the club, we'd hate for something to happen to it, especially if it happened while there were people in the building who could be hurt. I don't want to overstep, but wouldn't it be better to close off for a few days and have it fixed rather than risk something worse happening that would damage Allure's reputation and everyone's safety?"

"I'm going to message the bartenders to put a bucket down. A nice looking bucket," Lorne mumbled, already tapping away on his phone.

"You said you were licensed contractors?" Curtis asked, leaning against the wall with his arms crossed, observing us. "I'm sure you've already got jobs booked, but do you think you could rearrange some things to at least take care of the urgent stuff and make it safe to use the building? Then we can get the roof replaced when the weather warms up."

Ah, there it was. That sweet spot in the negotiation process where I had the upper hand.

"I can recommend water extraction services, which you'll need... well, at least five minutes ago. Unfortunately, we're booked through February—"

"We'll double your going rate, and add a bonus if you give us priority on this," Curtis interjected. "Water extraction is great, but we need at least a short-term fix as well. Usually, we only let mated alphas work on the premises, but you've already passed all the membership background tests, and our security would be on-site as well..."

Cha-Ching.

We *were* technically booked for the next couple of months, but our schedule was lighter than usual, given the holiday season and the general winter lull.

"I'll see if we can move some things around. One of my packmates would need to do a walkthrough during the day to assess the damage so we can price it up. If it is an ice dam, then getting that roof cleared is the highest priority."

"Whatever you need," Lorne agreed. "Come in tomorrow—at least one of us will be on-site anyway. Shit, we'll probably need to phone our insurance company too, but frankly, however much we need to pay to get the snow off the roof and the water out of the attic, we'll pay it. Do you have any examples of similar projects to give us an idea of what our options are?"

"Absolutely, though my phone is in the lockers, but I can talk you through some ideas." This was my dream negotiation—a client who just wanted the problem solved, and was willing to throw money at it until it did.

As we discussed the various benefits of them replacing the shingle with a metal roof, Roxy sighed. She climbed out of Lorne's lap and moved back to the sitting area where her brother and his packmates were.

There was a lull in the conversation between us as Lorne pulled up our company website on his phone, and in the silence, I eavesdropped on Roxy's conversation with her brother and his pack, mostly by accident.

"...I'm sorry she had to leave early. I didn't know her heat was so close, otherwise, I wouldn't have encouraged her to come at all. Pre-heat is *unbearable*. I'm glad she got to meet you, though."

The effort of keeping my growl repressed at the idea of Bubbles being pressured to come out when she was in pre-heat and uncomfortable made my throat ache.

Get yourself under control, I scolded silently, giving myself a mental slap across the face. Not my business. None of it was my business. I was a motherfucking professional. I wasn't about to start growling in the middle of this meeting.

"Do you think she liked the necklace?" Blondie whispered. "The way she perfumed when Asher was putting it on her—"

I ground my teeth together, loud enough to draw a glance from Lorne, and quickly pasted a smile that I hoped looked less forced than it felt.

"Let's get it done," Lorne said. "Honestly, I just want the problem solved with as little disruption as possible. Curtis? Sound good?"

Curtis shrugged. "I guess. Can we still use the stage for rehearsals while the work is happening? Maybe we could use this as an opportunity. Create some new shows, maybe even hire a few new omegas and give them time to learn without the pressure of performing..."

"We'll do our best to keep that area disruption-free," I hedged, not wanting to make any promises we couldn't keep. My instincts were already pressing against me, urging me to keep the omegas safe. "You'll need to have industrial dehumidifiers and fans going to dry the place out, though."

"I suppose that's all you can do," Curtis sighed. "There'll be alphas whenever you're on-site to supervise, and if we could keep the number of *unmated* alphas on-site to a minimum, we'd prefer that. The safety of the omegas is our top priority."

Except for the whole moldy ceiling, possible fire

hazard situation, I supposed.

"Of course. Arata will be here first thing tomorrow morning to assess the job, and I'll get in touch with the water damage guys we work with to start drying out the club."

I knew they'd been busy with the heavy snowfall causing issues, but I hoped I could convince them to make Allure their new number one priority.

Lorne and I stood at the same time, and he clapped me on the shoulder. "Come on. I'll walk you out. We should probably close the club early, if you think it's that much of a hazard."

"We can't close before midnight at a New Year's Eve party!" Roxy yelled from the office as we made our way back into the stairwell. This was huge—we'd be kicking off the new year with a big job and some lucrative new connections. Maybe we could even prioritize some of the projects around our own home with the unexpected income boost. My pack would be thrilled. Hopefully thrilled enough that they wouldn't mind leaving early so I could get a head start on rescheduling.

Besides, I'd seen Bubbles leave with my own eyes. There was no reason for us to stick around if she wasn't going to dance tonight.

We could be where we always were when the clock struck midnight at the start of the new year. In our perpetually omega-less home.

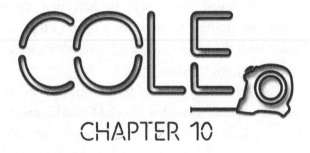

CHAPTER 10

"What's taking him so long?" I grumbled, not realizing I was bouncing on the balls of my feet until Zach put a hand on my arm, giving me a pointed look.

Right, right, be cool. Don't want to be bouncing around like a pup in case Bubbles sees us.

She'd disappeared from view after talking to the rich prick alphas, but the balcony was full, and I had no doubt there was some other swanky pack trying to woo my omega.

"He's back," Arata said, nodding towards the stairs that Kaito was descending, a totally unreadable look on his face. Not for the first time, I wished my packmate was, like, one percent more expressive. Arata for sure got all the facial expressions in utero.

The moment Kaito got close, I caught a whiff of something incredible, and pounced on him before he had a moment to speak, dipping my head to his chest and inhaling as though my life depended on it.

Oh my god. Oh my god, I'd never smelled

anything so good, not *ever*. Nothing on earth smelled this good. Well, this scent *without* Kaito diluting it would probably be better, but it was pretty close.

I was purring like a lawnmower and I didn't even care. *Could I somehow get the shirt off Kaito without touching it and getting my own scent all over it?* This was a strip club, after all, surely it'd be fine if Kaito was shirtless...

"Personal space, Cole," he snapped, trying and failing to shake me off. "I'm flattered, but you're not my type."

Kaito was my packmate and one of my best friends in the world, but instincts were instincts, and my hackles rose before I even realized what was happening. A warning growl rumbled out of my chest at the idea of someone taking this dream omega away from me, and my packmates froze.

"Whose scent is this?" I rasped.

There was a long pause from Kaito, and I contemplated forcing him to the ground in a show of submission.

"Easy, Cole," Arata said, using that smooth jazz voice that always settled us when our testosterone was making us stupid. "Kaito, stay still. Whose scent is it?"

"Bubbles," Kaito replied cautiously, his body language rigid as I leaned into him again. Bubbles. *My* Bubbles. Not that I'd needed Kaito to confirm it, not really. Call it instinct, but even though I'd never been able to catch her scent before, I still knew. I knew it in my bones that this was Bubbles' scent.

I greedily sucked down lungfuls of it, letting her delicious gingerbread scent overlaid with something syrupy and needy soothe the worst of my territorial irritation. Now I was feeling less Me Alpha, Hit Packmate, I could appreciate that Kaito was a lucky bastard, and that worked out in our favor. He'd *met* her. It was really happening.

"Her heat is approaching," I groaned, inhaling again, careful not to touch the areas where her scent clung to Kaito's clothing in case I accidentally covered it with my own. *Wow, I really went full unbalanced alpha there.* "Sorry for the growling, man. How attached are you to this shirt?"

If I got to sniff Bubbles' intoxicating gingerbread scent while jerking off tonight, maybe my knot would properly deflate for the first time since I'd caught wind of her. At this point, I probably needed medical attention. *If your knot lasts more than two hours, please call your doctor.*

"You're not jerking off to my clothes," Kaito deadpanned, grabbing the collar of my shirt and bodily removing me. Arata immediately took my place, leaning into his twin's space to get a good inhale.

"She smells like gingerbread and the kind of sex that throws your spine out of alignment," Arata sighed. "You know what I mean?"

"No," Kaito deadpanned, glancing away.

Liar.

"You talked to her. This is great, right? What did you say? What did she say? Did you get her number?" Zach asked, which were good, rational questions that I should have probably thought of. How did he even get Bubbles' scent all over his shirt? Hope bubbled up in my chest at the idea of her rubbing herself all over my packmate because she met him and just *knew* we were her dream pack.

I'd rub her so good if she'd let me.

"We crashed into each other, she apologized, I told her it wasn't necessary. Don't you want to hear about how the conversation with the owners went?" Kaito asked bitterly, like we were all raining on his business parade, though I sensed there was a little more to it than that. "We're going to have to reshuffle some jobs, but we'll be able to finish the basement at the house with this money. Maybe even put up drywall in the attic. I need to get to my phone and start making some calls."

Pop. RIP, hope bubble. It was good while it lasted.

How was he thinking about *work*? This was all the evidence I needed that Kaito was secretly a robot. He'd *touched* Bubbles—by accident, sure—but how could he be thinking about anything other than *that* right now?

"You told her that her apology wasn't necessary," Arata repeated flatly. "Then what, Mr. Ice King? Please tell me you made sure she was okay? Maybe even threw a compliment in there? Something about how beautiful she looks, like a normal alpha trying to woo an omega?"

Kaito frowned. "Of course I checked that she wasn't hurt, and the compliment was implied in the way that I looked at her. None of you seem particularly enthused about the project."

I groaned dramatically, while also dragging Zach into our huddle so he could get a good sniff of Kaito's shirt too. He was too polite to get all up in Kaito's grill without an invitation. Kaito growled irritably, but stayed in place because he was a good packmate, if not a little dense sometimes.

"Who cares about the project?" I asked. "Did you even introduce yourself? I swear, Kaito, if you were rude to her, I'll eat a chili cheese dog in your car again."

"The fuck you will," he snapped. I could still see the trauma in his eyes from the grease stains I'd accidentally gotten on the seat last time. Kaito would keep his car surgical theater-level clean if he could.

"Were you rude?" Arata pressed. "Was the other pack there? The one she was talking to?"

Kaito's brow creased in consternation, and I

felt a tiny bit bad even though Kaito did regularly need to be called out on his bullshit. On the one hand, it was his single-minded focus that had meant we'd bonded as a pack before we even graduated high school, well before a lot of our peers who'd hesitated, waiting to see if better packmate options came along. Kaito's determination had driven us to start our business, and had gotten us every job we'd ever had.

It probably also contributed heavily to us still being omega-less.

"They were there, and I wasn't rude. Arata, you'll need to come in tomorrow to do a walkthrough and figure out the extent of the damage, and I'm confident you'll be on-site for the next few weeks. You can tell her yourselves that she's beautiful and smells like an expensive physiotherapy bill, if you must," Kaito grumbled, cheeks flushing slightly red as he probably realized how badly he'd fumbled up there. "Though she'll probably be too distracted by the other pack courting her to notice you anyway. Pack Kennedy still wants the dancers to be able to rehearse here throughout the repairs. There will be alpha security on site to keep the omegas safe."

I groaned dramatically. I hated working on ceilings, and now I might not even get to see Bubbles? What was the point?

"Tell us more about the other pack," Arata

pressed. My boner *almost* went down at the reminder that we had competition. Shit, I hoped Kaito smelled as good to Bubbles as she smelled to us. "They're related to Pack Kennedy, the pack who owns the club. And they gave her a courting gift—an expensive-looking necklace. I think it had diamonds in it."

"Of course they did," Arata groaned. "We're so screwed."

"Though it sounded like they'd only met Bubbles for the first time today," Kaito continued slowly.

"They gave her a courting gift on the first meeting?" Zach asked, baffled. "That's so... presumptuous."

"More like *desperate*," I scoffed.

Zach shot me a totally uncalled for look of disbelief. "Yes. *They're* the desperate ones. Nothing *we've* done could be described as desperate. Nothing at all."

I opened my mouth to argue that coming to the club every night just made good financial sense, considering how much the membership fee was, but Kaito beat me to it.

"We should have a couple of weeks here to make an impression. If we're going to draw her attention away from the 'desperate' pack—ideally before her heat—then that's our chance," he said decisively. "Let's get home. I have to look at the schedule, and

110

Arata has to do a walkthrough tomorrow so we can put together the proposal."

He turned on his heel, just as the crowd in the club started counting down from ten.

"New Year's Eve..." Arata mumbled, a thread of longing in his usually relaxed voice. When the countdown hit 'one,' I understood why. While this was a club mainly designed for single alphas, there were still plenty of people here with dates—packs whose dynamic was more romantic than familial, as well as a few betas—and all of them were currently locking lips, ringing in the new year with their tongues.

Cool, cool, cool. Not jealous at all.

Definitely not disappointed about the idea of spending yet another New Year's Eve wishing desperately for an omega, for a sense of completion for our pack.

No, I wasn't going to let myself be disappointed about that. Not tonight. Not even Kaito's abysmal first meeting with Bubbles and the fact that some other pack was throwing jewelry at her could dampen my spirits. Soon, we would meet my dream omega and woo the hell out of her, it would be amazing. I'd woo her so hard, she'd forget all about that fancy necklace.

"Happy fucking New Year, Pack Knight," Arata said with a wry smile, bumping me with his shoulder. Kaito was already stomping through the crowd like a bull in a china shop, not caring about all the romantic interludes he was disrupting.

"Happy fucking New Year," I sighed. I might not have my dream omega yet, but I *was* going to steal Kaito's shirt out of the hamper the moment he took it off for reasons definitely not related to jerking off. Maybe, just maybe, I'd come hard enough to finally get a good night's sleep.

CHAPTER 11

After the disaster at the New Year's Eve party, I'd been too embarrassed to call Roxy. Just thinking about the fact I'd almost dry-humped my boss's younger brother in the middle of a work party filled me with mortification and had me seriously considering changing jobs.

Except, my family hadn't raised a quitter.

That, and Roxy herself had called me right past noon the next day to make sure I was okay—because that was the kind of person she was. She'd brushed off my apologies, laughing about the whole thing and telling me to stop worrying, even as I vehemently promised this would never happen again. According to her, Pack Carmichael hadn't been horrified by my behavior, either. In fact, Roxy said I'd left a good impression on them.

Go figure.

Pack Carmichael had given me a diamond necklace as a courting gift upon meeting me, and I'd thanked them by losing control of my hormones and fleeing, only to spend the next many hours fucking myself with my wide collection of sex toys while thinking about *another* alpha.

An alpha who'd been grumpy and rude and who'd smelled like expensive whiskey and cinnamon. An alpha who'd looked at me with dark, soulful eyes and whose body had been all hard edges under the slightly ill-fitting suit. I knew because I'd copped a feel when I'd bumped into him.

I didn't even know his name, and yet, it had been Cinnamon Growl Alpha's knot I'd dreamed about while I fucked myself to oblivion with my dildos. And when I'd finally come, my orgasm had been stronger than any I'd ever had.

A pity he was a grouch, though, but at least he'd made for good clit closet material.

During her call, Roxy had also given me a heads up that some new alphas might be seen around the building, but that we shouldn't worry and that we could feel free to rehearse as usual.

To say I was curious would be an understatement. Since I'd started working there, I'd never seen alphas around other than the mated ones who worked there—and the clients, of course, but those only frequented at night. Roxy hadn't gone into detail as to why there might be some strangers around, saying she'd explain it to all of us in person when she saw us on the second, and that only made me even more curious.

I supposed I was about to find out, I reminded myself, getting out of the car and heading to the club.

It was early, stupidly so, especially for a post-holiday workday at a strip club. However, I preferred it that way. Coming in early meant I was less likely to run into the other omegas, since most of them didn't come in until the afternoon. It prevented me from feeling awkward or having to compete for one of the poles.

With my head held high, I walked into Allure, refusing to show weakness or any of my inner turmoil. Nobody had to know I'd been extra awkward and acted like a hussy in front of Roxy's pack and her brother's. I already had no idea how the other omegas might react to learning Roxy had introduced me to her brother's pack, there ought to be some jealousy at the very least, and I wasn't going to make things worse. Or give them a reason to hate me even more, or mock me. I was Amélia da Silva Cavalcanti, and I cowered to no one.

Probably.

I greeted Jason, a bonded alpha in his late forties who worked security for Pack Kennedy. Jason was a nice guy who usually took the day shifts so he could spend his nights with the rest of his packmates and their lovely omega, Vanessa. He belonged to one of those lucky packs who met in high school and had found their perfect omega early. Their kids were now attending the same school they'd all gone to, and their oldest would soon graduate.

"Happy New Year, Bubbles," he said as I passed, beaming at me.

"Happy New Year, Jason." I stopped and smiled at him, feeling more like myself than I had in days. "Did you and the family have a good time?"

If anything, his grin got bigger. He slapped his belly. "Sure did. Kids were all home, and our Vanessa outdid herself. It's why we didn't come to the party." Everyone who worked at Allure, from the cleaning staff to the dancers, had been invited to the New Year's Party and encouraged to bring their families if they wanted to. However, I understood why some packs, like Jason's, had opted out. A strip club was hardly where they could bring their teenage kids. "How about you? Had fun?"

I blushed and averted my eyes, picking up a strand of my hair and playing with it. "Yeah. It was fun."

Way to go, Amy. Not even in the building and already going all awkward about New Year's.

Jason misinterpreted my reaction because he winked. "Bet a nice omega like you had her pick of the alphas, huh? Good for you. Make them work for it, girlie. Anyway, I better let you go inside and get to work. Don't want you to be late. Have a nice day, Bubbles."

"Thanks, Jason, you too. And once again, happy New Year!" I exclaimed, smiling brightly.

"Oh! And I almost forgot!" Jason said, his eyebrows raising. "The boss lady asked me to let you guys know there are some alphas on site today. Nice men, seem to know their business. They'll be doing some construction work around here, so you might see them."

"Oh." My eyes widened at the new info, my belly fluttering.

Construction workers, huh? I *loved* me a good, strong alpha who knew what to do with his hands.

Jason must've seen something on my face because he gave out a belly laugh. "Unmated, too, in case you were wondering." He winked conspiratorially at me once again. "Well, then, off you go. Don't want to be late, do we?"

Blushing, I scurried inside through the back door, trying to slow my steps so they'd resemble more of a power walk than a hurried escape. I walked through the omega-only area, heading straight to my locker, not really paying attention to my surroundings.

I was absolutely not hiding beneath my hair and hoping nobody would notice me scuttling by.

Not that there was anyone around to notice. The club was deserted, not an omega in sight. In fact, other than Jason, I hadn't run into anyone at all so far.

Once I'd changed into some workout clothes that consisted of high-waisted burgundy yoga shorts, a matching sports bra, and a loose white cropped top, I headed to the stage.

I knew I had to face Roxy soon and apologize in person, not to mention talk about the training schedule for the week, but first, I wanted to stretch my muscles and work up a sweat. Besides, she might not be in yet.

I headed to the pole at the furthest corner of the stage, noticing as I went that the glass was down—I didn't understand the mechanism behind it, but it was some high-tech thing that Pack Kennedy had come up with that kept the dancers from being overwhelmed with alphas' scent. The thing was usually down during the day, but all it took was the push of a button, and the giant glass panels would slide up from a nook on the floor right at the edge of the stage and block us in. At first, I'd thought it was weird, but now, I got a thrill off the whole window thing. It was like we were expensive, luxurious toys the alphas could see and covet but never have. Like window shopping when you were on a strict budget.

After sorting through my phone and finding the playlist I'd come up with for just such occasions, I put it and my water bottle down in the corner and started stretching.

Sandy and Junior blasted from my speakers. The

singers were siblings, both betas, and the duet had been *huge* when I was a kid. I'd grown up listening to it, and every now and then, I liked to play the songs for nostalgia's sake. Maybe not the sexiest choice of music for a stripper—most omegas preferred sexier songs to practice, usually the same one they'd dance to during their routine—but it wasn't like I'd dance to it.

I just needed something to get my blood flowing.

It didn't take me long to tune out everything but the music and my body's movements. The music changed while I stretched, and soon enough, a slow, sultry song was playing that was perfect for what I'd do next. Smiling, I walked towards the pole and repeated the routine I'd danced for Christmas.

Feeling sweaty, I took off my shirt and threw it in the general direction of my phone, turning once more to face the pole. Then I went through the routine I was supposed to have done on New Year's, since the moves were still fresh in my mind.

I knew I was better at the floor part of my routines than the aerial work at the pole, but the only way I'd improve was to keep practicing. It would help build core strength and muscle memory, and that would go a long way toward making my dance numbers even *better*.

I'd just grabbed the pole again when I turned and saw it.

Or rather, *him*.

Cinnamon Growl.

He was in the middle of the room, on top of a ladder, with a *tool belt* on.

I almost whined.

I was a sucker for a working alpha. In fact, I had this one very specific recurring fantasy that involved a strong, half-naked alpha with a hard hat and worn, ripped jeans.

And although Cinnamon Growl *was* in a pair of faded jeans, he was, unfortunately, wearing a shirt. Still, his clothes today made him look even more mouthwatering than what he'd worn the last time I'd seen him. The suit had given him a dashing, impeccable dressy look, and he'd seemed comfortable, but I hadn't been able to fully appreciate his body then. Would it be bad to hope his jeans were just loose enough that they'd ride down and show me his happy trail?

Cinnamon Growl had a screwdriver in hand and was messing around with a lightbulb. I couldn't see his eyes from this angle, but I could see his dark, straight hair, the curve of his jaw, and the way his muscles strained against the fabric of his shirt.

I imagined what it would be like to have those strong, capable arms wrapped around me, all over me. I bet his hands were big and callused, too.

I knew I was perfuming big time, but I was too

wrapped in my fantasy to care.

He moved on the ladder, his white shirt rising with the movement, and I was able to see the tiniest sliver of bare skin.

Suddenly, his nostrils flared, and his head whipped in my direction crazy fast.

Our gazes met, and I whined.

Actually *whined*.

And all he'd done was *look* at me.

I was so, so wet for that alpha, it wasn't even funny. And I was pretty sure it wasn't even the pre-heat speaking. I'd taken care of my wave well enough that I shouldn't be feeling new effects for another few weeks.

Still, the more I watched him, the more I wanted him to bend me over right here, right now, and impale me with his cock until I came so hard I lost consciousness.

No, I wanted him to pick me up, carry me until my back was against the wall, and then fuck me. I was wet enough that he wouldn't even need to touch me, though I wouldn't complain if he sunk his teeth into my neck and made me his.

The enormity of what I'd just thought finally sank in, and I was so surprised by it, I lost my balance on the pole and slipped.

I fell on my back, wincing at the pain in my ass and shoulder blades, but at least I hadn't hit my head.

Under normal circumstances, I'd be quick to get up, brush off my clothes and crack a joke about gravity, but not now. Now all I could do was close my eyes in mortification.

Twice now. Twice I'd seen Cinnamon Growl hottie, and twice he'd seen me make a fool of myself. Though the first time me bumping into him had been more of a happy accident, there was no brushing *this* off.

For the second time in as many days, I wished I'd just stayed home.

"Bubbles, hey, are you okay?"

I didn't have to open my eyes to know it was him. His voice wasn't what I'd expected. It was softer, kinder. But it was definitely him. The scent of cinnamon clung to him, and so did something else ... *apples*. Hmmm, apple cinnamon pie was one of my favorite desserts. I couldn't scent the whiskey, but he'd probably just been drinking that, and that was why I'd smelled it. Though not in a bad, "I'm an alcoholic who smells like stale whiskey" way, but just the rich notes of someone who liked the drink.

His hands were all over me. Poor alpha was probably trying to check if I was hurt and worrying about me, and yet, all I could do was focus on the way everywhere he touched; I came *alive*.

"Bubbles?"

My belly fluttered when I heard him say my stage name. He *knew* who I was. Even though I wasn't one of the more popular dancers, or had been here long, he knew who I was.

Had he been the one to ask about me to the waitstaff? One of the betas who worked here had given me a heads up that a pack had come every single day between Christmas and New Year's and asked about me. It had to have been Cinnamon Growl's pack.

"Are you okay? Do I need to call someone?" He rapid-fired the questions, growing increasingly concerned when I didn't answer, and I finally managed to get a hold of myself.

I'd revisit this memory, the scents, the feel of him, later when I was alone. Cinnamon Growl was definitely filling up my spank bank with all kinds of hot material. For now, though, I had to put him at ease. The need to comfort him was almost visceral.

I opened my eyes.

Shit. He was on his knees, his body all but covering mine as he examined me. His gaze was so full of concern, I reached a hand to his cheek before I even knew what I was doing.

"I'm okay. Promise. It was just a little fall," I said, blushing.

We were so close, if I moved my head just a little, I could lick his face and find out if he tasted like cinnamon apples, or if it was just his scent.

Hmmm, would his cum taste like apple pie? I

really wanted to find out.

Rather than pushing me away like I would've expected based on how he'd acted at the New Year's Eve party, Cinnamon Growl actually leaned into my palm as if seeking even more contact.

Something pulled at my heartstrings.

I perfumed so damn hard, they'd probably be able to smell me from backstage.

Cinnamon Growl inhaled deeply, his pupils blowing wide, and he purred.

There was just something about an alpha's purr.

I rubbed my legs together, desperate to feel any kind of friction.

His purring intensified, and I was ready to grab him by the neck and push my pussy against his mouth so I could feel the vibrations against my clit.

I'd probably come from that alone.

One thing was for sure, though, and that was another pair of panties, ruined. If this kept up, I'd have to start buying them in bulk.

"What the hell is going on here?"

Roxy's icy tone was like being dumped into a frozen lake mid-winter, and it managed to break us out of whatever spell we'd fallen under.

Not-So-Grumpy-Grump jumped back, offering me his hand to help me up, and I gladly accepted, pretending I didn't feel the tingles from where our palms met.

I gave him a quick, shy smile and pushed my shoulders back before turning to face Roxy.

Her lips were turned down in disapproval.

Not good. Not good at all. Here I was, thinking I couldn't afford to embarrass myself in front of Roxy again, having promised I definitely wouldn't make a repeat of the party, and failing miserably. *Fucking hell.* This was the second time she'd seen me throwing myself at an alpha. And the first one had been a member of her *family*.

I couldn't even blame this one on the pre-heat, either.

"Hey, N...Roxy! I'm so sorry. I came in early to practice, and I was going through my routine when I fell. C ... " I stopped and turned to Cinnamon Growl, realizing I'd almost used his nickname out loud. "I'm sorry, I don't know your name." I gave him a sheepish grin, and he smiled in return, putting his hands in the pockets of his jeans and drawing my attention back to his tool belt and the bulge of his ... other tool that his pants weren't doing a good job of hiding.

"Arata. Arata Knight," he offered.

Arata Knight. Even his name was kind of hot.

I was so doomed.

"Right. So, Arata was working over there," I pointed at the ladder like Roxy needed to know every single detail of what had happened. "And he probably saw me falling, and he came to check if I was okay. Which I am. I mean, my ass hurts a little, but it's nothing I'm not used to. Not that I have a habit of taking things up my ass that make it hurt. Not that I'm opposed to some butt stuff." *Shut the fuck up, Amy!* "Anyway, he was just about to help me up when you arrived." I finished lamely, my cheeks flaming and my eyes wider than saucers.

What the hell had I been thinking? Mentioning butt stuff like that? It was nobody's business whether I enjoyed being fucked in the ass or not.

Though maybe Arata wouldn't mind knotting me real good while another one of his packmates fucked my ass.

"Thank you, by the way," I remembered to mention to Arata, a little too late, and he nodded, winking at me.

My perfume went wild at the flirty gesture. There was definitely more to Arata than the Cinnamon Growl I'd taken him for.

Roxy's lips were still pursed, but I noticed her shoulders had dropped slightly, and she'd relaxed.

"I see. Well, I'm glad you're not hurt, Bubbles. Thank you for the help, Mr. Knight. I actually came looking for you," she told him, and I was *really* glad I knew Roxy was a bonded omega because, for a second, jealousy made me see red. "Curtis and I would like to talk to you about the timeline your firm submitted." Shiit. I hadn't even noticed Roxy's alpha behind her until she'd mentioned his name. This was just *great*. "He has a few questions. If you wouldn't mind following me?"

And then she turned and left, Arata hot on her heels.

I watched him walk away, adding the way his pants hugged his ass to my clit closet.

I seriously hoped I'd be seeing a lot more of Arata Knight around here. He'd definitely provide enough new material to make my pre-heat a lot more fun.

And if I bought a couple more vibrators with bigger knots, well, what was an omega to do?

CHAPTER 12

I hadn't seen Not-So-Grumpy-Cinnamon-Growl again. Not later that day, and not the days that followed. It was such a pity, too, because I was dying for another sniff of his scent. Often, I'd caught myself wondering if the rest of his pack would smell just as edible, but I hadn't seen any of the members of Pack Knight. And though Roxy had told all of us omegas that Pack Knight had started some construction work and were currently doing something on the roof—in the roof?—I hadn't seen them around at all.

I wasn't too proud to admit I'd even tried to catch a glimpse of them from outside, but either they were coming in at odd hours, or maybe my timing just sucked.

Honestly, if not for all the noise we kept hearing during rehearsal—which was, admittedly, pretty annoying—I would've thought I hallucinated the whole thing.

Get a grip, Amy. Just because one member of

the pack smelled like my favorite dessert and looked like sin, it didn't mean the other alphas would. And even if they were all as handsome as *Arata Knight* and smelled just as good, odds were they already had an omega they were courting. Sure, Arata had reacted to my scent, but considering how strongly I'd been perfuming, it wasn't like he'd stood a chance. Besides, he knew where I worked; he might even be on the roof *right now*. If he or his pack had been interested, they would've asked me out already. And they hadn't. That was all I needed to know to stop this little infatuation from getting out of hand.

I was also very aware that my job was unconventional at best, and Pack Knight might not like the idea of dating or courting someone who made a career out of dancing in skimpy outfits at a strip club. I couldn't even blame them. An omega working at all was unusual, but to work at a strip club ... Even if it was an omega-approved career, it didn't mean people had an easy time accepting it, especially when it was a pack that wanted to bond with the omega.

I needed to stop thinking about him, about all of them when I didn't even know the whole pack, and start thinking about work.

Sure, the club might be closed for a few weeks while renovations were going on, but rehearsal was happening in full-force. Roxy was determined to make Allure's reopening a whole thing, and if she got her way—which she usually did—it would be even bigger and better than the Christmas special. Every single omega was excited about it. After all, big events meant bigger tips.

This morning, I had a private lesson with Roxy before we did the group rehearsal, and that was what I should be focusing on.

So when I walked on stage and saw Arata Knight across the room, looking dashing in jeans and a light blue button-down shirt while he talked to someone on his phone, my heart pitter-pattered in my chest.

Smiling, I waited until he looked at me and gave him a little finger wave in hello. Arata frowned, scowled, and turned his back to me, leaving me hanging.

Confused, and more than a little hurt, I watched him leave.

Arata Knight was one confusing alpha. His hot-and-cold attitude was giving me whiplash.

How was it that this was the same alpha who'd helped me up and flirted with me a little not that long ago? He'd been so freaking nice! Now he was back to acting like Cinnamon-Growl, back to what he'd been like when we'd run into each other on New Year's Eve.

Whatever hope I'd had, whatever fantasies I'd

started to build up about Pack Knight, deflated like a balloon.

"Oh good, you're already here!" Roxy's words broke me out of my gloom, and I turned to watch the sultry omega walk towards me. I forced a smile on my face, and she answered it with a genuine smile of her own.

Roxy had tied her red hair up in a ponytail, and she wore a matching emerald green workout outfit that looked amazing on her.

"You ready to get started?" she asked, taking the pole beside mine. Two of Roxy's alphas—Lorne and Justin Kennedy—took their positions. Lorne stood near the backstage exit, arms crossed and a scowl on his face, while Justin sat at one of the tables in front of the stage, picking up his phone to give us the illusion of privacy.

Roxy never really went anywhere without at least one of her alphas. That was true to most mated omegas, really, but due to Roxy's past and the trouble she'd had once with a stalker, back when she'd been only an unmated dancer, her packmates struggled to let her out of their sight. Thankfully, though, Pack Kennedy was always mindful of us omegas, and they did their best to give us as much privacy as they could ... or at least the illusion of it. Regardless, the truth was, we all felt safer having them around. And it wasn't like any of us were shy around alphas, or that their presence here would prevent us from doing our jobs. We worked at a strip club that literally catered to alphas. We were used to having an audience.

"Sure! I just need to stretch a little first," I replied, raising my hands over my head, interlinking my fingers, and reaching my arms up to illustrate my point.

Absolutely not keeping an eye on where Arata had disappeared to see if he'd be back. Or thinking about him. Or worrying whether he was having a bad day and if I could help him.

Roxy copied my movement, winking. "Even better. It means I get to talk to you while we stretch."

Keeping my arms in the same position, I bent my body until I felt the burn on my side, mentally counting to ten.

"Uh, okay?" How did one respond to a statement like that? Did she mean just chitchat? An actual serious conversation? No, there was no way Roxy would want to hold a serious talk while we were in the middle of stretching, and somewhere the other dancers might show up or eavesdrop. Roxy always kept serious talks behind closed doors. She valued our privacy as much as she valued her own.

Roxy's throaty, musical laugh filled the room.

"Don't worry, Bubbles, it's nothing serious," she reassured me, bending her body to the other side and encouraging me to do the same.

Right. *Note to self: focus.*

"Listen, I hope I'm not overstepping, but my brother's pack, you remember Pack Carmichael, right?" she asked, and I nodded to let her know that yes, I did, in fact, remember them.

How was I supposed to forget the alphas who'd gifted me a diamond necklace and who I'd all but propositioned in the middle of a party less than a week ago? The embarrassing memory would live rent-free in my head until I died, probably.

"Good," Roxy said, straightening and lifting one leg over her head.

In her late thirties, Roxy was more flexible than I was, which was pretty amazing. I hoped one day I could build up to it and become an even better dancer.

"Well, would it be okay if I gave them your phone number? And your real name? They were quite taken by you, hun, as I'm sure you guessed by the courtship gift. They'd like to ask you on a proper date. Court you, if you're willing to give them a chance. I will, of course, act as a chaperone for the date if you want, or we can find someone else if that will make you more comfortable."

Speechless, I only stared at Roxy as she talked. For some reason, she was acting like she was making a hard pitch, rather than presenting me with a possible solution to all my problems.

Even if things didn't work out with Pack Carmichael, even if they eventually decided to pick another omega like all other packs had done in the past, they might still be interested enough that they'd be willing to help me through my heat.

I wouldn't have to go through it alone. No bouncing on silicone knots while pretending they were the real thing. No physically painful moments when I couldn't find my relief, no matter how many vibrators I used or how big their size.

I'd have real knots to bounce on, real dicks, and real alphas to make me feel good.

Just thinking about it made me perfume, and I glanced at Roxy, hoping she was far enough away she wouldn't be able to smell it.

"Sure," I heard myself say, the sense of relief so big, I felt I might cry. "I'd love that."

CHAPTER 13

"Today's the day," Arata whispered, bouncing on his heels in a distinctly Cole-like fashion. Oh good, the puppy-like enthusiasm was contagious.

Not that I *wasn't* excited that we were hopefully going to catch another glimpse of Bubbles today, but we were hardly going to impress her by bounding around like overexcited toddlers. Well, I didn't *think* so, at least.

"You don't *know* she'll be here," I pointed out calmly, not wanting him to get too excited. We'd spent the last few days ripping out the sodden insulation from the attic, and steering clear of the main part of the club completely, but today we were working downstairs, replacing some water damaged sections of the wall behind the bar, and Arata was hopeful they'd resume rehearsals, and he'd get another shot with Bubbles.

Another shot, because he'd already *had* a shot, and it sounded to me like it had gone pretty well.

Not that I was an expert in flirting or omegas or human interaction in general, but Arata had seemed confident, and the lingering scent of needy omega on his clothes was a good sign.

Right?

Right.

Cole had definitely interpreted it as a good sign—he'd practically tackled Arata the moment he'd gotten in the door, sniffing him all over while Arata patiently held still and waited for Cole to finish.

In our past weak attempts at courting omegas, Arata had always been the one they felt drawn to first—he was easy to talk to (unlike Kaito and me), and flirty without a startling level of enthusiasm (Cole). I had no doubt that if we were going to have any success getting to know Bubbles, it would be through Arata.

"I have a good feeling," Arata said absently, drawing me back into the conversation. He pulled out his phone as it buzzed in his pocket, and mine went off at the same time. I didn't need to look at the screen to know it was the group chat.

Cole: *I'll never forgive any of you for keeping me off this job.*

Cole: *I'm going to go find a new pack.*

Arata snorted at the empty threat—Cole's go-to when he was sulking about us ruining his fun.

Cole: *@Kaito, this is bullshit. Change the*

schedule! I'm the best plasterer, you know I should be there.

Kaito: *Sorry, I can't talk right now.*

"Ooh, he's breaking out the auto replies. He must be in a bad mood," Arata laughed, tapping away on his screen. It wasn't like we were going to keep Cole away forever, just until he'd learned to rein in his excitement a smidge. Arata had told us how the Pack Kennedy omega who owned the place had given him a death glare for helping up Bubbles when she fell. Though I imagined Arata had taken his time in helping her to her feet, given the way he'd strutted around like a peacock all afternoon, smelling like needy omega.

It wasn't like Bubbles' perfume had been subtle. That had probably distressed the Pack Kennedy omega too.

I was both incredibly jealous and incredibly grateful that it had been Arata there, not me. Who knew what I'd have done if Bubbles had fallen over in front of me? Panicked and frozen up, probably. Best case scenario, I'd have rushed to her aid, tripped over my own feet, and knocked myself unconscious.

Not that I was a particularly clumsy person, but my brain had helpfully decided to fixate on that idea.

Arata: *@Cole, you're not helping your case. Try those breathing exercises we practiced the other day.*

Cole: *I DON'T NEED AIR; I NEED BUBBLES.*

"He's going to terrify her," I murmured. Arata snorted, his phone suddenly lighting up.

"Let me go talk him down," Arata chuckled, used to being the moderating presence in our pack. "I'll be back in a second."

I nodded, unpacking the equipment we needed for today in the corner of the club we'd commandeered while Arata ducked out the emergency exit to the alleyway we'd parked our van in. The doors would usually be closed, and the fact that the club had stationed bouncers on them today was our best indicator that the omegas would be coming in.

I was on the fence about whether or not it mattered if the omegas did show up. If *Bubbles* showed up. When Arata had come home a couple days ago, with Bubbles' scent all over him, and given us the details of their chance encounter, I'd started to feel hopeful. Cole was all but planning our bonding ceremony and singing love songs under his breath, but I still worried. I couldn't help thinking about all the ways this could fall apart. In the past, other omegas had promptly moved on to greener pastures whenever a wealthier, more sophisticated pack appeared. Bubbles already *had* that kind of pack circling her. There were too many things we didn't know, and I didn't like it.

Bubbles was an unknown. How Bubbles felt about the mystery pack who showed up with a courting gift at their first meeting was unknown. Bubbles being in pre-heat and what that meant for the possibility of *dating* her was an unknown.

Ugh, stupid Cole, using up all of Arata's time. I needed Arata the Emotional Support Alpha for a while.

I stiffened as I caught the faintest whiff of gingerbread behind me. *Shit, she's here. She's standing behind me.*

Why was she standing behind me?

Did I have something in my hair?

Where the *hell* was Arata? I wasn't the talker of the pack. I needed him and his social skills here if we were going to make a good impression on Bubbles. Besides, he'd already met her! Talked to her! *Touched* her even. Shit, shit, shit. I couldn't do that stuff.

Was I supposed to say hello? Hi? No, 'hi' sounded stupid. No one said 'hi' anymore, did they?

Fuck.

It wasn't like I could delay this any longer either—I could *feel* Bubbles' stare, burning into my back. Was she waiting for me to turn around? Oh god, she definitely was. That was what normal people did.

Why had she even come over to this corner, as far away from the stage as possible? Was I not meant to be here? We'd been here for days and no one had said anything.

Okay. Okay, this is fine.

Stop freaking out.

Don't say "hi".

I cleared my throat, turning around as nonchalantly as possible, like I had no idea that the world's best smelling omega was standing right there.

She was *so* pretty up close. I mean, she was pretty from far away too. She was pretty *all* the time. But up close, I could really appreciate the lighter caramel strands in her dark brown hair, pulled back into a ponytail on top of her head. She had big brown eyes and pretty eyelashes, and her lips looked *so* soft, tipped up into a gentle smile. There were a few freckles dotting the bridge of her nose, and I had a sudden, embarrassing urge to kiss every single one of them.

Say "hello" like a normal person. Don't say "hi."

"Hi-lo." *FUCK.* "Hello. I meant hello."

Smooth as silk, you fucking moron. I was blushing so hard, I was surprised I wasn't casting a red glow around the room.

"Hi-lo," Bubbles replied cheerfully, grinning broadly and giving me a wave that was almost as awkward as I was. "Sorry, I didn't mean to, er…"

She trailed off, her own cheeks flushing. Didn't mean to stand behind me and stare a hole into my back? I wasn't complaining. Especially when her nose was twitching ever so slightly, her body swaying toward mine.

Please find me as delicious smelling as I find you.

"No need to apologize," I said quickly, not wanting her to feel uncomfortable. "Bubbles, right? I'm Zach. Zach Knight."

"Knight?" she repeated. "Like Arata Knight?"

"Right, my packmate," I replied, barely suppressing a grin that she remembered his name. That was a good sign, right? Definitely a good sign. "You met him the other day."

"Yeah, I remember. He seemed, um, nice." Reading people's expressions was basically my kryptonite, but if I had to guess, I'd say Bubbles' smile seemed more polite than genuine, which made *zero* sense. Everyone liked Arata. He was impossible *not* to like.

"Is he all right?" Bubbles continued, tilting her head to the side. "Last time I saw him, he seemed kind of upset."

"He did? Arata is fine... I think. He's around here somewhere." Somewhere around here, *not* helping me with this conversation. Shit, Kaito should have swapped Cole and me. He'd come on too strong for sure, but there wouldn't be any awkward pauses.

"I like your hair thingy," I blurted, vaguely gesturing at the glittery silver thing holding her hair up.

Please, floor, feel free to swallow me whole at any moment.

Bubbles blinked at me, self-consciously touching her hair. "My scrunchie?"

I nodded stiffly, not trusting myself with words anymore.

Bubbles shot me a beaming smile that threw me slightly off-balance. "Thank you. Sometimes, you just need a little sparkle in your life, you know? That's why I love the costumes here so much."

"You look really good in them," I replied hoarsely. Bubbles perfumed almost instantly, her gingerbread scent turning syrupy sweet with arousal. Arousal in response to *me*. I'd never smelled anything more mouthwatering in my life.

I adjusted my tool belt as discreetly as I could to hide my growing erection, trying not to wince at the uncomfortable pressure on my dick.

"Thanks," she said breathily, catching her lower lip between her teeth for a moment. Fuck. Me. Sideways. She was so *cute*. Omegas could be aloof, but Bubbles didn't seem to have any of that. She seemed *kind*. She hadn't looked down on me for butchering something as simple as saying hello. "Um, do you mind if I warm up over here? The other omegas find my scent a little overbearingly cloying right now," she added, gesturing vaguely at the stage where a couple of dancers were stretching. "Oh, never mind. You probably find it overbearing too—"

"No," I blurted way too loudly, before clearing my throat. How could anyone find her scent anything other than *mouthwatering*? I was hard as a rock from getting an up-close whiff of it. If Cole were here, he'd be making jokes about using our dicks as hammers. "No. No, it's not at all. Your scent, I mean. Of course you can warm up here. Oh, you probably want me to leave—"

"No." It was Bubbles' turn to clear her throat. "Stay. I don't mind."

"Okay. Yeah, cool. No worries."

The glitter of her scrunchie glinted in the light as Bubbles raised her elbows, twisting her body from side-to-side, drawing attention to her lithe figure in tight navy workout clothes. Pack Kennedy was probably going to fire us for perving on one of their dancers, but Bubbles had told me to stay, and I wasn't about to ignore her commands for anything.

"Do you come here often?" Bubbles asked, her voice husky as she moved into a lunge, stretching her legs. She winced almost instantly at the cheesy question, and a little of the panic that always made my chest tight when I was talking to new people eased. "Not to work. I mean, I know you're here to work. Have you been to Allure before, you know, *not* working?"

"We joined Allure right before we got the

roof job. Our first night was the Christmas show," I replied hurriedly because that sounded a lot better than 'yes, we come here all the time. We're actually semi-stalking you.'

"Oh, that was an amazing show, don't you think?" Bubbles gushed, her entire face lighting up as she switched legs. "All the omegas sharing one stage! It was so much fun! I'm so happy I got to be a part of that number."

"Uh huh, it was amazing," I agreed instantly as Bubbles brought both her legs together and bent over at the waist, her pert ass high in the air. She had a great ass. A fantasy of me walking up behind her, peeling those skintight leggings off, and eating her pussy from behind while she held onto her ankles played out briefly in my head before I got myself under control. "I mean, we couldn't take our eyes off you. At the show. You have a really pretty accent. Can I ask where you're from?"

Flawless subject change. Well done me.

"Brazil," Bubbles replied, a slightly wistful look in her eyes as she slowly straightened.

"Brazil?!" I repeated, finally feeling like I had something we could talk about without me second-guessing every second word. Maybe just every third word. "I've always wanted to go to Brazil. Their Beta Soccer League is totally unmatched. I still can't believe they lost the last Championship, but they really put up a fight. This year's games should be amazing—some of the new players look really promising."

I stopped talking for long enough to realize Bubbles was giving me a slightly bewildered look. "Sorry. I get excited talking about soccer. My packmates don't get it at all."

"No, no, that's okay," she reassured me quickly, moving like she was going to touch my arm before pulling her hand back. "I mean, I don't watch soccer, but ... I guess, I'm surprised you keep up with the *beta* league, since you're an alpha and all."

I shrugged. "Alpha matches are more aggressive, but the real skill and technique are happening in the beta leagues."

Besides, I'd always had an affinity for betas. Maybe because, as far as alphas went, I was quieter and less domineering than my peers. I loved my packmates, and I hoped we could find our omega— and the more I talked to Bubbles, the more I wondered if she could be that omega—but I also thought that if fate had made me a beta, I would have gotten married and been happy that way too.

"That's really cool," Bubbles said softly. "My Aunt Lu is a beta and used to play beach volleyball professionally. She's always saying how beta leagues are criminally underrated. Have you ever watched volleyball? I have a whole game day ritual to watch my aunt's old team."

For the first time in my life, I contemplated going full Cole and dropping to my knees, begging Bubbles to fall in love with us and join our pack.

Fortunately, before my mental break could fully take hold, Arata strolled back into the club, tucking his phone into his pocket and beaming brightly when he spotted Bubbles. She paused her stretching routine, looking over her shoulder to see where my gaze had gone, and I didn't miss that she beamed right back at him. That knot of nerves in my chest loosened a little more. We could totally do this.

"Bubbles, it's so good to see you," Arata said smoothly, coming to a halt next to me. I felt myself relax slightly, always more comfortable in the presence of my pack. "On your feet this time," he added teasingly. "I hope you're all recovered from your fall?"

Bubbles blinked at him for a moment. "Oh! Yes, that. Did I ever tell you that you're my hero? Thank you for coming to my rescue."

The briefest hint of a purr rumbled out before Arata could quash it, not that he had anything to worry about, it seemed, because Bubbles' response was an immediate burst of perfume.

I was about ready to burn this tool belt.

"I'm glad you weren't hurt," Arata replied eventually, his voice deeper than usual.

"Totally fine," she laughed, not missing his alpha response. She gave Arata a long look, tilting her head to the side. "Are you feeling better?"

"Better? I feel great, yeah," Arata replied, flashing her an easy grin, though I had no doubt he was as confused as I was.

"Oh, good! Sorry. It's just ... you seemed kind of off yesterday, and I was worried something bad had happened. Or maybe it was just an off day? We all have those. Off days and off nights. Well, I'm glad you're feeling better. I like your smile. I'm going to stop talking now."

Arata laughed. "No, please go on. I could listen to you talk all day. Though I can assure you, I don't have off *nights*," he added with a wink that appeared to be directly connected to Bubbles' scent gland, given the way she perfumed.

The polite thing to do would be pretend we hadn't noticed, but both Arata and I were gulping down the thickly scented air with absolutely zero subtlety whatsoever.

"I'm sure you don't." Bubbles was inhaling our scent right back—pupils dilated, her head tilting to the side to expose her neck. All signs pointed to a very *interested* omega.

"Bubbles!" a male omega—one with wavy brown hair who I recognized as one of the lead dancers from the Christmas show—called from the stage, breaking us out of our trance. "We're running through group routines."

"Group routines," she repeated hazily, still staring at us. "Group routines! Shoot, I barely even stretched! Okay, I have to go. It was really nice talking to you, though," Bubbles added shyly, giving us a little wave before jogging toward the stage.

Could I bottle her scent somehow? Every step away from us took some of it away, and I'd already developed an addiction in the brief moments spent talking to her.

"All I want to do is go jack off for several hours straight, but Roxy is going to fire us if we don't get moving," Arata muttered, inclining his head toward the unimpressed omega club owner standing with her arms crossed and glaring at us across the room. "Let's get to it. That went well, right? I think it went well. In fact, I think we should see if she's interested in grabbing a drink when she's done with rehearsals with whoever she wants to bring along—friends, chaperones, whatever. Something real casual, no pressure, you know?"

"Yeah? You don't think that's too fast? What about Cole?"

"Ideally, I'd take him for a run first, tucker him out," Arata laughed. "It's not too fast—the worst that can happen is she says no, right? I know you like to over-analyze for several weeks before making a decision, but if we don't shoot our shot, we might be too late. We all like her. She seems at least a *little* interested in us. Let's take a chance."

"Okay," I agreed, blowing out a heavy sigh. It went against every one of my instincts to make a decision without thoroughly assessing the pros and cons first, but Arata was right. Bubbles was worth putting ourselves out there for. "As soon as she comes out of rehearsal, we'll see if she wants to grab a drink."

———————

After a full day of ripping out and replacing drywall, I had more than enough time to work myself into a full-blown panic about the idea of asking Bubbles out. We didn't even know her real name! Besides, we were covered in dust, and probably stunk. This was the stupidest idea Arata had ever had, on par with the time he'd insisted we buy Cole a trampoline for his birthday. The birthday boy had immediately decided to try jumping from the roof, breaking both the trampoline and his clavicle.

"You smell like a ball of stress," Arata groaned. "Please, *please*, attempt to chill out. Do you want to try Cole's breathing exercises?"

"No, I want to make a list and practice what I'm going to say," I muttered, taking a few deep breaths anyway. "You do all the talking, okay?"

Arata laughed. "I got you, you know by now that you don't have to ask."

That was true, I did know. My packmates weren't perfect, but in the more-than-a-decade that we'd been a bonded pack, I'd never had to talk on the phone or order food, because they all knew I hated it and would pick up the slack for me.

We were packing up our tools slower than strictly necessary. The guys we'd subcontracted for the industrial sized-fans and dehumidifiers were parked in front of the private exit the omegas normally used, which meant we could see the omegas trickle out from the backstage area through the main club, chatting to each other with their workout bags slung over their shoulders as they made their way to the stairs that led up to the foyer.

Come on, Bubbles. Where are you?

Pack Kennedy was going to show up at any moment to kick us out for loitering.

"Did we miss her?" Arata murmured, frowning as a couple of omegas disappeared into the stairwell, leaving the club empty.

"I don't think so. We really need to go before we get arrested for trespassing."

Arata snorted. "Your paranoia is showing."

"Your lack of paranoia is showing," I mumbled. Before he could reply, three alphas walked confidently into the empty club space. Dressed in *suits*. Adjusting watches. Slicking back styled hair without a speck of ceiling debris in it.

"Shit balls, is that the pack from New Year's Eve?" Arata hissed. I nodded glumly, shoving the rest of my stuff in my backpack and hitching it over my shoulder. There was no way the presence of the courting-gift pack here was a coincidence.

Whatever chemistry we'd had with Bubbles this morning was obviously just that. Chemistry.

A light trill of laughter from the backstage door caught our attention, and Arata and I stood there as silent spectators while Roxy emerged arm-in-arm with Bubbles. Bubbles, who definitely was not dressed in sweats with a workout bag slung over her shoulder like the other omegas had been.

No, Bubbles was in a skin-tight emerald dress with a slit up one thigh and thin straps that showed off her tanned shoulders, her hair pulled back loosely to expose the long line of her neck. Her face was fully done in makeup that she hadn't been wearing when we'd talked to her earlier.

Bubbles was dressed for a date.

A date with alphas who weren't us.

It was like Arata and I had blended into the wallpaper. Roxy enthusiastically dragged Bubbles towards the alphas, greeting them with familiarity, while Bubbles smiled, nodding along with what Roxy was saying. That delicious pre-heat gingerbread scent wafted our way as the group headed toward the stairs, leaving us standing in the dim corner of the club where we'd been packing up, covered in filth. I thought I caught a glimpse of Bubbles' glossy dark hair before she ascended the stairs, her head turning back to where we were standing, but then she was gone, leaving us alone in the silent club.

I knew I had a tendency to jump to the worst case scenario, and sometimes—often, even—those thoughts were disproportionately negative. In this situation, I was pretty confident they were warranted. Bubbles had definitely felt some kind of attraction to us—her scent didn't lie—but she'd *chosen* to go out with that other pack. Maybe she had an even stronger attraction to them. Maybe she liked that they were related to her bosses' pack, that they were obviously wealthy, and had given her an expensive necklace as a courting gift.

What were we bringing to the table aside from sexual chemistry? We didn't even have a finished nest at home. What were we thinking, even *trying* to get to know Bubbles?

"Well, fuck," Arata sighed, rubbing the back of his neck.

"Yeah. Fuck."

"It's just a date," he reasoned, ever the cool-headed one in our pack. "I mean, it might go terribly. Hopefully they're boring as shit and talk about the stock market or something the whole time. I'm not giving up hope," Arata finished decisively.

"Right," I said flatly, shoving the last of my tools away and yanking on my jacket.

"You're not giving up either," Arata instructed, giving me a pointed look. "Focus on the positives. Remember how well this morning went."

I wanted to argue, but Bubbles' warm smile when I'd totally botched our introduction this morning floated back into my head. Maybe I could be optimistic and hope her date was boring too.

But I'd still be picking up a pint of cookie dough ice cream on the way home to soften the blow for Cole.

CHAPTER 14

Pack Carmichael surprised me by choosing a little French bistro that was known for its delectable pastries and long waitlists.

I'd always wanted to come here, but the one time I'd tried to book a table, they'd only had an opening months from now. That was how popular this place was.

However, the second Caleb told the hostess their pack's name, we were led inside.

The restaurant was spectacular. From the outside, it didn't look like much, but no sooner had we entered it, it was like we'd been transported to a magical place.

Cast in shadows, most of the illumination at the bistro was due to candle lights over the table and in strategic places. Low, instrumental music played from somewhere, helping set the mood, but not loud enough to interrupt or disturb conversation. Each one of the dark wooden tables was set far enough apart to provide the diners plenty of privacy.

The hostess took us to a table at the farthest corner, giving me a knowing smile. Asher pulled out my chair for me, like a true gentleman. Caleb sat beside me while Asher and Connor sat at the other side of the table.

Roxy, true to her word, had come to chaperone with her pack, however, the hostess led them to a table far enough away that it would still seem like Pack Carmichael and I were alone for our date.

They really had thought of everything. My little omega heart was all happy at their attentiveness.

"Would you like some wine?" Caleb asked, looking up from the menu.

I smiled at him. He looked incredibly dashing in a dark-blue well-fitted suit and white button-up, with the first button open. Caleb didn't wear a tie, adding to the boyish look and showcasing just a little bit of skin.

Out of all three alphas, Caleb looked like the most easygoing, while Connor was the one that intimidated me the most. He was just so ... quiet. It was as if he was taking everything in, analyzing it, before any and every action.

Basically my polar opposite.

"Yeah, I'd love some!" I exclaimed, subtly wiping my palms on my dress and hoping it wouldn't stain.

I may or may not be a tad bit nervous about this date. I couldn't help feeling the pressure for it to go well. I absolutely could not afford to embarrass myself in front of them and my boss yet again.

I needed Pack Carmichael to like me.

"They have a delicious Bordeaux red that we usually get when we come here. Unless you'd prefer something else?" Asher offered. His dark eyes glowed in the candlelight, making him look just a tad bit dangerous. Contrary to Caleb, Asher's suit was gray—or maybe even black—and not only was his shirt completely buttoned, but he'd matched it with a black tie.

Bordeaux? Was that a grape? My knowledge of wine vintages was basically reserved for Cabernet Sauvignon and Tannat. Oh! And Sauvignon Blanc, though that was a white wine. That just about summed it all up. Not that I could tell the difference in the taste, just that those were the things I looked for in the labels along with the word "sweet."

"That's fine? Whatever you guys think is good is fine by me. I'm afraid I don't know much about wine," I admitted, shrugging. All red tasted the same, not that I was going to say that out loud. It was clear they knew their business. "Oh! Maybe just something not too dry?"

Caleb chuckled. "All right, then, Amy. One bottle of not-too-dry wine coming up." He winked at me to let me know he was just teasing and then ordered for us.

I watched in fascination as Caleb did the whole fancy wine routine I'd only ever seen in movies, before nodding in approval. Only once he'd done that did the waiter serve the rest of us.

This really was like being chucked into a whole new world.

I smiled at the waiter when he offered me a menu, thanking him.

"Everything looks so amazing. I can't decide what to order." I seriously wished I could have two stomachs so I could try everything.

The Carmichaels chuckled.

"Well, we wouldn't want to deprive you of anything good, so how about we just order everything that's appealing to you? There are four of us. I'm sure we can handle it," Caleb offered while Connor and Asher nodded their agreement.

I just stared at him. At all of them. They were giving me carte blanche to pick anything and everything. I absolutely had seen how pricey the stuff here was, and they were telling me to pick all the things?

Damn, Pack Carmichael really knew how to woo an omega.

I just hoped they wouldn't come to regret that decision.

The food had been even more impressive than what I'd expected, and that was saying a lot, because the reviews online *raved* about this place.

We'd barely talked as we ate our meal, mostly just complimenting how good it all was and enjoying the experience. It wasn't until the waiter took away our plates—Caleb had been right; we really had managed to eat it all—that the conversation started again.

"So, Amy, Nicole told us you're from Brazil?" Asher asked from across the table.

"Yeah. Kind of. I was technically born here, but I moved there when I was eleven and only came back last year." I shrugged, not wanting to go into detail about my big tragic story. "What about you guys?"

Caleb half-smiled. "Asher and I are from here. Connor's family is British, but he's been here since he was a kid, too. That's why he always sounds so posh."

"Oh! That's awesome. I love your accent," I told Connor. There was just something about a British accent that made a girl's ears super happy. I knew there was a multitude of varieties even amongst them, but any and all of them just did it for me.

I wasn't picky.

"Thank you. I like yours." He flashed me a seductive smile.

Yup. He was definitely the dangerous one.

"To amazing accents." Caleb raised his glass for a toast, and we all clinked our glasses.

"So, what do you guys do for a living?" I asked once I'd taken a sip of my wine.

Connor smiled at me as if pleased with my interest.

"Oh, we mostly invest in startups; give them what they need to really get going."

That was pretty vague. "Any company I might be familiar with?"

"Do you know the app, Nest Fest?" Asher asked, and my eyes widened.

"Yes! I love that game. I play it whenever I have a chance. It's seriously good!"

Caleb chuckled. "Well, I'm afraid we can't take credit for making the game; we just saw an idea we thought was good and chose to invest in it. But I'm glad you like the game."

The waiter brought our desserts, and just the smell made me salivate. The plate he placed in front of me was like a work of art. The mille-feuille had layers of puff pastry, raspberries, pastry cream, and chocolate drizzled all over it. Beautiful, delicious, and *all mine*.

I closed my eyes at the first taste, enjoying the explosion of flavors on my tongue.

Maybe I didn't need a pack to see me through

my heat. Maybe all I needed was a box full of this mille-feuille, and some macaroons.

"Never in my life have I caught myself wishing I was dessert before," Connor commented under his breath.

I opened my eyes to find all three alphas staring at me, gazes fixed on my mouth, pupils dilated.

Blushing, I looked down at my food.

Tonight had been fun. Pack Carmichael had kept the conversation flowing easily enough. They'd been thoughtful, attentive, and spoiled me all the way through.

And yet, I'd felt a stronger desire for a plate of sweets than I had for the alphas who were trying to woo me.

Even now, as Connor was clearly flirting, I couldn't reciprocate. There was none of the heat I'd felt the first time I'd met them, none of the attraction.

As the date went on, I'd been forced to acknowledge that maybe my initial reaction to them had been my pre-heat talking and nothing more.

And yet, here I was, still in pre-heat, but this time, I felt nothing. Why *didn't* I feel like before? What had changed?

Was it the fact Pack Knight had been added to the mix, smelling like Christmas and spice?

Pack Carmichael were nice, sweet, caring, well-off alphas looking for an omega to complete them. They should be everything I was looking for in a pack and more. But there was no thrill, no belly flutters, no chemistry.

They didn't make my heartbeat speed up the same way the two alphas from Pack Knight had.

I just wished I'd realized this before I'd agreed to go out with them. I would never have led them on if I'd known it was a lost cause. They were damn good alphas, and they deserved an omega who'd fully give themselves to them.

Unfortunately, though, I couldn't be that person.

Not only that, but Roxy was obviously invested in this pairing—she wouldn't have introduced me to them otherwise, or pushed me to let her give them my number—and I didn't want to raise her hopes just to crush them later. I didn't want to disappoint someone I saw as both a boss and a mentor of sorts.

The realization sat heavily in my stomach, almost ruining my appetite for the dessert.

"So," I started, wanting to change the subject to a safer topic. "I never really asked. What's your story?" We'd talked about music, books, and traveling, but hadn't touched on any deep topics.

At my deflection, Connor awkwardly looked down at his plate, and I winced internally.

I didn't want to be mean, but flirting would only lead them on, and that would be worse.

"Our story?" Caleb asked, tilting his head to the side.

I shrugged. "Yeah. You seem like a great pack. How come you're still unmated?"

The alphas exchanged a look, and Asher was the one to answer my question. "I suppose we were too focused on work and building something for ourselves. We always assumed a relationship would come later. Then one day, we stopped and realized we'd basically married our work rather than mated an omega like we'd originally planned, and it felt ... lonely."

"All our achievements and money meant nothing when we had no one to spend them with. No one to spoil or lavish with gifts. Now we're back in the swing of dating, so to speak, but it feels like we missed our moment," Caleb continued, grimacing.

"Just a little too old, or a little too wrong. We've traveled enough with work, seen the world, and now all we want is to settle down, honestly. Then my sister told us about you, saying how she'd found a perfect match for us, and we couldn't help getting our hopes up. It's why we were so bold by giving you a courting gift when we met." Then he paused, flashing me a smile. "No pressure or anything. But you should know this is what we're hoping for. We're willing to go as slow or as fast as you want, if you want. Set your own pace. But we're definitely interested. What do you say, Amy?"

I blinked at him, feeling more than a little overwhelmed.

We'd literally only met, and they were already talking about forever? I knew some packs liked to move fast, but just. Wow.

I had not seen this one coming at all.

"I. Erh... As slow or fast as I want?" I sounded about as panicked as I felt.

I seriously regretted all the food I'd just eaten, that was for sure.

After an awkward goodbye to Pack Carmichael, I entered Pack Kennedy's car so they could drive me home. Part of the whole chaperoning deal was that they had driven me to the restaurant and would be the ones to see me home. It wouldn't do for an unmated pack to learn where the omega they were courting lived. At least not for a few dates. I was also not supposed to be alone with them until I made up my mind on whether I wanted to take the courtship further or not, as a protective measure to avoid unwanted bite marks.

There had been cases of packs with not-so-good intentions who'd asked an omega out on dubious terms and mated them against their will. Not that I thought Pack Carmichael would ever do that, but following protocol cost me nothing.

Besides, things had been quite awkward near the end, after my realization that we might not be a good fit, and their statement that they thought otherwise.

I should be elated, but I just felt sick to my stomach.

Even with my lukewarm reaction, they hadn't seemed discouraged. In fact, they'd assured me I could take as much time to think things over as I wanted to.

They were really, *really* nice alphas.

"Oh, Amy, how marvelous!" Roxy bumped my shoulder with hers, all but vibrating with excitement. "I'm so happy for you. I knew you'd hit it off right away, and you all look so good together."

Oh no.

"And just in time for your heat, too! Absolutely *nothing* beats heat sex." Roxy half-whispered, conspiratorially, not giving me time to properly form an answer to any of this. All I could do was sit there, blushing and wishing her pack wasn't hearing any of this. "You'll see! Don't worry, though. You don't have to mate them before the heat. You *could* and *should* make them work for it; maybe have them help you out and only mate them once your heat is over. Take them off for a spin, so to speak. It'll help you make a level-headed decision that won't be overshadowed by hormones."

I wasn't a prude, not by a long shot. I mean, I worked at a strip club and made alphas horny for a living, for goodness' sake. I was an omega, too, which meant sex was definitely one of the biggest things on my mind at any given time. And yet, hearing my boss so casually tell me to take her brother and his pack for a "spin" was making me blush so badly, I probably resembled a lobster. Somehow, this was worse than when Aunt Raquel had sat me down for my first sex talk as a teenager.

Maybe because Aunt Raquel was a doctor and she'd made it all sound very clinical and natural.

Justin chuckled. "Sweetheart, you're embarrassing her," he said from the passenger seat, and I flashed him a grateful smile. "We know you're excited, but this needs to be Amy's decision. She's young. She should meet a few different packs, and see which one appeals to her more. Don't think we've forgotten how long you held us off before you finally admitted we were the perfect pack for you." The light admonishment held nothing but love and affection towards their omega, and it made my heart feel all happy and full for them.

Beside me, Roxy sighed. "I know. I know. You're right. I'm sorry, Amy," she told me, her green eyes serious. "I just get excited about these things, and seeing my brother's pack finally courting someone who I know would be good for them makes it so hard for me to be objective! I won't speak any more of this, promise. Unless you want me to. And if you do decide to shop around with other packs and need us to chaperone you again, we'll do it. I know you don't have family nearby to chaperone, and we don't mind filling in."

Then she mimed zipping her lips and throwing away the key.

"Thank you," I told her honestly. "And thank you for agreeing to chaperone me. I know how busy your schedule is."

Roxy waved my words off. "Oh, don't worry. This was fun! We love a chance to go out and eat well. Besides, now that the club closed down for renovations, we have a lot more time on our hands."

The club's renovations were in full swing, with all the snow cleared off the roof and giant fans all around the place to dry out the bar area. Something about water damage and light fixings.

I was just grateful we were able to keep rehearsals going, because it meant we'd still get paid, even if we wouldn't be making the extra in tips. And since, for some reason, I'd never been one to make much from tips anyway, it didn't make that big a difference for me. Some of the other omegas had complained, but all it had taken was one gentle reminder from Roxy that it was either come for rehearsal and get paid, or close the club altogether, and they'd suddenly agreed this was for the best.

I'd take advantage of this opportunity to focus on practicing even more, and if I made some moon eyes at a certain pack that always wore jeans, tight shirts, and tool belts to gather new finger vault material, well, nobody could blame me for it.

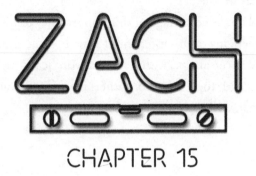

CHAPTER 15

"Okay, I need you all to get your heads in the game," Cole announced, pacing back and forth in the kitchen while the rest of us sat at the breakfast nook, observing him with various degrees of amusement and/or frustration.

Safe to say, Cole had *not* taken the news that Bubbles was out on a date right now with Pack Early Courting Gift well. Not even the cookie dough ice cream had soothed his ire. He'd gone to dramatically throw it in the garbage, before changing his mind and shoving it in the freezer instead.

"I don't want to point fingers, but this is all of your faults," Cole continued.

Kaito rolled his eyes.

"*I* haven't met Bubbles yet! All three of you have! We'd be halfway to mated by now if you'd put me on the Allure job, but nooooo. I'm stuck at the Hayes' house, redoing a bathroom, while all of you met Bubbles and *didn't* ask her out."

I glanced at Arata to see if he was going to do one of his calming-yet-motivational pep talks, but he took a swig of his beer and shrugged a shoulder at me, letting Cole get it out of his system. Cole was a great packmate, and I loved him like a brother, but he was garbage at handling disappointment.

And we were *all* disappointed. Arata was trying to remain optimistic, and I was doing my best to hold on to that good feeling I'd had when I talked to Bubbles this morning, but Kaito looked like he'd given up hope altogether—if he'd ever had any.

Where was Bubbles now? Had they gone out to dinner? Maybe a show? She had been super dressed up. Was she home by now? Would she go home tonight?

For all we knew, the next time we saw Bubbles, she could have a mating mark on her neck.

"We need to debrief and make a game plan," Cole insisted, vacillating between blame and action.

"We've already debriefed," Kaito snapped. Oh good, now they were going to be at each other's throats on top of our existential crisis.

"Don't you start," Cole ordered, pointing his beer bottle at Kaito. "You're at the top of my shit list. You met Bubbles first and then just wandered off to do business boy shit instead of asking her out like you should have."

"Business boy shit?" Kaito repeated incredulously.

"I said what I said."

"None of you would have met Bubbles if it wasn't for my *business boy shit*," Kaito grumbled under his breath. Fair point.

"*Debrief,*" Cole insisted, ignoring him. Arata shook with silent laughter, shaking his head. "What do we know about Bubbles?"

I sighed heavily, twisting the bottle I was holding between my hands. "She's really kind. Her Aunt Lu is a beta who played professional beach volleyball in Brazil. She likes sparkly scrunchies and the glittery dance costumes she gets to wear. She loved dancing with the other omegas in the Christmas show. She smells like gingerbread and sin."

"I *thought* my first conversation with her went really well," Arata added, looking contemplative. "But then she seemed to think I was in a bad mood? So now I'm not sure."

"She got an expensive courting gift from the pack who she's probably still with right now, at some swanky restaurant with a waitlist a mile long. The pack who is related to her boss," Kaito said flatly.

"Forget about them," Cole replied impatiently. "They only met for the first time on New Year's Eve, that means this is probably their first date, which means *there's still a chance*. I bet Bubbles doesn't care about things like fancy restaurants."

"You're basing that on nothing but naive hope,"

Kaito shot back.

"I thought you *wanted* an omega. Why are you determined to be so miserable about this?" Cole challenged, slamming his beer down on the counter a little harder than necessary.

Welp, here we go again. Kaito had always been our undisputed pack leader, and it was normal for a pack to test their leader occasionally to make sure they were meeting expectations, but nobody tested Kaito like Cole did. It was probably the universe's way of balancing the fact that Arata lived in a perpetual state of relaxation, and I had a mostly healthy aversion to confrontation.

"I don't want my pack to get hurt." Kaito set his drink down, standing up and bracing his hands on the table, pinning Cole with the full force of his alpha glare.

Cole's muscles flexed, a hint of a growl escaping, though not enough to be considered an actual challenge. Kaito's eyes flashed dangerously, and I rested my forehead on the table with a groan. They hadn't actually come to blows since the twins' twenty-first birthday, but a dominance fight was always a possibility.

"Put your dicks away," Arata laughed, clapping me on the back and encouraging me to sit up. "Kaito, you know you want an omega, and you know that there's always a risk of getting hurt when we put ourselves out there. You can't protect us from our own feelings."

Cole blew out a breath, some of the tension in his posture dissipating. Deep down, he knew Arata was right—Kaito was just looking out for us, in his surly, overbearing way.

"If you put me on the Allure job, I'll ask Bubbles out tomorrow," Cole suggested hopefully.

Kaito sat down slowly, shaking his head. "Even if I wanted to—which I don't, because it was difficult fitting the Allure job into the schedule and everything is running tight right now—I have to get sign off from Pack Kennedy for all alphas working on-site. I'll send them your information, Cole, but I doubt they'll have time to review it before tomorrow."

"Ugh, fine," Cole groaned, pulling open the top drawer and grabbing a pad and pen. "I'm going to write a speech, and you are all going to carry a copy in your pocket at all times. Whoever sees Bubbles next is in charge of delivering said speech, asking her out for dinner at that new Brazilian restaurant."

"Or risk having all their saved games deleted," Arata added, looking around our group with a mischievous twinkle in his eye.

"That's harsh, A, and I like it." Cole gave him a mock salute. "Okay, here we go. Dear Bubbles..."

———

"What do you mean, you're not coming with

me?" I asked Arata as he slid a to-go cup of coffee across the kitchen island for me. Kaito and Cole had already left for the day, and I'd assumed that Arata and I were heading over to Allure together like we had every other day since we'd started the project.

"Relax, Z. I just need to do a supply run across town, it won't take long. We'll go in separate vehicles, and I'll meet you at the club by noon."

"I could just come with you?" I suggested, my panic ratcheting up as Arata pocketed one of the notes Cole had written, handing me the other.

"Nope, one of us has to be on-site to manage the subcontractors—Pack Kennedy's rules. And Kaito's," he added. All of the alpha subcontractors we were using had to be mated, too, as per Pack Kennedy's rules. They were definitely making exceptions for us. "You'll be *fine*. Bubbles went on a date last night. What are the odds she'll be in at the crack of dawn to rehearse? And even if she is, you have a script." He tucked the paper into the chest pocket of my jacket, patting it twice with an unrepentant grin on his face.

"Arata," I warned, giving him my sternest 'this is a bad idea' face. "I *will* screw this up. I'll forget how to read, or throw up, or maybe just pass out and hit my head on the floor—"

"You've never passed out from nerves, and you haven't had a panic puke in *years*. And you're not going to forget how to *read*." He gave me an indulgent look. "But if it's too much, don't worry about it, I'll just read her the letter when I see her instead, okay? I won't even delete your games." He paused, looking thoughtful. "Cole might."

"Helpful," I muttered, grabbing my coffee and heading to the door to pull on the rest of my winter gear before heading to the van.

This is fine. I'm going to be fine, I told myself on repeat as I drove, blasting my most motivational rap playlist for courage and checking my pocket to make sure the note was still in there at every intersection. *Why,* today, of all days, did I have to go in on my own?

I'd be annoyed if Cole deleted all my saved games, but that wasn't what was truly bothering me. I just didn't want to let my pack down.

The moment I parked in the alleyway and jumped out of the van, my phone started buzzing in the pocket of my work pants. I accepted the call, tucking the device between my face and shoulder so I could carry in my equipment, glad I didn't have to store it in the locker while we were working here. It had taken some pushing from Kaito to get Pack Kennedy to allow it, but everything would take us twice as long if we didn't have our phones.

"Hey, Cole," I greeted while nodding at the Allure security manning the door today. "What's up?"

"Have you seen Bubbles yet? I called Arata and he said you were there on your own."

"I literally just walked in the door, give me a minute," I scoffed, setting down my stuff in the usual corner I'd commandeered and taking a look around the place at all the work yet to be done. All the big fans had been taken away last night, and it was eerily quiet compared to how loud it had been the rest of the time I'd been on-site here.

"You've already called Arata and me this morning? How much coffee have you had?" My one cup was definitely feeling insufficient.

"I called Kaito too, but he's stopped answering because all I do is ask him about getting onto the Allure job. But that's what voice messages are for," he added in a singsong voice.

Cole sounded smug, but I was ninety percent sure Kaito wasn't listening to any of those voice messages.

"If you want to be here so bad, shouldn't you be busy, you know, working? Finishing up at the Hayes' place?"

"Don't you worry about me. I am *ahead* of schedule," Cole replied smugly. "And Mrs. Hayes made me orange snickerdoodles, so I know she loves me and thinks I'm doing a great job."

I snorted, having worked for Mr. and Mrs. Hayes before. They were an aging beta couple, slowly renovating different areas of their beloved home to make them more accessible as they needed them.

Cole was working on the bathrooms, but I'd done the front and back porch last summer and gained three pounds in cookie weight.

"I know full well that Mrs. Hayes is only feeding you under the misguided impression that alphas need to eat more often than betas."

"We do," Cole agreed, because he always ate like he was on the verge of going into hibernation for the winter.

"We don't. You're just taking advantage of the cookies—"

My words failed as I caught a whiff of gingerbread. No. Surely not. It was still *dark* out; there was no way Bubbles could be here already.

"Helloooooooooo," Cole asked. "Earth to Zach. Where'd you go?"

The gingerbread scent was growing stronger. And without the hum of the fans in the background, there was no disguising the light sound of footsteps either.

"Bubbles is here," I whispered, gripping the phone a little tighter as my palms started to sweat.

"Speech time!" Cole replied excitedly. "Put the phone down so I can listen."

"What? No, you weirdo—Oh, hey! Bubbles," I stammered, turning around the moment I felt her gaze on me. I aimed my thumb blindly for the 'end call' icon, shoving the phone into my pocket.

"Hi-lo Zach," Bubbles said brightly, rocking back and forth in her bright white sneakers, eyebrows shooting up in surprise. Probably because I'd identified her by scent before even looking at her, and had completely forgotten to play cool about it.

It was cold in here today, and she was wearing thick cream leg warmers over her dark leggings, with an oversized cream sweater that made her look like an adorable marshmallow. Especially with the pale pink beanie, complete with pompom, that she was tugging down over her ears.

"Hi-lo Bubbles," I replied softly, some of my nerves fading now that I had my eyes on her. Something about her presence was just so soothing. Weirdly, for a moment, I was glad I was alone. That Bubbles and I had formed a little greeting that was just our own. It made me feel... seen, somehow.

"How are you?"

"Me? Oh, uh, I'm good. How are you?" I asked. *Cool, calm, totally got this. I am under control.*

"Oh good! That's great! I'm good too, thanks! How about you? Oh wait, I just asked you that. Sorry." Bubbles winced, and I forced my hands to stay at my sides instead of reaching out to comfort her. Boundaries. Boundaries were important.

"That's okay. It's pretty early, I need at least one more coffee before I can make real conversation," I joked. That was a lie; all the caffeine in the world wouldn't make me a conversationalist.

"It is super early," Bubbles agreed. Were her cheeks a little flushed? It was hard to tell with her hair down and her hat pulled on tight, but it kind of seemed like she was blushing. "I, er, wanted to get a head start on rehearsing."

"That's cool. You're obviously really dedicated to dancing, that's awesome." I swallowed thickly, a pause extending on longer than what was probably comfortable as I dug deep for the courage that I hoped existed way down inside me. "So, um, I wanted to ask you something."

My one coffee churned uneasily in my gut, but I forced myself to keep my gaze on Bubbles, because despite being the reason for my nerves, she soothed them at the same time with her presence.

"Oh, sure. What's up?"

Damn it, I should have memorized the speech.

"Uh, my packmate wrote down what I'm supposed to say." I fumbled with my jacket pocket, pulling out the paper and unfolding it.

"Dear Bubbles." I cleared my throat. "How have you been?" *Oh my god, this was stupid. I feel stupid.*

"I hope we're not overstepping by saying this, but our pack has been captivated by you—" *Did Cole break out the thesaurus for this? He totally did.* "—since we first saw you. Pack Knight would love to take you out on a date. If you're open to it, of course. We'd love to get to know you, and for you to get to know us. Honestly, we'd like to court you, if you're okay with it. But if not, no pressure. Maybe we could just hang out and see where things go? If so, we wondered if you'd like to join us for dinner at the *Braz*, it's a Brazilian restaurant near here, which we hope will give you a little taste from home. Or it could be somewhere else, too, whatever you want. What do you say?"

Why was Cole like this? Why was *I* like this? I should have at least read the note beforehand, so I knew what I was in for.

Or better yet, ditched the note and just came up with a speech on the fly. Except I'd never been able to do that, so I don't know why I was even entertaining the thought.

"You're inviting me ... on a date?" Bubbles clarified, her eyebrows raised. She was probably confused by all of the unnecessary words Cole had jammed in that speech.

"Yes. A date." I shoved the piece of paper back in my pocket, making a note to ceremonially burn it later.

"I'd love to!" Bubbles said, with enough excitement that I immediately stopped planning the note-burning bonfire in my head. "But—"

No. Please no. No buts.

"—would it be okay if Pack Kennedy chaperoned us? Just, you know, to follow the rules and all? I could see if they're free tonight, if that's not too soon?" she added with a nervous laugh.

Right. Single omegas weren't in the habit of going on dates with alpha packs alone. Still, she wanted to go out *tonight*. That had to be a good sign.

"Of course. We can pick you up from here if you like?" I asked, remembering the way the other pack had showed up yesterday to get her. We cóuld totally do that. Be all ... gentlemanly, and such.

"Oh, no, it's okay. Pack Kennedy will probably want to drive me, so we could just meet there?" Bubbles sounded apologetic.

"That's totally fine," I assured her. She probably wouldn't want to drive around in one of our branded company vehicles anyway. I told her the restaurant address, and we agreed to meet at seven. *Shit.* Would we have enough time to make a reservation? I should have thought about that before agreeing to tonight. What if they were fully booked for seven o'clock? What if they were fully booked *all night*? It was a Friday, for fuck's sake. What had I been *thinking*?

"So I'll see you tonight?" Bubbles said, shooting me a smile so bright that my internal panic dimmed for a moment.

"Great, yeah. Yep," I added, popping the 'p.' *Why am I like this?* "We'll see you tonight, Bubbles."

"Amy," she corrected shyly. "I mean, we're going out to dinner, you should at least know my real name."

Amy. It suited her. As much as I loved her stage name, there was an immediate sense of intimacy in knowing her *real* name.

"Amy," I repeated gently. "We'll see you later."

She gave me a short wave, walking backwards for a few steps before turning and heading toward the still-empty stage area. I blew out a quiet breath, closing my eyes for a moment. I'd done it. I'd asked Amy out.

We were going on a date with her, and hopefully, we wouldn't entirely screw it up.

Okay, first things first. Book a table.

I pulled out my phone, intending to pull up the restaurant's website, my eyes widening when I realized I was in the middle of a phone call.

"Cole?" I hissed, pressing the phone to my ear. "Did you just eavesdrop on that whole conversation? What is wrong with you?"

"What is wrong with me? What is wrong with *you*? If you didn't want me to eavesdrop, you should've hung up the phone!" he countered. "Anyway, that is irrelevant. I'm messaging the group chat right now so everyone knows that it's happening. It. Is. Happening. Hey, should we get her a first date courting gift? Like that other pack? I'll ask in the group chat." He paused for a moment, finally taking a breath. "Arata said no with a bunch of exclamation points. Maybe I should buy one, just in case..."

"You definitely shouldn't," I replied instantly. "That is so weird and presumptuous. She hasn't even *met* the whole pack yet."

"And whose fault is that?" Cole grumbled before falling silent for a moment. "Oh weird, I tried to book a table at the restaurant, but I couldn't find a booking button for some reason. Never mind, I'll look again later. Right, what are we going to wear? Nothing *too* fancy—"

"What do you mean there was no booking button?" I slumped against the wall, hoping Pack Kennedy wasn't watching from some camera room somewhere, noticing how unproductive I'd been this morning. "Maybe we should pick somewhere else. Somewhere a bit fancier—"

"This isn't about being *fancy*; it's about giving Bubbles—Amy—an authentic taste of home, which is way more meaningful than just some generic fancy restaurant."

Okay. Okay, that was solid logic, even though I couldn't help but remember Amy leaving for her date last night and how dressed up they'd all been. I should have asked her if she'd enjoyed her date, except then maybe I'd have come across like a creepy stalker. Or would I? Was it bad manners that I *didn't* ask?

"Don't you freak out on me now, Zachary Knight," Cole warned, sounding alarmingly like Kaito when he did his serious voice. "We all like Amy. We all want to get to know her, and maybe— just maybe—she wants to get to know us too. This is our opportunity."

"Right. No, I know. It's just that ... don't you think it's a little risky to take a Brazilian to a Brazilian restaurant? What if the food sucks?"

"What? No way, there was a whole blog post raving about it. It'll be fine! I'm hanging up now. The group chat is going wild. Apparently Kaito *can* respond to my messages when he wants to," Cole snorted. "It's going to be fine, Zach. It's going to be *amazing*. We'll all be declaring our love for one another by the end of the night, you'll see."

CHAPTER 16

Zach was *super* cute.

And not just because of the slightly long dark hair, short, well-maintained beard, and those dazzling blue eyes that were so gorgeous, they didn't look real.

Those were very nice bonuses, but the main thing that pulled at my heartstrings was just how adorably awkward he was.

I just wanted to put him in my pocket and carry him everywhere. It was a pity he was so damn tall; otherwise, I might just see if I could lift him.

He'd carried around a *letter*. Well, not really a letter; it had been more of a script another one of his packmates had written so he could ask me out. Just how cute was that?

Feeling like a million bucks, I all but skipped as I went backstage, through the omega-only area, heading towards Roxy's office.

I'd only met two members of Pack Knight,

and while Arata sometimes confused me with his mood switches, Zach was always endearing. And both of them smelled good enough to eat. Just one sniff of Zach's caramelized cashews scent or Arata's cinnamon apple scent were enough to speed up my heart rate and make my panties go damp.

So much so, I'd taken to wearing the pre-heat pads at all times. There was only so much washing I could do before I ruined all my underwear.

If the other alphas—or alpha, for all I knew, there was only one more—of Pack Knight were as sexy and amazing as Arata and Zach, I was pretty sure I'd proposition them to help me with my heat.

Ideally, the alphas would be the ones to initiate that type of thing, but that didn't mean an omega couldn't. So long as I made it clear from the start I wasn't ready to mate and I wasn't sure I would be anytime soon, it should be fine.

If they agreed, I'd bounce *so good* on their knots over and over while inhaling their delicious scents until I was high on their alpha pheromones.

But I was getting ahead of myself. First, I had to talk to Roxy, ask her to chaperone our date, and actually *meet* the entire pack.

I skidded to a halt in front of Roxy's office, and just stood there, suddenly feeling awkward.

This felt weird. Like, really freaking weird. As excited as I was about the idea of the date—and could I just take a moment to appreciate the fact that there was not one, but *two* packs interested in me—I didn't want to mess things up with my boss.

Because as friendly as Roxy might be, here, she *was* my boss. Pack Kennedy owned Allure, and Roxy had been the one to hire me. I didn't want to jeopardize my relationship with her.

Not that I thought she'd do that. Technically, she'd been the one to tell me I should "shop around" with other packs. She'd also volunteered to chaperone me on future dates if I wanted.

That didn't mean she would've expected me to actually take her up on the offer, though.

I wrung my hands, bit my bottom lip, and stared at the black door as if it would tell me what to do.

Should I try to find another chaperone? No. There were no other options. I had no family here, and I didn't know a lot of mated packs who could play chaperone. I supposed I could always try to see if Jason's pack could do it, but I only knew Jason himself, and while he was friendly, they had a bunch of kids, which probably made it hard for them to have a night out to chaperone me. I definitely should've thought about this before I suggested we go out tonight, but Zach's shy half-smile had messed up my brain.

Roxy may have introduced me to Pack

Carmichael and hoped I would mate them, but that didn't mean I had to.

I may have given Pack Carmichael a shot, but a date wasn't a promise of forever. Just because I'd accepted their courting gift and gone out with them, it didn't mean I was required to take things further. Not to mention, we'd only gone out *once*, and while Roxy and I had varying opinions on how the date went, it didn't mean I had to commit to anything.

The truth was, I didn't think we'd be a good fit at all. Not that there was anything wrong with Pack Carmichael, but if I was going to one day mate with a pack, I didn't *just* want them to be nice people. I needed there to be chemistry. I needed them to make my blood boil and my vagina sing.

I didn't know if Pack Knight would be that for me—though they definitely made me horny enough that I needed pre-heat pads, and we hadn't even gone out yet—but I knew for sure Pack Carmichael wasn't.

You're not doing anything wrong, Amy. She offered. Just knock on her door and get this over with. You need time to go home and get ready.

It's going to be fine. Chin up.

I raised my hand to knock on the door, but it opened before I could.

Roxy's green eyes widened in surprise, and I quickly dropped my hand before it connected with her face.

"Bubbles?"

"Roxy, hi," I squeaked, blushing.

"Hello," she smirked as if amused by me. "Do you want to come in? I assume you want to talk?" Roxy asked, stepping back slightly to let me in.

"Oh, no, it's okay. You were on your way out, right? I can come back later!" I offered, still just awkwardly standing right outside her office.

I actually couldn't wait and did, in fact, need to talk to her now, but I was trying to be polite.

"Nonsense," Roxy replied, "Come on in and close the door behind you. Would you like something to drink?" she offered, heading to a white mini fridge and opening it to show me the options.

"Oh, some water would be nice, thank you." I finally entered, closing the door behind me.

Roxy's office was as soft and feminine as the omega herself. Pale gray walls, white furniture, with splashes of gold or pastel pink here and there for color. On her desk, there was a crystal vase with fresh pink roses, and the wall behind it was covered with pictures, most of herself dancing.

The mini fridge was installed on a cupboard that went from wall to wall, connecting the office area to a small but cozy sitting room with a couch and a couple of chairs.

When she turned and saw I was still trying to figure out where I was supposed to go, she smiled. "I assume this isn't a work talk? If not, then why don't we sit over there?" She gestured towards one of the beige armchairs. Sitting on it was like being hugged by a cloud; it was that soft.

Roxy gave me a bottle of water on her way to the couch.

"Thanks."

I watched as she sat on the couch, crossing her legs. She flung her red hair over her shoulder and, keeping her posture straight, linked her fingers above her legs. Her every move was well-mannered and effortless, making her look like a queen. Or maybe a prima ballerina.

"So, what did you want to talk about?" she asked, flashing me a smile. "Is this about Pack Carmichael? Do you want me to tell you more about them? I'll be happy to answer any questions you have, but just know that you could also text or call them, and they could tell you everything themselves. They really were quite taken by you, you know."

Oh, I absolutely should not have come to ask her what I was about to. Hindsight and all that.

Too late for that, Amy. Time's ticking.

"No, erh. It's not about Pack Carmichael." I gave her an apologetic smile. "Actually, I was wondering if your offer to chaperone was still on the table?" I nervously played with the bottle in my hands, wishing I'd sipped some before I started talking. My throat was dry, and my belly was staging a protest that had me regretting all my life choices.

I was pretty sure my scent was all over the place, too, a clear sign of my nerves, but Roxy was polite enough not to mention it.

At my question, though, her eyebrows rose and she pressed her lips together. "Of course!"

Even I could tell the enthusiasm was a little forced. But then, I really should've expected it. It didn't matter, though. Roxy was a great omega, and I knew I could trust her, even if she might disapprove of some of my choices.

"Who is the lucky pack? Anyone I know? Or have you been giving those dating apps a chance like some of the other omegas around here? I know Henry swears by one of them. Heat something, he says it's the best way to find partners to help him with his heat without having to worry about the bite."

"No, I haven't really met anyone on dating apps. It's actually Pack Knight. They were the ones to ask me out."

Roxy frowned. "Pack Knight?" Then a light seemed to dawn on her because she stared at me like I'd grown a second head. "You mean the help?"

I bit my tongue so I wouldn't point out I was technically the help, too, if she was going to put things that way.

She's just trying to look out for you, Amy. She

doesn't mean to sound so judgmental.

"The contractors who are doing the renovations here at the club, yes," I gently corrected.

Roxy was still staring at me as if I'd just told her I wanted to put on a banana costume for my solo dance at the great reopening show.

"Are you sure you want to let them court you? They might not be able to provide you the type of life an omega deserves."

"Yeah, I want to get to know them. They seem really nice." And hot, and they smelled amazing.

"I mean ... sure. Okay, if that's what you want, then, of course we will chaperone you. When is the date and where?"

"Thank you so much! And I'm sorry if this puts you in an awkward position, but I remembered your offer and, well. I trust you." My smile was so big it hurt my cheeks a bit. "It's tonight. Seven pm, at Braz. They chose a Brazilian restaurant so I could have a taste of home." Just how adorable was that? I had never gone to Braz before, but they'd been spot on in guessing I missed the food from home. Usually, when I had enough time, I could cook some of the things, but there were some pastries and dishes that were too much of a hassle to cook for myself. I hoped they had some of those.

Roxy was still frowning. "Tonight? They didn't give you a lot of time to get ready, did they?"

I stared down at the unopened bottle in my hands, fidgeting. "It's fine. I was actually the one to suggest we go tonight. It was an open invitation of sorts." I admitted, avoiding her disapproving gaze.

"An open invitation for a date as a way to start courting an omega? How ... *cute*."

"Is it still okay? If you and your pack had plans, I'm sure I can talk to Pack Knight and reschedule," I offered, realizing I wasn't the only one who would have little time to get ready.

I also didn't have their number, but maybe they were still around here somewhere.

"No, it's fine. Seven, right? We'll pick you up in front of your building at six-thirty, then. I'll call my alphas and let them know."

I got up. "Thank you. Seriously. I can't thank you enough. Not only for this but for everything you've done for me and all the other omegas here. We're lucky to work at Allure."

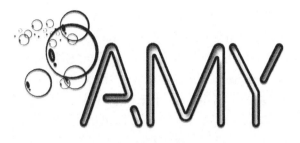

AMY

CHAPTER 17

"Hi! Thanks for doing this!" I said, sliding into the backseat of Pack Kennedy's expensive SUV and closing the door behind me.

"No worries. We didn't really have any plans for tonight, and we're all curious about trying Brazilian food," Justin answered from the driver's seat, smiling at me.

Justin and Sean were my favorite alphas out of Roxy's pack. They tended to be more easygoing and smiley than both Curtis and Lorne.

Luck was on my side, too, because since there were five people in Pack Kennedy who were chaperoning me, Alphas Curtis and Lorne were in the other car tonight. That meant Roxy and I had the backseat to ourselves, with Sean and Justin in the front.

They'd done the same when they'd chaperoned my date with Pack Carmichael. I should probably bake something for them to say thank you.

Beside me, Roxy tilted her head closer, took

one sniff, and wrinkled her nose, frowning.

I had to resist the urge to lower my own head and smell myself. I was absolutely not stinky, though. I'd only just had a shower. Maybe she was reacting to my scent? Usually, another omega's scent could be quite unpleasant for us, but working at a place filled with other omegas, I'd learned to just breathe through my mouth and tune out most of it.

"Amy, when is your next heat?" Roxy asked, her face still scrunched up like she'd smelled something sour.

"Not for another month, at least. My last one happened right before I started at Allure." I could say the exact date and time it started, too, because it had been hell. My first few heats had only lasted a couple of days and been easily handled with an assortment of toys, but the one right after my twenty-third birthday? It had lasted a week, and it had been *painful*. No amount of silicone toys or finger rubbing had been able to quench my need, and I was pretty sure the only reason I hadn't gone out to find the first available alpha to knot me was the fact I'd been sequestered away at one of the heat centers. They were dedicated places that provided a haven for omegas who chose to go through their heat solo. Padded, soundproof walls, locked windows, and locked doors with an en suite bathroom. Each unit had its own well-stocked kitchen and supplies, and only omegas were allowed inside the whole building. Another layer of security and a way to ensure we would go through our heat solo. Sometimes, depending on how bad one's heat was, things could get ... hazy.

Once we went in, we were only allowed out again when our heat was well and truly over. It seemed barbaric, but it wasn't. It was the safest way to get through it without accidentally being mated. Or worse, being forced into a pack bond against our will.

If things didn't go well with Pack Knight today, I'd have to either consider asking Pack Carmichael for help or finally cave and book a room at the nearest heat center. I couldn't put it off much longer, either, or I'd risk not finding an empty unit.

That would be much, much worse.

"A month? Are you absolutely certain? You've been going through pre-heat since New Year's Eve, haven't you? Is it possible you miscalculated?" Roxy asked, still frowning at me. From the rearview mirror, I could see even Justin was frowning.

Embarrassed, I stared down at my lap and played with the buttons of my heavy winter coat. "Yeah, I'm sure. My pre-heat tends to come a lot earlier than most. It should settle in a couple more years, though. At least, that's what the doctors said." Aunt Raquel had taken the time to explain that an omega's first heats could be a little irregular, and the lead-up to them could vary, too. It all depended on a lot of things, including our specific hormonal balance and even whether we went through the heats solo or bonded. She'd also cautioned me that my mother had gone through much of the same, and only after she'd taken her mates had things settled for her.

Roxy didn't seem convinced, but she let the matter drop, and I was grateful for that.

Instead, we drove the rest of the way to the restaurant in silence.

———

"They're late. What kind of alphas are late for their first date with an omega they're trying to court? Are we just supposed to stand outside and wait for them? In this cold?" Roxy glanced around us, her gaze filled with disgust as she bundled up even more in her pastel pink trench coat. Hearing the distress in her voice and seeing her shiver, her alphas crowded in around her, forming a physical barrier as if that would keep the wind and snow from their omega.

I shivered in my puffy purple winter gear, my hands deep in my pockets, wishing I'd remembered to put on a scarf.

The cold wind was killer on my throat.

I liked snow. No, I *loved* snow. It was pretty and fluffy and made me think of all the Christmas movies I'd seen growing up.

However, I'd spent the last ten years in a tropical place where the coldest recorded temperature had been like sixty-four degrees Fahrenheit. I wasn't used to feeling like a human popsicle. I loved winter and snow, but I loved them from inside my apartment, with the heater full blast and a warm cup of tea. Actually being outside in the middle of it all was nonsense.

"Should we go inside and wait for them there, then?" Curtis suggested, just as one of those big tourist buses stopped in front of the restaurant and a group of betas talking animatedly stepped out, entering the very same restaurant we were standing in front of.

Oh no. Pack Knight had chosen a tourist trap for our first date.

I could tell Roxy was thinking the same thing because she gave me a pointed look, eyebrows raised as if to say, "I told you so".

I pretended I hadn't seen, choosing instead to watch the betas rush into the place so they could escape the freezing cold. They spoke a mix of different languages, but when I caught some of them speaking in Portuguese, I smiled, wondering which part of Brazil they were from.

Well, if there were Brazilians coming here, then the food should be good, right? If this was a steakhouse, like most of the Brazilian restaurants here seemed to be, then even that big a number of clients shouldn't be a problem. They probably had reserved half the place, sure, but it was all-you-could-eat meat, and so long as we sat closer to the kitchen and, therefore, to where the servers would be coming out of with the steak on skewers, it wouldn't make a difference.

I hadn't been to a steakhouse in *years*, really, so that was even more exciting. Granted, the fact Pack Knight was running late was far from ideal, but I was sure they had a good reason for it. Maybe one of them had gotten sick?

Or maybe they'd been stuck in traffic or something. We had run into some traffic ourselves, but Pack Kennedy had picked me up early enough that we'd still made it here in time.

Maybe Pack Knight had given up?

I bit my bottom lip, nerves making my stomach cramp. Could that be it? Maybe they were worried about my choice of profession and had decided they didn't want to date an omega who worked at a strip club, even if that was one of the jobs omegas were actually allowed to do. Maybe they'd met a tinier, curvier omega and decided they'd rather court her?

I really should've remembered to give them my phone number. Now, even if they'd chosen to cancel the date, I wouldn't know because they had no way of contacting me.

As one, all the Pack Kennedy alphas stared at me, their faces stern, and I realized I was probably sending out some major distress signs.

That was further proved when a random older alpha started to walk closer, a broken, weird purring noise coming from him.

Shit. I had to get my scent under control.

Lorne and Sean Kennedy broke out from their places around Roxy and intercepted the random alpha before something could happen, and I closed my eyes, trying to focus on clearing my mind and just taking deep breaths.

It's all right, Amy. They're probably just stuck in traffic. It hasn't even been fifteen minutes. That's an acceptable delay. They'll be here soon.

Roxy placed her hand on my shoulder, startling me into opening my eyes. She must have approached me while I was trying to talk myself into calming down, and her alphas were now forming a barrier that closed both of us in.

I tried not to breathe in the scent of Roxy's alphas, because they smelled all wrong for me and would probably only drive me deeper into my freakout.

Roxy looked at me with pity. "Let us drive you home, Amy. We can stop somewhere along the way and buy you some comfort food. I think your pre-heat is getting worse, and being exposed like this won't do you any good," she offered kindly, reminding me that despite some of her previous comments about Pack Knight having rubbed me the wrong way, she really was only trying to look out for me.

"Five more minutes. Let's give them five more minutes; if they don't arrive, we can leave."

Even if I was being a bit pathetic, I wanted to give Pack Knight a chance. Arata and Zach Knight had been super nice and sweet when I'd interacted with them—well, Arata sometimes acted like Cinnamon Growl, but the two times I'd actually talked to him, he'd been nothing but friendly—and I really wanted to meet the rest of their pack. I wanted to meet whoever had written that cute invitation note that Zach had read. I wanted to get to know them better, see if I'd have as much chemistry with the rest of them as I had with Arata and Zach.

If Roxy was right with her concerns about my heat, then now, more than ever, I really needed to find a pack to help me. I didn't care if I came across as a little desperate.

I couldn't go through another heat at the center. Not when for the first time I seemed to have some actual prospects.

Roxy's lips formed a thin line, but she nodded, conceding.

"They're here," Lorne said, not hiding the disapproval in his tone.

As the tourism bus drove away, and a pickup truck covered in Knight Construction branding pulled up in front of the restaurant. Three alphas stepped out before the truck drove away, probably so the fourth alpha could look for a parking spot.

Arata Knight's dark hair was styled neatly back, off his face. The only other time I'd seen him this nicely dressed had been when we'd run into each other at the New Year's party. However, tonight, rather than a suit, he wore an open, dark blue woolen trench coat that made him seem just as dashing. When he saw me, he sent me an apologetic smile, which was enough to tell me he was in a good mood tonight, none of the Cinnamon Growl for our date.

That was a good sign, right?

Next to him stood Zach. His black hair fell a little over his eyes, giving him a more boyish look. His already pale skin looked even paler, as if he was about to come down with something. He wore a black shirt that looked just a little bit rumpled and probably helped make him look even more ghostly. It didn't help that even his coat—which was also open; what was it with these alphas and not buttoning their jackets?—was black as were his jeans. Basically, he could've stepped right out of a *Men in Black* movie ... or a vampire romance novel.

The fact that only made me want to show him my bare neck and beg for his bite made all sorts of alarm bells blare inside my brain.

The last alpha, and one of the two I hadn't met yet, looked like he'd just stepped out of a fashion magazine. Under his black trench coat, he wore a tight, white turtleneck sweater that helped show off his tanned skin and tight blue jeans. His slightly curly hair was longer even than Zach's—and messier—and his beard was less well-trimmed. His eyes were hazel, and they lit up when he saw me, a huge smile covering his face.

"I'm so sorry we were late!" he said, rushing to me as if Pack Kennedy wasn't currently creating a human barrier between us. "Our car broke down on the way here, and we had to grab a cab, go back home, get the truck, get the car towed... We would've called, but—" He made a gesture, and I knew what the rest of his sentence would be. They would've called, but they didn't have my number. "We did call the club and ask them to let you know," he added, looking at the alphas from Pack Kennedy. I was pretty sure I caught Lorne averting his gaze, as if guilty, but I was probably reading too much into this. "But I guess they couldn't get through."

As he spoke, he walked closer until Justin and Curtis had to step aside to make way for him. As they did that and he closed the distance between us, I took a deep breath.

My eyes widened, and my mouth watered at his scent, even as I grew wet. Mulled wine. This alpha smelled like red wine and spices, like the perfect hot drink to have during a cold winter night.

I didn't have to see his pupils dilating to know

I was perfuming.

The heat in my center was enough of a tell.

"I'm Cole, by the way. Cole Knight." His words were a mixture of a growl and a purr. "It's a pleasure to finally meet you, Amy."

He offered me his hand, and I took it, loving that I was about to be carrying a little bit of his scent with me and wishing I could rub all over him like a cat to get even more of it. "Hey, Cole! It's nice to meet you." My voice came out all breathy and sexy, and I was actually pretty proud of it.

Then I looked behind him and noticed Arata and Zach were right behind him. I smiled at them. "Hi-lo, Zach! Hey, Arata! Nice to see you two again!"

Cole turned to look at his packmates, and I was pretty sure he'd just mouthed "hi-lo?" to Zach, who blushed.

"Hey, Amy! We're so sorry we were late. Have you been waiting long?" asked Arata.

Roxy scoffed from beside me.

"Yes, because we were here on time."

I winced but didn't protest at her words. The truth was, even though I understood they had a perfectly good reason for being late, and I wanted to be the filling of a Zach-Cole-Arata sandwich, I *was* a little upset that they'd been late. We'd waited out in the cold for over twenty minutes, and that meant I'd had twenty minutes to spiral into nerves and worry that they wouldn't show up at all.

For an omega, that type of stress—especially during pre-heat season—was torture.

All three Pack Knight alphas averted their eyes, looking chagrined. "We really are sorry. We'll make it up to you guys, we promise. Thank you for not giving up on us and waiting." Cole's eyes were so damn earnest, it was impossible to stay upset at him.

"How about we go inside? We can wait for Kaito there. He should've parked the car by now, and I don't think we'll wait long, but the least we can do is get you out of the cold," Arata offered.

"Finally." Roxy didn't waste time in turning her back on us and heading to the restaurant, her alphas hot on her heels.

I sent Pack Knight an apologetic look.

"Are you sure? We can wait for him?" I didn't actually want to keep standing outside, especially now that most of their pack was here, but it felt kind of rude to leave Kaito Knight out in the cold.

Plus, I was curious to see what the final member of Pack Knight looked like.

"Oh yeah, it's totally fine. He won't mind," Cole assured me, shooting me a boyish grin.

Then he surprised me by placing his palm on the small of my back, escorting me inside.

I knew it was wishful thinking, but I could've sworn I felt the heat of his hand all the way through my layers of clothes.

Cole Knight was a walking temptation, and I loved it.

———————

I bit my bottom lip to keep from laughing when I walked through the doors.

Oh, this was a traditional Brazilian restaurant, all right, but it was no steakhouse.

The furthest corner of the room had one big wooden counter with multiple dishes—not that we could currently see any of it since the group of beta tourists was all there, filling up their plates.

A self-service restaurant. I wasn't entirely sure if it translated the same way into English, but it was just a place you went to where you could eat whatever and pay by the kilogram. The closest thing I could think of was to call it a buffet.

Pack Knight had just chosen what was probably the least romantic place in the world for a first date. Or for *any* date, really.

Roxy's pack stood frozen just inside the door, probably shocked beyond belief.

Nothing said, "let me get you naked," like going through a line and filling up your plate, knowing the clerk would be judging you by how much or little you put there. Or your food choices.

It was taking everything I possessed to quelch the ridiculous need to laugh at the disaster that tonight was proving to be.

And the date had barely even started.

"I can't find the hostess," Lorne commented, glancing around in confusion.

It was getting really damn hard to hide my amusement. "There isn't one. See where the tourists are standing?" I tilted my head in the direction of the buffet, which was beyond crowded right now. "We just have to head there, grab a tray, a plate, and fill it up with the food. There's probably someone right at the end of the buffet with a little scale, and we have to weigh our plates, and they'll give us a slip with the weight and price. Oh! And if we want something to drink or whatever, we can probably ask the person weighing the food for it. If not, then there might be a server somewhere, but I wouldn't count on it." I glanced around and found a little cashier window right to our left with a couple of people in line to pay. "Then, once we're done eating, we can go there, give them the slip and pay for it. Easy peasy summer breezy." I all but sing-songed the end, making Cole snort behind me.

Roxy swirled around to stare at me, mouth agape and green eyes wide. "Amélia," she emphasized the *e* to try to copy the way I pronounced my name, and it was probably the closest anyone had ever gotten. "*You cannot be serious.*" She sounded like she was on the verge of having a crisis.

Her alphas all crowded around her, purring, trying to soothe their omega.

Meanwhile, Zach and Arata were staring daggers at Cole, who rubbed the back of his neck. "The reviews raved about it! It had a four-point-seven star average!"

If I bit my bottom lip any harder, I was going to draw blood. Poor Cole.

"Did you actually *read* any of the reviews?" Zach asked his packmate, crossing his arms in front of himself. "I knew this restaurant was a bad idea," he added, muttering under his breath.

"Yeah. I mean, sort of?" Cole shrugged, flashing me a smile that was more of a grimace. "Most of them were in other languages."

"This *can't* be happening. Let's call this what it is and leave." Roxy's distress was growing by the minute, and it started to permeate her scent.

Pack Knight exchanged a glance, and then they all just stared at me, expecting me to decide what we should do.

On the one hand, Roxy was doing me a favor, and she was clearly regretting it pretty hard. I felt like I owed it to her to just leave and call it quits on tonight. Maybe try some other time with Pack Knight.

On the other hand ... Pack Knight had the insane ability to make me wet with just a look, and I really wanted in their pants.

Okay, so Roxy might have a point. Pre-heat was definitely riding me harder than it should, which was all the more reason to follow through with the date.

I'd find a way to make it up to Roxy later.

"I mean, we're already here, right? Let's give it a go! I'm sure the food is amazing."

Justin Kennedy nodded. "Yeah, it'll be an adventure. C'mon, babe, let's find you a seat, and Curtis can fill up a plate for us. You won't even have to get close to the buffet, promise."

"There's an empty table right there," I suggested, pointing to a spot to our right with a couple of empty tables right by the wall. It was one of the few places not currently occupied, and I was pretty sure if we didn't hurry to score it, some of the betas in the tourist group might.

"Perfect. Why don't we go secure the seats while you guys get the food?" He gently guided Roxy towards the empty seats, Lorne at their side, leaving two of their packmates with us.

"Seriously, we don't have to do this. We can find another restaurant if you guys want. I'm sure there's an Italian place somewhere around here that's a little less crowded," Cole offered, running a hand through his hair and messing it up even more.

I shook my head. "Nah, this is fine. You guys did promise me a Brazilian restaurant, and this *is* one. I've been to places like this before. Don't worry about it!" I didn't add that I hadn't stepped foot in a self-service restaurant since I was in my teens and still in school before I'd started to perfume as an omega, but that was okay.

They were embarrassed enough as it was.

Just then, the door behind us opened, and Arata walked in.

Wait a minute.

I fully turned, my eyes going from Arata One to Arata Two. They had the same hair, styled the same way. Same color clothes and eyes. The only difference I could note was that Arata Two was scowling, whereas Arata wasn't.

"There's two of you! Oh, this explains *so much.*" Was it possible that every time I'd seen Arata and thought he was Cinnamon Growl, he was actually his twin!? And the times I interacted with him, when he was nothing but nice, he was the real Arata?

"Yeah," Arata One smirked at me. "We're twins, and I'm the better-looking and much nicer one. This is Kaito, our pack leader."

Arata Two—Kaito, whatever—took one look around the place and his scowl deepened even more. "Cole, what the fuck? A *buffet*?"

Rude. He was totally going to be forever known as Cinnamon Growl. The nickname fit him quite well.

"Well!" Cole exclaimed, clapping his hands

and pointedly ignoring his packmate. "We're all here now, so let's check out the food!" Once again, he placed his hand on the small of my back, gently guiding me forward.

I loved the way he kept touching me as if needing the proximity and his scent all over me. I knew I shouldn't be allowing this much contact to an alpha who had only just begun courting me, but his scent and proximity were addictive.

We made our way through the tables, straight to the buffet. Knowing they would all follow my lead, I grabbed my tray first, a fork and a knife, and my plate.

As I made my way through the line, picking up a little of this and that, I noticed Cole was pretty much getting the exact same things I was, and so were most of his packmates.

They were probably scared of getting something they wouldn't like the taste of, which was fair. Not every food was for everyone. Even I had traditional dishes I didn't care much for, one of which was Aunt Lu's favorite.

Still, the fact all of Pack Knight was following my lead almost made me want to put something super different on my plate just to see what they would think of it. *Almost.*

Then I saw the cheesy bread, and I decided to be nice.

I freaking loved *pão de queijo*. Should've put less actual food and more of the good stuff. Oh well.

I could always come back for more if I had the room.

Once I was at the end of the buffet, I placed my plate to be weighed and winced at how heavy it was. I may or may not have gotten carried away, but they had so many great options!

"Here you go, dear," the beta clerk said, writing down the info on a slip of paper. "Would you like something to drink? We have soda, water, or juice," she offered, smiling at me.

"Hi! I'll have a Coke, please."

She nodded, grabbed a can from the fridge behind her, and placed it on my tray with a plastic cup.

"Have a great evening!"

"Thanks, you too!" I replied, turning and carrying my tray to the table Pack Kennedy had scored for us.

Roxy watched my approach with pursed lips, disapproval radiating off her in waves.

I didn't need her to tell me what she was thinking; it was written all over her face.

I was determined to see this date through, though. We may have gotten off to a bumpy start, but that meant the only place to go from here was up, right?

CHAPTER 18

Oh man, my packmates were going to *kill* me, and I wasn't even entirely sure I'd blame them.

I should have read the reviews. Maybe translated some of them? That would have been wise.

Hindsight is 20/20 and all that jazz.

We all set our trays down on the two long tables we'd commandeered, taking a moment to shrug off our winter coats that we basically had to sit on because there was nowhere else to put them, and getting situated on the uncomfortable plastic benches.

Positive: I was sitting next to Amy.

Negative: Zach was on my other side, pumping out anxious pheromones like this was a trial by fire instead of a date. A not-so-well thought-out date, but a date nonetheless.

Kaito and Arata sat on the other side of the table, while Pack Kennedy squished at the neighboring table. There were only a few inches of space between the two, which meant Amy and Roxy were practically shoulder-to-shoulder, and I had no doubt that was intentional.

Firstly, to keep the alphas they knew between them, and the tables of betas and other alphas squished in on every side. Secondly, so Roxy could easily access Amy's ear and remind her of all the ways she clearly disapproved of this date.

Whatever. I didn't care if everyone at both tables disapproved—Amy looked stoked with her plate piled high with all kinds of foods, some of which I recognized and others I didn't. And she was *beautiful*, and smelled *incredible*. Getting her scent firsthand was roughly a billion times better than inhaling scraps of it off my packmates' clothes.

She was wearing a fitted dark green dress with long sleeves and tall black winter boots. Her dress had slid up a little when she sat, exposing toned thighs in sheer black pantyhose, and I was having some thoughts that probably weren't appropriate for a by-the-pound buffet filled with tourists and families.

"This looks so good," Amy said, shooting us a beaming smile. "I haven't had *pão de queijo* in forever! It's such a hassle to make. It just isn't worth it, you know?"

"Well, then I'm glad I chose this swanky joint for our date so you could get your fix," I teased, winking at her. Arata snorted from across the table, and Amy's laugh loosened a small amount of the tension.

At our table anyway, Pack Kennedy didn't look so easily convinced.

Zach's nervous scent had even mellowed somewhat, and I hoped he was back to his baseline stress level rather than his first-date stress level. First-date-on-steroids level, since he'd been agitated all day that we couldn't make a reservation at this place.

It was possible that his panic had been warranted.

I'd tried to convince him to go shopping with me to chill him out, but he insisted on wearing the black shirt he always wore when he was worried about sweat patches, or somehow forgetting how cutlery worked and spilling food all down his front, but Amy seemed to like his vampire-chic style.

I'd stopped at the mall on my way back from the Hayes site, bought myself the tightest sweater I could find that showcased my muscles without looking obscene, found a pair of jeans that drew attention to my ass—I had a *great* ass—and gone through my full curly boy hair routine in preparation for tonight. Curl cream, plop, diffuser on cold, *the works*. My hair was runway-ready.

Did Amy like my hair? Was it too soon to ask?

"When did you move to America?" Arata asked, sitting directly opposite Amy.

"I was born here, actually. I moved to Brazil

when I was eleven, and then came back here last year," Amy replied, giving him a small smile because Arata always had that soothing effect on people. "I'm due to go back for a visit this year to see my aunts. I can't wait."

Huh. Aunts? I'd assumed she'd want to go back and visit her parents, since she was being chaperoned by a pack that wasn't related to her. Arata kicked me under the table as though I needed a reminder to not ask overly personal questions on the first date.

I twisted slightly to get my shins out of the firing line, only for my knees to knock against Amy's under the table. We both froze for a moment before I grunted out an insincere apology and moved my legs to give her more space.

I did not want to give her more space. I wanted to eat up all the space between us. I wanted to feed Amy her dinner while she sat on my lap, then I wanted to eat her for dessert.

Too soon?

Maybe too soon.

I shoved a cold fry in my mouth before any of those words escaped me.

When Kaito grunted quietly and sent his twin a glare, I knew Arata had given his shins the same warning message. Fortunately, the restaurant was loud enough that Amy didn't seem to notice.

"What about you guys? Are you from around

here?" Amy asked, reaching for her Coke.

"Oh yeah, we grew up here," I said, scrambling in my head for a way to make that sound more interesting. We'd worked for Kaito and Arata's parents until they were ready to retire and sold us the construction business, which we'd continued to grow ever since. Shit, Amy was a lot more well-traveled and interesting than we were.

"Oh, that's nice! How did you all meet? Did you live close to each other or something?" Amy asked, sipping her Coke.

"High school," I replied instantly. "Specifically, an alpha academy not too far from here. I met Zach on the first day of school when he was, er—"

"Hiding in the bathroom, so nervous I was contemplating throwing up," he supplied wryly, relaxing a little on my other side at this familiar story.

"Aww!" Amy leaned over to give him a sympathetic look, patting his hand on the table. Her upper body was basically in my lap, drenching me in her scent, and I wanted to inject that gingerbread smell directly into my veins somehow. Was that a thing? *Come on, science. Don't let me down.* "No judgment. I was a total mess my first day of high school, too—I walked into the wrong building, the *alpha* building, and I was so nervous I didn't even notice the scent right away. I nearly caused a riot."

"I can definitely believe that," Arata replied

smoothly, giving Amy a flirty smile that made her blush. *Yes! Go, Arata!*

Amy straightened, and I immediately missed her closeness. I promised my pack I was going to be on my best behavior tonight—they were convinced I'd come on too strong for some reason—but Amy's body language felt pretty flirty. What was I supposed to do? Leave her hanging? Fuck that noise.

"So, then what happened?" Amy asked, glancing at Zach again and breaking me out of my internal debate on first date etiquette.

"I dragged Zach out of the bathrooms and swore I'd be his bestest buddy and wouldn't abandon him—" I began.

"—he then promptly abandoned me—" Zach scoffed.

"—at which point Arata adopted him in the cafeteria, not five minutes after Kaito and I had met for the first time in English class and got in a *heated* debate about ... I actually don't remember, but it really made an impression on our new teacher." I paused to take a deep breath and shot Amy a grin. "I came into the cafeteria, looking for my new buddy, Zach, only to find him hanging out with the asshole I'd just been arguing with in class."

"He really came in all guns blazing," Arata laughed while Kaito smirked, silently observing the conversation. "Marching up to me, telling me what a stubborn dickhead I was. Fortunately, I've been on the receiving end of twin confusion many times before, and I knew what was going on."

"I'm glad it wasn't just me," Amy admitted, shooting Kaito a shy look. Not for the first time, I wished he wasn't quite so unreadable. He wasn't doing his grumpy face, but he wasn't exactly shooting Amy bedroom eyes either.

"So, as you can see, we were really meant to be a pack right from the very beginning," I said hastily, drawing attention away from Kaito's indecipherable expression.

"Love at first ... awkward bathroom meeting?" Amy laughed.

"Something like that," Zach scoffed. "Honestly, I'd probably still be hiding in that stall now if Cole hadn't taken pity on me."

"*Befriended* you," I corrected, not taking my eyes off Amy.

"Kaito encouraged us to bond as a pack a few months later," Arata added.

Amy scooped up a spoonful of rice, accidentally bumping me with her elbow in the process because this bench was definitely not designed for three people—especially when two of them were alpha-sized. "Oh, I'm so sorry—"

"That's okay," I assured her, twisting to the side and switching my fork to my left hand. "Here, you can move over a bit if you want."

Zach jabbed his elbow into my rib—one hundred percent on purpose, definitely giving me a *'don't scare her, Cole!'* lecture in his head—but Amy didn't hesitate to shift into my personal space, her shoulder brushing against my chest. There was no misreading this signal—we were totally scent marking each other, and that fact was *not* lost on Roxy, who looked about ready to stab me with the blunt knife she was holding.

"Well, I'm glad you put high school behind you and decided to form a pack," Amy said after pausing for a moment to eat, surveying our table with a small smile.

"Yeah, it worked out. Now we just need our omega to complete our pack," Kaito said mildly, as though he hadn't just dropped the most awkward bomb ever on the table.

My dude had zero subtlety.

"Right," Amy agreed slowly. "You, uh, never found her, I guess?"

"It's okay. You can ask," I assured her. "It's not a sensitive subject. It just ... is what it is. We've never met the right one."

And none of them were interested in pursuing things with us, but I wasn't about to announce that. Especially when Roxy was already looking down her nose at us.

Amy gave me a soft smile. "That's fair. And in

the spirit of being honest, and since the subject was brought up, and we're on a date and all ... I should probably mention that I'm not entirely sure I'm ready for a mate bond, or if I'll ever be." She laughed a little nervously. "Right now, my biggest concern is getting through my heat. Without accidentally bonding a pack."

Oof. I mean, I got it, but that didn't mean it didn't feel like a blow to the sternum.

"If all you want is a pack to help you through your heat, we can be that to you," Arata said smoothly, leaning forward. *What?!* This was not what we'd talked about at all; Arata was going way off-script. "If all you want is to have dinner tonight, then that's fine too. You're in charge, Amy. There's no pressure."

Amy leaned forward too, ensnared by Arata's soothing attention that had her immediately relaxing. I silently thanked Arata for always knowing how to pass his chill on to those around him. Unconsciously, my hand rested on Amy's lower back, my thumb rubbing circles meant to soothe her before I even realized how wildly bold I was being.

She didn't seem to mind.

Zach jabbed me with his elbow again, catching my kidney since I'd basically turned my back on him to snuggle up to Amy, and Kaito was giving me a *look*, but I didn't think it was related to me touching Amy. No, it was a *warning* look, telling me to be careful about how I responded to her declaration.

Obviously, I hoped that Amy hadn't written off the idea of a mate bond entirely, but I heard loud and clear what Arata had been telling us while he was reassuring Amy—there was nothing we could do if she had, so just let it go and enjoy her company.

Cool, cool. Totally cool.

Why was my pack looking at me like I was about to throw a tantrum at the dinner table? They were so dramatic.

I was disappointed, but my disappointment wasn't Amy's problem. Actually, if anyone looked like they were about to have an explosive reaction to her statement, it was Roxy. Her jaw was practically on the table as she stared at Amy.

Well, well, well. It looked like a certain someone hadn't known that before throwing her brother's pack into the mix.

"Thank you for being so understanding," Amy said eventually, and the last dregs of my disappointment faded because Amy's comfort was more important than anything else.

Amy and Arata were still staring at each other, pumping out let's-get-naked pheromones like the world was going to end if they didn't personally repopulate it right this second. They were having a whole silent, sexually fraught conversation with their eyeballs that none of us were in on, and it was kind of turning me on. I had less than zero interest in banging my packmates, but seeing them connect with an omega was sexier than I thought, in a voyeuristic kind of way.

Roxy cleared her throat with absolutely zero subtlety, breaking the moment, and Amy startled backward. I hooked my arm around her waist completely, so she didn't topple off the bench, hugging her into my side.

If Roxy's eyes got any bigger, they were going to bulge right out of her head. Pack Kennedy's alphas seemed more divided—two of them looking stern and disapproving, the other two doing their best to hide their smiles by looking down at their plates.

"Thanks, Cole." Amy twisted to look up at me, giving me a soft smile that faded into something distinctly less *sweet* when she realized how close our faces were. There was only an inch between our lips, and both of us froze, the moment drawing out for what could have been seconds or hours.

Did I want to grab Amy with both hands and taste all that sweetness I knew she possessed?

Yes. Hard yes. Absolutely yes.

But I also wanted to brush soft, chaste kisses over those pouty lips. Not to seduce, but just *because*. Because I liked her and I wanted to, and I thought it might make her smile.

I wouldn't—*couldn't*—I didn't have the right

to be that affectionate, we'd only just officially met. I'd just dream about it, mixed in with the far *less* chaste fantasies I'd been having about Amy since that first night I'd seen her on stage.

"You have something ... right ... here," Amy breathed, reaching up with her thumb to brush the side of my lip. My tongue darted out at the same moment, catching the side of her digit, and we both sucked in a surprised breath.

Fuck.

Fuck.

Fuck.

"Amy," Roxy said loudly, startling our whole table, who'd apparently also been holding their breaths. "What is this I'm eating?"

Amy jumped, nearly cracking her skull against my nose before turning to face Roxy, looking very much like a kid who'd got caught with her hand in the cookie jar. She didn't seem inclined to put any space between our bodies, though, and neither was I. Besides, Amy's perfume signaled loud and clear that she was just fine with our seating arrangement.

Why had I worn such tight jeans? As great as my ass looked in them, my knot was doing its best to make an appearance, and there wasn't even an inch of space free.

My packmates seemed to be having similar struggles, shifting awkwardly in their seats. The tables around us must be miserable with the scent-bombing we were inadvertently doing, but there was no way we could rein it in now. I was vaguely aware that Amy was explaining the food to Roxy, but my attention had mostly zeroed in on where my hand rested on Amy's hip, my fingers spanning the top of her thigh.

Roxy glanced down, lips pinching at the slightly possessive hold, but it was only a chaperone's place to intervene if the omega wanted them to. Amy's hand came to rest over mine for a moment before she returned to eating, further mixing our scents together.

Did she know what she was doing to me?

I shoveled my food into my mouth, barely tasting it as I battled to keep the steadily increasing sexual tension in check. Fortunately, Arata easily slid into the role of the entertainer, regaling both tables with stories of our younger, less responsible years, and he always nailed punchlines, so even Roxy looked amused, despite her best efforts. Zach had relaxed on my other side, and even Kaito was almost smiling. His body was still slightly angled away from the group, though, as if he expected this all to go to shit at any moment, and he needed to be ready to run.

It was probably a side effect of Amy saying she wasn't necessarily looking for a mate bond. Kaito would be on high alert, ready to run rather than risk any of us getting our feelings hurt.

"I'm so full." Amy half laughed, half groaned, slumping against me. "That's probably a very unsexy thing to admit on the first date."

"Nothing unsexy about enjoying a good meal," Kaito grunted. Amy turned into me to look at him across the table, eyebrows rising slightly in surprise. *You and me both, beautiful.*

"Well, it's getting late," Roxy announced, standing up and making a show of grabbing her coat. Her alphas followed her lead, and as much as I wanted to pick Amy up and wrap her around me like a koala, it was probably time to go. Amy may have enjoyed the food—and hopefully enjoyed the company—but I doubted this crowded, noisy restaurant was anything resembling comfortable for an omega. Especially an omega approaching heat.

"Here, let me go pay," Kaito said as he stood, collecting our tickets before arguing with Pack Kennedy for a bit until they relented. It would be poor form to make the chaperones pay for their own meals, even if they clearly hadn't wanted to be here and didn't approve of us in the slightest.

One of Pack Kennedy's alphas—the one with a dark tan and green eyes, who'd been looking like he was trying not to smile the whole meal—cleared his throat. "Why don't we go get the car? We'll swing around the front and pick you up, Amy, if you'd like?"

"Oh, yes, please," Amy replied, beaming at him, her leg shifting slightly under my palm.

Oof. Roxy was totally reaming her alpha out with her eyeballs.

"Come on, darling," one of the other alphas murmured. "We're chaperones, not prison wardens. Give them a moment."

With a not-insignificant amount of complaining, Roxy finally agreed, pulling on their coats and winding through the packed tables to the front table. Kaito rejoined us before we did the same, my hand resting on Amy's lower back the entire time. It didn't escape my attention that she attracted a few stray sniffs as we passed the tables, but my pack was on-point with their 'fuck off' glares, and Amy didn't hesitate to stick close to us.

It wasn't an insignificant gesture. She was trusting us—unmated alphas—to keep her safe. That was huge.

Amy hurriedly pulled on her gloves as we got out onto the snowy street, fumbling with her beanie before I gently plucked it from her fingers and pulled it over her head, pushing a few strands of hair falling over her eyes behind her ear.

In my periphery, I saw my packmates standing with their backs to us, hiding Amy and me from the world, sandwiched between them and the brick wall of the restaurant.

"Thank you for coming out tonight," I told her, letting my fingertips linger on her jaw, not quite able to pull away yet.

Amy's eyes twinkled. "Thank you for inviting me. You wrote the note, didn't you?"

"It's a burden, being the most eloquent and best looking member of my pack," I teased. Arata snorted, blatantly eavesdropping.

"Best looking, huh?" Amy replied with a light laugh, waggling her eyebrows at me.

"Mmhm. I'm not above bribery to get you to admit it," I murmured, leaning in closer, my lips tipped up in a half smile. I was close enough to see the faint freckles dotting the bridge of her nose, and it may have been the cutest thing I'd ever seen in my life.

"And what are you going to bribe me with, hm?" Amy murmured back, tilting her head to the side.

"A kiss?" I suggested, my breath feathering across her lips. It was a request, framed as a flirtation. *Please, omega. Let me kiss you.*

Amy's eyes dropped to my lips. "Skip the bribe. You can have the kiss for free."

Mine.

I cupped her jaw, my other hand finding her waist to pull her in close, the first brush of my lips against hers setting off a rumbling growl of need in my chest that was impossible to suppress. Amy's hands found my jacket, pulling me closer, and I cursed the thick layers of winter clothes between us.

There was no shyness, no hesitation. Amy's lips parted, her tongue swiping against mine. I sucked on her lower lip, dragging my teeth gently over the sensitive flesh, giving her a taste of what it would be like if she had me in her nest. I'd give her *everything*.

"Cole," Arata warned quietly, careful to keep his tone soft and even so as not to trigger my territorial instincts. "Pack Kennedy are pulling up now."

Amy's whine of protest made it almost impossible to pull away. Her perfume was sharp with need, and if we had even a sliver more privacy, I'd have made her come right there and then. I brushed a couple of light teasing kisses over her lips, a promise of what was to come. *This is just our first kiss, Amy, not our last.*

My packmates were staring at Amy, entranced, pupils dilated, sucking down lungfuls of her scent. She didn't look intimidated at all to have them all fixated on her like that. If anything, she was reveling in their attention.

But Pack Kennedy's SUV was crawling closer, and our time was running out.

"Shoot, let me get your numbers," Amy said quickly, fumbling for her phone with her gloves on.

"Here, I'll get yours, and we'll message you, okay?" Arata replied smoothly, pulling his device out of his pocket. I kept an arm wrapped around

Amy's shoulders as she rattled off her phone number, squeezing her into my side before reluctantly releasing her as Pack Kennedy pulled to the curb; Roxy's nose practically squashed against the glass as she peered out from the backseat.

"Message me," Amy demanded, giving Arata a stern look before breaking into another infectious smile.

"Promise," he assured her, the three of them parting so she could walk to the waiting SUV.

Amy climbed in, and we all stood in the freezing cold, watching until the tail lights had disappeared around the block. I wanted nothing more than for Amy to be riding home in our vehicle, to be able to carry her upstairs to a completed nest, lay her down on the bed, and do unspeakably filthy things to her body while she begged for more.

We weren't there yet, but I knew we could be.

Amy liked us. We liked Amy. Nothing was going to keep us apart.

CHAPTER 19

"Good morning, Lia!" Aunt Raquel's cheerful greeting immediately had me smiling.

"Morning, Aunt Raquel. How's it going?" I asked, walking to my window nook and sitting there, making myself comfortable.

It was just before noon here, which meant Aunt Raquel had once again gotten out of bed early, but not as early as she'd done on Boxing Day, even though today was a Saturday.

Or maybe she had, but decided to wait before calling me. Both options were equally as likely.

"Oh, you know, same old, same old. I'm more curious about *you*. How are you? Is the cold weather making you sniffly? Have you been wearing enough layers? You went on your first date with the other pack last night, yes? How did *that* go? Is your contraception shot up to date? Did you remember to take one last month like you were supposed to?" She sounded way too eager. Aunt Raquel wasn't even trying to pretend Aunt Lu was the one interested in the gossip as she usually did. That told me how invested she was in my love life—or lack of.

"I'm alright. Yes, I have been wearing enough layers. No, I'm not coming down with a cold, don't worry. And yes, I did remember to take my contraceptive shot last month. You sent me an email reminding me." One of the downsides of having a doctor in the family was that she knew too much, and there was no question quite "off limits."

"That's good! What about the date?" She pressed, all but ignoring everything else I'd just said even though I'd been answering her questions.

"It was really nice."

"*Nice*? Lia, a pair of shoes on sale is nice. A rain-free day in August is nice. A date should be much more than just that. Tell me everything! Where did you go?" Before I could reply, I heard muffled voices on Aunt Raquel's side of the line. "Oh, actually. Hang on. I'm putting you on speaker. Lu wants to hear it too."

Oh great. Now both my aunts would get to grill me for details.

"Hey, Lia, good morning!" Aunt Lu sounded even more cheerful than Aunt Raquel.

"Hey, Aunt Lu. You done with the morning exercises?" Yes, I was deflecting, but so what?

"Who cares?" Protested Aunt Raquel, and

I didn't have to be there to know she'd just earned a glare from Aunt Lu. "You two can discuss the benefits of being fit later. The date, Lia. Spare us no details. Where did you go? How was it? Did you take any pictures of them?"

"Yeah, sure. I totally made the alphas pose for multiple pictures in the middle of our date just so I could show my aunts what they looked like. Got some of them naked, too, by the way."

My sarcasm was deep enough that Aunt Lu laughed.

"Just tell us how it went, Lia. You know the more you put it off, the more curious Raquel will be. Unless it really was a bad date, and you don't want to talk about it?"

I sighed. "No, it's not that. I mean, there were certainly ... moments. But Pack Knight was charming, and they were super eager. I had fun." Once the initial hurdles had passed and we'd actually sat down to eat, it had gone pretty well. Arata, Cole, and Zach were easygoing, communicative, and they made me laugh a lot. Kaito was... well, the Cinnamon Growl nickname was going to stick forever, and I didn't know how I felt that one of their packmates didn't seem to like me. It certainly put a dampener on my hopes that Pack Knight might be game to see me through my heat. Though, since it wasn't like I had to bond them, maybe I could have Arata, Cole, and Zach help, and Kaito could bow out? It was far from ideal, but I couldn't force him to like me.

And I really was growing desperate.

Still, I wanted to get to know them a little better before I asked if they would let me bounce on their knots when my heat came. Maybe have dinner again, or buy them coffee. Something, at the very least. Preferably a second date where things went well and Roxy wasn't constantly making little snide comments to make the alphas uncomfortable. Even though they'd offered, I felt I needed more time before I said yes.

Besides, Cole had kissed me until my toes curled and my mind blanked. I'd probably stunk up Roxy's car the whole way home. We'd even had to keep the windows open because of me. It had been … far from ideal. At least Roxy hadn't been sick over it, though, as I'd heard some did when another omega was perfuming as badly as I'd been.

I didn't regret it, though, and if given the chance, I'd kiss Cole all over again. And Arata. And Zach.

I'd kiss Zach so good he would forget to be nervous about it.

"Lia? You still there?" Aunt Raquel's question had me blushing.

"Yeah, sorry, I was just remembering last night."

"Ohh, that's good, then. How about you do the remembering out loud? Preferably starting from the beginning. Where did you guys go?" Aunt Raquel pressed.

"They took me to a Brazilian restaurant, actually. I thought I told you this yesterday?"

"Awww, they wanted to give you a taste of home? That's sweet!" Aunt Lu sounded like she was halfway in love with the pack already.

"What *type* of Brazilian restaurant? How was the food?" Aunt Raquel's rapid-fire questions were a direct contrast with her mate's response.

"One that served actual Brazilian food that I didn't have to cook?" I joked, trying to evade the question while technically answering it.

Aunt Raquel's huff told me she wasn't falling for it.

I sighed.

"A self-service place," I mumbled, talking fast in the hopes this would soften the blow. "The food was okay, not super great, but it wasn't terrible, either. It's a really popular place here in Seattle, too."

"A SELF-SERVICE RESTAURANT? They took you to a pay-by-the-kilogram place on YOUR FIRST DATE? Lia, tell me you left! I can't believe this!"

I had to pull my phone away from my ear so Aunt Raquel's loud rant wouldn't permanently damage my hearing.

"Oh, Lia. I'm sorry." Aunt Lu's response was

a lot quieter, but she couldn't mask the pity in her tone.

I didn't *want* them to pity me. Pack Knight had been lovely, and they'd made me laugh more than I had in ages. They'd looked at me like I was the most beautiful omega in the world, and when they did it, I actually believed them. They gave me hope that maybe, just maybe, I might have found a pack who saw me and liked me for who I was and not just because I smelled a certain way.

"It wasn't their fault," I protested, but Aunt Raquel cut me off before I could say much more.

"Not their fault? Lia, child of my heart, of course it *was* their fault! They asked you out, did they not?"

"Yes, bu—"

"No buts. They asked you out. They picked the place. They should've done a better job of researching it before taking you there."

"The restaurant is apparently super well-rated, though! How were they supposed to know what it was like?"

"They clearly didn't do a good enough job of looking it up, as they should have. There's no excuse for this, Lia. I don't care how good looking or nice they are; this just isn't done. Every alpha takes *multiple* classes in high school with the proper ways to court an omega. I'm not talking just one or two, either. I think I had at least five. And that was in high school alone. Not to mention all the classes on how to properly soothe your omega, how to move from the courting period to mating. There was even one on making sure they had the perfect nests. This pack's behavior is a dishonor to all alphas."

I winced. Aunt Raquel was sounding a lot like Roxy had, and both women had *nothing* in common. This was bad.

"Lia, honey, your aunt is right. I mean, I'm a beta, not an alpha, but even I know they committed all kinds of faux pas from their choice of venue alone. I'm also pretty sure you've left a lot out, including how packed the restaurant probably was, considering you said it had such high ratings online. I know you want to find a pack to help with your heat, but maybe it's best to book a room at a heat center?" Aunt Lu's gentle pity had me fighting back tears.

I was unable to stop myself from whining. "I don't want to go through it alone. Last time was *hell*."

"Oh Lia, I'm sorry. What about that other pack? The one who gave you an early courting gift? Your date with them went better, right?" Aunt Raquel coaxed, her voice a lot gentler than before.

"Pack Carmichael? They were nice, but ... there was no chemistry," I admitted, sounding just as miserable as this conversation made me feel.

"Well, I don't have to remind you that this type

of thing won't matter when you're in the middle of your heat and desperate for a knot, but since neither of your current options seem ideal, how about you try one of those dating apps? Book a room at a heat center, too, just in case, but maybe you can find an alternative pack with whom you have a little more chemistry?"

If even Aunt Raquel was trying to campaign for me to use a dating app, that truly did mean she'd lost all hope.

"I ... I'll think about it," I replied, unwilling to cave just yet. I knew I was being stubborn, but I knew no other pack would make me as horny as Pack Knight had.

Not only that, but Pack Knight had made me laugh a lot. They'd been sweet and caring, and Cole had scent marked me constantly as if desperate to have me carry his scent. Arata had known just the right thing to say whenever one of his packmates had seemed a little nervous, and they'd even managed to make Roxy laugh, even though she'd clearly disapproved of them.

I couldn't tell my aunts that, though. They'd never approve. They'd already made their minds up about Pack Knight, and no matter what I said now, nothing would make them good enough in their eyes.

"All right, Lia. You do that. Get some rest, too. You've been working a lot. We love you!"

"I love you guys too. Have a good day."

A.R.A.T.A

CHAPTER 20

"So," Cole began brightly, holding an enormous spoonful of cereal just below his mouth. We'd all taken advantage of having today off and slept in, gathering in the kitchen for "breakfast" close to noon. "How do we think last night went?"

I took a sip of my black coffee, waiting for someone else to burst his bubble. He'd gotten lucky that none of us had properly ripped into him last night, but we'd all been eager to go our separate ways the moment we got home.

To masturbate.

I mean, that was definitely why *I'd* wanted some privacy.

"It was a disaster," Kaito deadpanned, spooning a truly disturbing amount of sugar into his coffee. "The restaurant sucked. Roxy hates us. If we were any worse at our jobs, Lorne Kennedy would have fired us on the spot."

Cole wrinkled his nose. "They're not going

to fire us, they need the repairs done too urgently. Besides, a couple of the Pack Kennedy alphas seemed to like us okay, and their opinions aren't even the ones that matter."

That was true, though it was a little naive of Cole to think that Pack Kennedy's view of us wouldn't impact Amy's, at least a little. They were her bosses, and at least friendly enough for Amy to consider them chaperone material.

And ultimately, we *had* fucked up with the restaurant, so it wasn't like the complaints Pack Kennedy might have about us were unfounded. Even if it had been super fancy, it was overcrowded and not omega-friendly in the slightest.

"The food was okay," Zach offered tentatively. "Kind of cold, but it tasted good? If you don't think too hard about all those people breathing on it in the line..."

"Way to look on the bright side, Z," Cole agreed, lifting his coffee toward Zach in a toast. "The only opinion that matters is Amy's, and I think she liked us. She *kissed* me," he added smugly.

That was true, and that kiss—admittedly, it was a *hell* of a kiss—was currently sustaining all of the hope we had. That, and the fact she'd given us her phone number.

"I think you should message her first," I told Cole, pulling out my phone. "You and Amy really had a moment last night—a lot of moments, actually—and it might be overwhelming for all of us to message at once."

Cole nodded his head vigorously, curls bouncing up and down. He and Amy had been scent marking each other like horny teenagers all throughout dinner; the car ride home with him had been torture. "Yes. Yes, I should absolutely message her first. Gimme her number."

Kaito groaned, and I was about to tell him off, but surprisingly *Zach* beat me to it.

"Dude, you do not get to complain. You barely said two words to Amy last night! You know it's bad when *I* don't look like the least talkative one in the pack."

Kaito scowled, not objecting because he knew Zach was right.

Cole looked at me, subtly nodding toward Kaito with wide eyes, clearly wanting me to intervene, but I shook my head. My pack had gotten used to me mediating, and most of the time, I didn't mind, but in this case, I wasn't sure it was necessary.

I couldn't mediate Kaito into *not* being scared of courting an omega, into not being scared of failing again, and I *knew* that's where his insecurities were. Call it twin intuition. They were Kaito's hurdles to overcome in his own time, with our support.

We just needed a second date. One where Kaito sat next to Amy instead, because there was no way he could keep up that icy mask if he actually spent any real time getting to know her.

Kaito cleared his throat. "Cole, you message her first. Arata, say hello in the evening. Zach, tomorrow morning. Sound good?"

"What about you?" Zach pressed while I forwarded Amy's number to each of them.

"I'll go last. I'm going to head out. Is anyone free to come with me? I need an extra pair of hands," Kaito replied gruffly.

"I'm free," I volunteered, downing the rest of my coffee. Cole was already totally absorbed in his phone, and Zach clearly hadn't found Kaito's evasive answer satisfactory, judging by the glare he was shooting my twin. "Where are we going?"

I raised an eyebrow at Kaito as we pulled up at the home improvement store where we usually bought supplies for jobs, wondering what exactly we were doing here on a Saturday and why *he* was the only one who knew about it. For all his control freak ways, Kaito didn't actually go out and pick up all the material. Those sorts of tasks generally fell to us.

"Okay, Mr. Mysterious, what's the deal? Have we got so much work going on that you've decided to get your hands dirty again?" I teased.

Kaito rolled his eyes, jumping out of the truck and waiting for me to do the same before locking up. "I'm picking up drywall. I ordered it last night."

"You did?"

Okay, maybe we *hadn't* all been masturbating last night. Apparently, some of us had been ordering *drywall*.

Grim.

"And what exactly is this drywall for?" I asked casually, jogging to catch up with Kaito as he headed through the automatic doors, striding toward the pickup desk. This place was packed with families on the weekend, picking up supplies for projects, and I narrowly dodged a toddler who was sprinting down the aisle, pushing their own stroller at NASCAR-level speed.

"The attic."

The attic?

I stopped dead in my tracks while Kaito approached the pickup desk, pulling up the order confirmation on his phone. Our attic? Where we were planning on building the *nest*?

The decently-sized attic was accessed by a spiral staircase, but was completely unfinished. It had exposed insulation in the roof and walls, and a giant HVAC duct running along one wall, under the window. We'd always talked about turning it into a proper nest one day, but without an omega, every other project around the house had taken precedence. Cole had tried to steal supplies from our yard to finish it himself after the first time we'd *seen*

Amy, but Zach had convinced him to wait until we'd at least discussed it as a pack.

Kaito and Cole could be so alike in their bullheadedness.

"They'll help us load up," Kaito said nonchalantly, wandering toward the exit to wait by the vehicle, easy as that.

"I'm sorry, you're going to need to explain this like I'm five. You ordered drywall last night? For the nest? Do you even know how much we need?"

"I do know how to measure," he replied dryly.

"So we got home from that date, and everyone went to their rooms to jerk off"—Kaito shot me a withering look—"except you, who went up to the creepy attic and took measurements for drywall?"

"Apparently."

I let out a slightly exasperated laugh, following him into the parking lot. "You don't think it would have been easier and made more sense to just tell Amy you like her?"

"She doesn't want a pack. She wants help with her heat," Kaito grunted. "We can't help with her heat without a nest."

I hummed, not buying his explanation at all. No, I was pretty sure that Kaito *like-liked* Amy, and this was his emotionally stunted way of expressing it. The nest was a gesture for him, but if it all went to shit, he'd still have plausible deniability and claim it was just meant for her heat anyway.

My packmates were going to give me gray hairs one of these days.

———————

All four of us could hang drywall in our sleep at this point, so between us, we'd gotten the walls and ceiling done in one afternoon, and the joint compound was now drying.

I hopped out of the shower, toweling off and pulling on comfy sweats to join my packmates downstairs, ready to finally sit down after spending my day off doing anything but relaxing. It was worth it, though—the nest wasn't anything close to nest-like, but it was at least a *room* now.

"Arata, your turn to message Amy," Cole announced the moment I entered the living room, tapping his fingers impatiently on his phone even though he'd been in contact with her all day and barely helped out with the attic at all.

Fair enough, I'd also rather message Amy than hang drywall. Except, despite me having twenty-four hours since our date to think about it, I still wasn't entirely sure what I wanted to say.

"Arata," Cole prompted, the faintest hint of a whine in his voice. In an alternate timeline, I was convinced that Cole was a pampered omega sustained purely by attention. "It's your turn. How are you going to open? Do you need some tips?"

"From you, who asked her out by proxy via an awkward letter?" I laughed, flopping down in the gray armchair Kaito and I always fought for and arranging the cushions behind my back to get comfortable. "Zach is still recovering from that, you know."

"That was from all of us, and Amy *loved* it," Cole shot back, just a touch defensively.

"Cole," Zach yelled from the kitchen. "We're on dinner tonight, remember?"

"Totally forgot," Cole replied cheerfully, climbing off the couch and disappearing through the dining room where Kaito was sitting, working on his laptop. It was a rare moment of peace, and the perfect opportunity to come up with a witty, flirty-but-not-skeevy opening line.

So why couldn't I?

The golden street light filtering through the blinds cast a shadowed pattern on the pale living room wall, and I stared at it, drumming my fingers mindlessly against my phone case.

I wanted to get to know Amy, but I also wished I knew her *already*. To have inside jokes, and share memes I thought she'd like, and know all about her day because she'd have been messaging me throughout it anyway.

"Are you messaging Amy yet?" Kaito called from the other room, furiously typing on his laptop.

"Sh, I'm thinking," I yelled back. Save me from

impatient packmates, rushing my process.

By force of habit, I pulled up the Nest Fest app, my go-to when I needed a mindless distraction. Zach and I had both downloaded it to keep up with trending designs, but we'd also gotten a smidge addicted to playing it in the process.

New Friend Found! Add: Amy?

I blinked at the alert for a moment. It must have synced from my contact list. I hit 'add,' opening the newest nest design challenge to occupy myself while I waited for Amy to either accept or reject my invite.

And maybe to get some ideas for the attic. Just in case we needed to urgently get that job finished.

Say Hello To Your New Friend!

Before I could, a message popped up within the app with Amy's name and a bunny wearing a sparkly stripper costume avatar next to it.

Amy: *Arata! You play Nest Fest?!*

Arata: *Of course. All the best alphas play Nest Fest (aka, me and Zach)*

Amy: *I just added him!*

Shit, note to self to give Zach a heads up before he saw the invitation and deleted the whole app in a panic.

Arata: *What challenge are you doing? I'm working on this one...*

I shared my in-progress design with Amy of a

nest with dark emerald walls and a large rectangular bed covered in jewel-colored cushions. Dark, cozy, and luxurious, or at least I'd hoped it was.

Amy: *I'm doing the same one! Hold on, let me figure out how to share it...*

It took a minute, but eventually, Amy's project came through. In contrast to mine, Amy's design was light and airy, with pale wood paneling on the walls, polished off-white tiles, and a circular bed covered in cushions in a variety of neutral shades.

Huh. It was a lot simpler than what I'd gone for, but somehow it didn't look *too* simple. It looked balanced. *Right.*

Did Amy like circular nest beds? I made a mental note to grab Kaito's attic measurements and check out the dimensions of circular beds for... reasons.

I didn't want to get too ahead of myself when it came to courting Amy—at this stage, helping her through her heat was really all she seemed to be looking for. That being said, she probably lived in an omega-only building, and the heat centers didn't allow alphas in, either. Having our nest finished was a matter of practicality.

Arata: *That's really nice. You have a real eye for this stuff.*

Amy: *Thank you! I like my apartment, but sometimes living in a rental sucks, you know? This is my way of painting walls without losing my security* *deposit.*

Arata: *I'll be sure to message you whenever we're standing in the paint aisle, agonizing over which exact shade of white to choose. You're going to regret telling me you like this stuff.*

Amy: *I find that hard to believe, though I'm always partial to a good eggshell white myself. Maybe oatmeal, if I'm in a spicy mood.*

She sent a winky face emoji, and I chuckled to myself. I was definitely in danger—I liked Amy more every time I spoke to her.

Like my laugh had summoned him, Cole came bounding into the room, skidding along on the floor in his socks and grabbing the back of my chair to stop. He had no concept of personal space, so it was no surprise that he leaned right over my shoulder to look at my screen.

"You're chatting in your weird game thing?" Cole laughed, unbothered when I lightly pushed his head away from my ear.

"We're bonding over it," I replied smugly.

"Mm, sexy. Paint colors," Cole teased. "Hey, Amy, check out my *semi-gloss finish*. It's so *durable*, and *scuff resistant*—"

He dodged the cushion that I chucked at his face.

"Was there a reason you came out here, or did you just want to tell me about your paint kink? No judgment."

"Shut up," Cole laughed. "Quesadillas are ready."

I sent Amy a quick message to let her know we were grabbing dinner before eating with my pack and handling the dishes with Kaito afterward. Zach and Cole were playing video games in the living room, and Kaito immediately excused himself to go back to his laptop and finish up some work. He never unloaded on us if he was feeling stressed about something, but I guessed that unexpectedly slotting the Allure job into our schedule had caused him some headaches.

"You sure I can't help with anything?" I asked, setting a cold beer down next to his laptop as he settled back in at the dining table, cracking his neck.

"No, thank you." Which translated roughly to *'I have control issues, and you might mess up my lists,'* but that was fine. Kaito had been like this our entire lives. "Go play games if you want."

I considered joining my packmates in the living room, but in the end, the only game I wanted to play was another round of Nest Fest with Amy. I headed up the stairs off the dining room to my bedroom, flopping down on the mattress and pulling out my phone. *Maybe Amy would enjoy decorating my room,* I thought. I'd bought a matching dark wood bed, nightstand and dresser, and had two sets of the same plain navy comforter. It wasn't like I spent a ton of time in here, but it was a pretty impersonal space.

Arata: *Hey, Eggshell, you still around? Ready to flex your Nest Fest skills?*

Amy: *Eggshell?! No way. Pick something else. Your nickname choice has been denied.*

Arata: *Got it, got it. Sorry, Oatmeal.*

Amy: *So you think I'm plain and healthy? I see how it is.*

Arata: *I'm totally kidding, but if you ever get sick of being Bubbles and need a new stage name, I'm clearly your guy.*

Amy: *Never. There is no greater stage name than Bubbles.*

I smiled all goofy at my phone, glad I'd taken some time away from my packmates for this chat because they'd totally be ribbing me right now otherwise.

Arata: *I agree. Bubbles is peak stage name. Did you eat dinner?*

Amy: *I did. I'm lying down now.*

Arata: *Same here. I could call if you wanted to keep talking without staring at your screen?*

Maybe I was being too bold, but the idea of lying back, closing my eyes, and hearing Amy's voice in my ear was too tempting not to at least ask.

Amy: *Go ahead!*

I grinned to myself, closing the app and pulling

up Amy's details. It rang twice before she answered, and only then did I really register what she'd told me.

That *she* was lying down.

In bed...?

"Hi, Arata," Amy said, and I swore I could hear the smile in her voice. She had such a bright, infectious energy that I could feel it even through the phone.

"Hey, Amy, how are you?"

I didn't *mean* for my voice to drop an octave lower than usual, or for the faintest hint of purr to rumble out. I was going to blame it on alpha instincts.

"Good." Did she sound a little breathy? Was that just wishful thinking? "Tired."

My alpha instincts flared up in full force. "Are you okay? Did you have a long day?"

"Not really? I had a home day, chatted to my aunts, tidied my apartment a little..." She laughed a little awkwardly. "Pre-heat is just tiring, you know?"

I mean, sort of. From textbooks and stuff.

"What do you need during pre-heat? Do you want me to send more food over? Soup, maybe? Do you have to rehearse next week? Surely, they can take a break from all the rehearsing since the club isn't even *open* right now," I added under my breath.

"You're sweet, Arata," Amy replied softly. "I'm okay, really. I had the day off, and I promise I've been eating and resting and doing all the right things. I'll

251

be on heat leave soon. It's been fun getting in extra rehearsal time—I've been working on a bunch of new moves that I can't wait to show off when the club reopens!"

"I can't wait to see them." My cock swelled in my sweatpants at the memory of her prancing around the stage in that itty bitty elf costume at Christmas.

There was a long pause, long enough to make me nervous.

"Amy? You still there?"

She made a noise of assent, sounding wary.

"What is it? Did I say something wrong?"

"No! No, it's not that. It's just ... There's something I've been wondering about. Does it bother you? That I'm a dancer? You know, that I work at a strip club for a living?"

I frowned at the ceiling. "No, of course not. That's where we *met* you, of course it doesn't bother us. I know you said you're only looking for a pack for your heat, but even if it went beyond that ... I mean, Roxy is a mated omega and still dances, right?"

"Right," Amy agreed instantly.

"You're dancing behind the glass, no alphas are actually allowed to touch you. *That*, I'd struggle with." Fuck, the idea of Amy dancing on the Allure stage in nothing but a thong, a pair of heels, and a collar of bite marks courtesy of Pack Knight was actually hot as hell. They could look, but only *we* could touch.

But that was getting way ahead of myself.

"I'd struggle with that too," Amy assured me quickly. "Are you sure? The costumes can be pretty ... nonexistent."

"And you look phenomenal in them. It's really fine, Amy. I promise, I'll always be truthful with you."

She exhaled a long breath. "Right. Okay, good. It's just that ... I like my job. I love dancing, and Allure has given me a chance to be independent while doing what I love. That's important to me, you know? And something I don't want to give up."

"I understand," I assured her immediately. And I did. While alphas shouldered a lot of expectations that weren't always fair when it came to courtship and pack life, it was *nothing* compared to the sacrifices omegas had to make.

Maybe this was why she'd mentioned not looking for a mate bond at dinner? If so, hopefully I'd alleviated some of her worry.

"Tell me about your day," Amy commanded softly. There was a rustling sound—like she was getting comfortable in bed—and I silently sent my dick a strict "stand down" order.

"My day? Well, our house was a real fixer upper when we bought it a few years back. Most of the big projects are done, but we started renovating the attic today," I told her.

"Oh, of course," she laughed. "Cole mentioned

that when I was messaging him. I guess I've kind of forgotten what pack life is like—you're always doing things together." She sounded a little wistful, and I wondered not for the first time where her parents were and when she left their pack. "There's always someone to talk to."

"Well, that's definitely true," I admitted. "It means it can be tough to get a minute alone sometimes, but we are all very respectful of each other's spaces. The other three are downstairs, and I'm in my room right now. I know they won't bother me here."

"Are you lying in bed too?" Given Amy's teasing tone, the question had probably been asked innocently. I reminded myself of that before answering, and yet my voice still came out like I was auditioning for a job narrating porn.

"Yeah, I'm in bed too."

Get it together, Arata.

"Is this where I ask what you're wearing?" Amy joked in a breathy voice.

I paused, wondering if this was about to be the best moment of my life. "Do you want to know?"

"Yes. Please," Amy rushed out, a faint needy quality to her voice. *Well, duh. She's in pre-heat, you idiot.*

"I'm totally down for a game of what are you wearing. Should I lie? Pretend I'm in a really suave suit or something?" I replied with a quiet laugh, the bulge in my sweatpants growing more prominent by the second.

"I mean, if you were going to pretend, I'd suggest faded jeans, no shirt, and a tool belt," Amy teased. *Well, shit. Definitely filing that little tidbit away.* I was down to play sexy contractor and horny client whenever she wanted. "But no, tell me what you're actually wearing."

"Sweatpants and a long-sleeved tee," I sighed dramatically. Should have left dust-covered jeans on from when we were working in the attic.

Amy hummed. "What color sweatpants? Please tell me they're gray."

"Black. Is that a deal breaker?" Fuck me, were we actually doing this? I was *so* glad I'd decided to come up to my room.

"On the phone? No. But I won't lie, I'd be totally down to see all of you in gray sweatpants in person," she laughed.

Note to self: Make sure we all own a pair of gray sweatpants.

"What about you? What are you wearing?"

"A silk sleep set—loose tank and matching shorts. Usually, I'd wear more in winter, but I'm running a little hot right now."

I palmed my cock over my trousers, imagining Amy in little silk shorts. "What color?"

"Eggshell white," she replied instantly, that addictive teasing tone back in her voice.

"My favorite," I hummed. "Though I'm guessing they look better off."

"So cheesy," Amy teased breathlessly, fabric rustling in the background.

"Are you taking them off?" I asked in a low voice. *Please be taking them off.* Fuck, just the thought of her bare pussy had my knot beginning to swell.

"Mmhm."

I paused for a moment, slightly amazed that the intense chemistry we had even came through over the phone, and vaguely worried that I was getting carried away. "Amy, are you okay if we go further? I don't want to make you uncomfortable."

"I'm not uncomfortable," she assured me, her voice husky. "Keep going. I love listening to your voice."

Snap. There went the tether on my self-control.

"Are you going to tease that sweet cunt while you're on the phone with me, hm? Has pre-heat got you feeling needy?"

There was the faintest hint of a whine. "*Yes.* I can't sleep unless I come, and your voice is driving me *crazy*."

I couldn't even pretend like I wasn't smug about that.

"We can't have that now, can we? How do you

usually get yourself off before bed, Amy? Tell me exactly how you're going to please that pussy while my voice makes you ache."

She swallowed thickly. "It depends on the night. At the moment ... well, it's pretty much impossible unless I use one of my fake knots. My body very much knows what it wants right now."

I scrunched my eyes shut for a moment, struggling to keep my breathing under control. Fake knots were all well and good, but they didn't expand in response to an omega's need, it wouldn't fill her the way she truly craved to be filled.

And I had a perfectly good *real* knot right here.

But that wasn't what we were doing right now.

"Go get it," I rasped, pushing my pants down over my hips and wrapping a fist around my cock. "I'm going to fuck my hand and pretend it's half as good as your pussy, and you're going to fuck your dildo and pretend it's half as good as my knot."

"Yes, alpha."

Oh man, I was so fucked. *So* fucked. I was going to hear that needy "yes, alpha" on repeat in my brain every time I felt even the least bit horny for the rest of my life.

I waited as Amy shuffled around quietly for a moment, sliding precum over the head of my cock with my thumb and giving my shaft a long, slow squeeze. There was the sound of a bottle popping up, and a squirt of liquid that had me sinking my teeth into my lower lip to suppress a groan.

"I got it," Amy said quietly, a rustling sound in the background as she pressed the phone back to her ear.

"Good girl. Tell me what you're doing while I stroke my dick and try not to feel jealous of silicone."

Another swallowed whine. I wished she was here so I could capture those whines with my mouth.

"I'm rubbing my clit," she breathed.

"How does it feel?"

"It's good. But ... it's a little cold. I'd rather have your cock here instead. Filling me up." Amy sucked in a quiet breath. "I bet you could fill me up *so* good..."

"We'd be nowhere near you feeling my cock just yet if I was there, gorgeous. I want to taste you first. I want to lie down while you rub your pretty cunt all over my face. You'd ride me so well."

"You're really good at this dirty talk ... thing. I can barely ... *speak* ... right now."

"You don't have to talk if you don't want to. Put me on speaker and hold the phone next to your pussy. Let me hear how wet you are for me."

Amy let out another small whine but followed my instructions beautifully. I squeezed my dick *hard,* thumb teasing the head, as the wet sound of the toy moving slowly around her clit filled the phone.

"That pussy sounds needy, Amy. I can tell from here."

"It is needy. *I'm* needy," she all but sobbed. "I wish you were here."

The words made my chest constrict. I wished I was there too, and not just because we were both horny and I knew I could make Amy feel good. I also just wanted to be there for her, to hold her and keep her happy and comfortable.

But I couldn't do that. So right now, I was going to give her an orgasm so good that it'd put her straight to sleep.

"Imagine I'm there, gorgeous. Push the tip in—just the tip—and imagine it's me. Imagine it's my cock pressing into you, teasing you with shallow thrusts until you're desperate and panting beneath me."

I heard the tip of the toy pressing into her soaked entrance in excruciating detail, and let out a low alpha growl before I could help it. The kind of growl that encouraged an omega to go pliant beneath them, and Amy's responding whine of need sounded almost pained.

"Ignore me, gorgeous. Fuck, it's hard to keep myself under control listening to you." I picked up my pace, stroking my shaft faster, my breath sawing in and out of my lungs. "Want you so fucking bad."

"I want to present for you, alpha," Amy panted.

More precum leaked rapidly out from the tip of my cock. The idea of Amy rolling onto her front, head down, ass up, presenting herself for my knot ... Shit, I wasn't going to last.

"I want nothing more than to see you present for me," I rasped. "Can you use the toy comfortably on your front? Get in position, however you want, gorgeous."

There were more rustling noises in the background as I attempted to get my breathing and my dick under control. Not even on the phone was I going to come before Amy did.

"Okay," Amy said, her voice louder and clearer. "I'm on my front. The dildo has a, um, suction base. It attaches to my headboard."

I groaned before I could help it. "Fuck yourself on it while I memorize everything about this moment so I can replay it for all eternity."

My omega didn't keep me waiting, and I closed my eyes, holding my breath so I heard every second of her impaling her soaked pussy on the toy. With each shift, Amy let out a small sound of satisfaction, resulting in a breathy moan as she held still for a moment.

"Did you take the knot?" I grunted, my hand working my cock roughly.

"No," Amy moaned, the wet sounds of her fucking the toy in earnest playing like the sweetest symphony in my ear. "Not yet, but it's right there, I just need to stretch a little more. I'm rubbing my clit, wishing it was your fingers on me instead of mine."

Another growl escaped me, the base of my spine tingling and my balls drawing tight as I imagined Amy beneath me, her cunt squeezing me as she came before stretching to take my knot.

"I'm going to need you to come for me, omega," I commanded, my voice rough. "Come for me, and press yourself down on that knot *now*."

"Yes, alpha," Amy gasped, her moan muffled by what sounded like the bedsheets as she found her release. I followed barely a second later, hastily shoving my tee up to spill over my hand and stomach, muscles contracting fiercely. My knot swelled to its full size, and I moved my fist down, squeezing it as tightly as possible, wishing it was buried in Amy's pussy instead.

I blew out a long breath, trying to clear the haze of desire in my head.

"Still there, alpha?" Amy teased with a breathy laugh that turned into a soft moan.

"Oh, I'm not going anywhere, sweet omega," I promised, meaning it more than she could ever know. "How's that knot feeling?"

"Good." There was a tired quality to her voice now, and I hoped the orgasm had been enough to take the pre-heat edge off so she could sleep. "The knot isn't as, um, girthy as a real one, I believe. I don't know, I've never seen a real one in person, but the toy is standard-sized and meant to come out without too much difficulty."

My knot didn't usually last long without an omega to bury it in, but I swore it was deflating slower than usual, like if it just held on long enough, I could get to Amy.

"Is that super weird that I've never been with an alpha?" Amy asked, sounding suddenly vulnerable.

"No. No, of course not. We've never been with an omega."

"Oh." There was a world of meaning in that one word, and I wasn't sure I caught all of it. If I had to guess, she sounded ... pleased?

Please be pleased. Please let us be the pack for you, Amy. Give us a chance, and we'll make you so fucking happy, you'll never regret it.

AMY

CHAPTER 21

I woke up the next morning after one of the best orgasms of my life feeling pretty good.

For probably the first time since I'd gone into pre-heat, I felt settled, under control. *Satisfied*.

And it was all thanks to Arata Knight.

He'd managed to make me come harder than ever before, and he hadn't even been in the same room as me. I couldn't help imagining what it would be like if he had actually *been* here. If it had been his knot swelling up inside of me, filling me up to the point of bursting.

Just thinking about it, remembering his filthy words, made me wet all over again. I grabbed my phone from under my pillow, contemplating texting him and having some morning fun.

Would Arata still be in bed like I was? Had he slept in like me, feeling sated and dreaming of all kinds of ways we could have sex? Had he woken up all hard and ready, burning for more of me?

If we'd been *together* together last night, I'd totally have woken up rubbing all over his dick, needing more of him. I was already so wet, I knew if he were here, I wouldn't have needed any prep for him to slide right in and fuck me real slow and good.

Biting my bottom lip, I started to slide my free hand under the covers so I could touch myself, when my phone vibrated.

Hope soared in my chest, thinking Arata had been feeling the same way I was, and decided to text me.

I unlocked the phone, and my smile faded a little.

Zach Has Accepted Your Friend Request! Say Hello To Your New Friend!

It was like being doused with a bucket of ice water.

I knew I wasn't being entirely fair to Zach. He hadn't done anything wrong, really. I'd just been desperate for more of a connection, especially after last night, maybe a cute good morning text, anything to indicate Arata had enjoyed our moment as much as I had, but I'd gotten nothing.

With a frustrated sigh, I kicked the blankets off and got out of bed, leaving my phone there.

It was almost noon on a Sunday. Of course Arata wasn't still in bed. Of course he'd gotten up and done other things. He was probably back to working on his attic, like he'd been yesterday.

I was dying to know what that looked like or what they were going to turn the space into. I should've asked yesterday, but I'd been too damn horny for that.

And I had zero regrets.

However, I couldn't spend my Sunday moping in bed, waiting to see if he'd text or call me again so we could have a repeat of yesterday, which meant I had to get started with my day.

After changing into some leggings and a comfy sweater, I went to the bathroom to fix my hair and take care of business, then headed to the kitchen. I could make myself some brunch and then maybe go out, and … I had no actual idea of what I could do. The truth was, I shouldn't be going out alone when I was this deep in pre-heat. No matter how many pads I put on or how much I tried to dampen my scent with products, I had no way of knowing when a big wave might hit.

Going to Allure was one thing. The club was packed with omegas and bonded alphas, and it was a safe environment for me. Even if the worst happened and I went into full heat there before taking my heat leave, one of the other omegas or even a beta could drive me to the heat center and drop me off there. Not that I was planning on allowing things to go that far.

I'd already called Roxy and scheduled my heat

leave. She'd even suggested I take more time than usual, and we made it so my leave would start a full week before my heat was due. *Just in case*, she'd said, since my pre-heat had begun a little earlier than expected.

Oh! I knew what I would do! I was going to reorganize my nest! Some of the new pillows I'd ordered had arrived, and I wanted to ensure I had the best place for them. Hopefully, some of the soft sheets I'd ordered online would also arrive next week. Aunt Raquel and Aunt Lu had given me a pretty generous sum for Christmas, and I'd splurged on all types of fancy new things for my nest.

I'd just finished making coffee when my phone chimed in the bedroom. I made a mad dash for it, picked it up, and smiled.

Zach: *Hi-lo, Amy.*

Aww, I loved that we had our own special greeting and that it had helped him feel less awkward about his initial blunder. The first time I'd done it, I worried he'd take offense, but he'd given me the cutest little smile instead, and I'd known I had hit the jackpot.

Amy: *Hi-lo, Zach! Thanks for accepting my friend request. I hope it's okay I added you. How are you guys doing?*

I may not know Pack Knight very well, but I was starting to. Yesterday, before Arata and I had gotten frisky, Cole and I had spent most of the day texting, and he'd entertained me by giving me a play-by-play of what the entire pack had been up to. He'd even managed to sneak in some pictures, which I'd promised never to mention to his packmates.

The fact Zach was the one texting me this morning, though, confirmed my suspicions that they were taking turns between themselves.

Which meant Kaito would be next, and I'd be lying if I said I wasn't curious to know how that would even work. Out of all the members of Pack Knight, Kaito was the only one I couldn't quite figure out. The mysterious, broody vibe worked for him, but it also made me worry about my chances with the guys as a pack.

Not that I was looking for forever with them or anything, but I couldn't help wondering.

Zach didn't reply right away. In fact, I waited so long, I started to worry he wasn't going to.

Maybe he's just busy, Amy. Not everyone has their phone glued to their hand.

I went back to the kitchen but placed my phone on the counter, just in case.

With nothing but time on my hands and feeling in the mood to cook, I made scrambled eggs with cheese and bacon and even took the time to make some french toast. Not exactly the most balanced breakfast—or brunch—but it smelled delicious and would be even tastier, so I didn't care.

I was just plating everything up when my phone chimed again.

Zach: *I'm happy you added me. We're doing good, thank you. How about you?*

Amy: *I'm doing all right, thanks!*

Zach: *Good. I'm glad.*

I stared at my phone for a good five seconds to see if he'd say anything else or try to start some more conversation but got nothing.

Well then. Great chat?

I supposed it was too much to hope that Zach would be more talkative over text, and that was okay; he more than made up for it in person.

Not that he was more talkative in person, just that he got all flustered and awkward, and it was clear I made him nervous. I liked that I had that effect on him, too. It was quite endearing.

Still, I'd have liked to get to know him better, but I supposed that would have to wait.

———

Kaito still hadn't texted me.

All week, I'd chatted off and on with the rest of Pack Knight—mainly with Arata and Cole—and Zach had even shared some of his Nest Fest designs with me and complimented mine. Yet, I hadn't heard from Kaito at all.

I also hadn't been able to see the guys in person.

Rehearsals had been picking up, with Roxy demanding more from all the dancers. The club was going to be reopening soon, and she was adamant we all have our numbers *down* before it happened. She wanted it to be our way of making up to the members for the time we'd been closed. I'd even started to have some more tutoring from her to improve my aerial routines. Not only that, but the glass separating the stage from the seating area had been up. I had a pretty good idea of why that was, but I was trying not to think badly of my boss.

I was antsy, frustrated, and more than anything, I *ached*.

My pre-heat was growing worse, my temperature was spiking, and my scent was getting so strong, some of the other omegas at the club were starting to refuse to go to Allure when I was there.

And even though I'd been chatting and flirting with most of the alphas from Pack Knight, there had been no more phone sex or sexting. I had my suspicions that they were trying to be respectful and not pressure me to choose by putting me in a constant state of horniness, but it had the opposite effect on me.

They also hadn't even invited me on a second date, which didn't help with my insecurity.

Pack Carmichael, however, had contacted me. They'd called, asking how I was doing, and wanting to take me out again, but I'd refused. Instead, I'd finally given in to my aunts' not-so-gentle coaxing and booked a room at the heat center near my apartment.

I felt miserable. Horny and miserable. Not the best combination, really.

At least Roxy had given me the day off yesterday, and today was Saturday, which meant I got to stay home, hide in my nest, and wallow.

Why hadn't they asked me out? Why hadn't Kaito even texted me? Had he convinced his packmates to find another omega instead? Someone who was willing to let them properly court her, someone who was interested in mating right from the start? Maybe Arata had lied? Were they not as okay with my choice of profession as he said they were? Or perhaps it was that I'd confessed my independence was important to me and that I wouldn't want to stop working even after I mated—if I mated at all?

My eyes burned as I grabbed the biggest tub of ice cream I'd managed to fit into my freezer and a spoon, and headed to my nest.

I knew my entire unit smelled of distressed omega, and I didn't care. Not like anyone would come in here anyway. Even if I'd wanted to, even if Pack Knight had decided to help me with my heat, they still wouldn't be allowed in the building, let alone my apartment.

I was truly and completely alone in here.

Not bothering with the lights, I padded across the soft carpet, relying on memory to find the comfiest spot in my temporary nest. The pillows made it seem like I was sitting on clouds as I settled and opened my food so I could eat my feelings.

It was okay. I was okay.

I'd chosen this. Chosen this path and this life. I'd chosen to turn down Pack Carmichael's invitation for a second date, even when they'd already told me they were willing to take things as fast or slow as I wanted.

All my choices.

I had the independence I'd always wanted, so why was it that didn't make this any easier?

Why was it that, deep down, I'd still been hoping Pack Knight would sweep me off my feet and choose me? Maybe even *keep* me.

Not because I was just *an* omega, but because I was *the* omega.

Their omega.

CHAPTER 22

My eye twitched at the near constant buzz of phones.

It had been a whole week of this. I'd practically forgotten what my packmates looked like because their faces were always buried in their screens.

Arata and Zach had foregone their usual Saturday morning sleep-in to wake up at the ass crack of dawn and play that design game with Amy, messaging her their creations and smiling goofily the entire time from the corners of the couch they'd commandeered.

It really was the perfect way for Zach to get to know an omega. With the game as a buffer, he was far more relaxed than he normally would have been talking to someone outside the pack.

And I knew Arata was getting to know Amy *just fine*. His pheromones had clogged up the hallway landing for days after that phone call. We'd practically had to restrain Cole when he found out that Amy might have even a passing interest in phone sex. Not wanting to exploit her pre-heat state of mind, all of us had agreed *not* to go beyond innocent flirting unless she explicitly asked to.

I sighed heavily. As irrationally annoyed about the whole constant texting situation as I was—*jealous* might be the better term—at least the three of them were making progress in connecting with Amy. The problem was me.

For some reason, I'd confidently asserted that I would arrange a second date with Amy. My packmates were used to me taking charge and being true to my word and assumed I'd do it.

But I hadn't.

They'd *asked* me if I'd done it. I'd been vague. I wasn't going to get away with being vague much longer.

"What's the app store password?" Cole demanded, wandering into the kitchen where I was washing up the breakfast dishes, his eyes glued to his phone. "My message game is strong, but I want to get in on the flirting-via-house-game thing."

Damn it. I'd been counting on Cole not participating. Now I'd be the odd one out. Even *more* the odd one out, because Cole had at least been messaging her. I was more into first-person shooter games than some room designing app. I'd only make myself seem more closed off in Amy's eyes if I tried to engage with her the same way the others were.

"I'll check," I lied, drying off my hands and picking up my phone, immediately pulling up Amy's contact details. We'd all exchanged numbers, made a schedule to contact her, and yet my message thread with her was empty. I hadn't known how to start a conversation. I didn't *do* this kind of thing.

Maybe the worst part was that no one had brought up my radio silence, because they'd all *assumed* I'd messaged her, and I hadn't corrected them.

But that also meant Amy hadn't mentioned my lack of messages to any of them either.

What did that *mean*? Was she glad I hadn't messaged her? Was she only interested in getting to know my packmates and *not* me? It wouldn't be unheard of, especially if Amy was only considering us for her heat. When the time came, she would choose who she invited into her nest, and no alpha should ever assume they'd be welcome.

The idea of sitting outside the room, knowing my packmates were knotting her through her heat without me, was agony.

So do something about it. You're never going to know if she's interested in you or not otherwise. If this starts and ends with her heat, or if there's a possibility for something more.

Something that wouldn't break my packmates' hearts. Theirs and mine.

I drummed my fingers against the back of my phone, hoping Cole didn't notice my indecision.

My heart pounded erratically in my chest every time I opened this message thread, my palms growing damp in a way that I refused to acknowledge was nerves. That would be stupid. There was nothing to be scared of.

Zach was the anxious one in our pack. Not me.

I had to do something. To make a gesture of some kind before Amy made the final call about her heat. What if she hadn't asked our pack to help her yet because of me?

Zach and Arata would be finishing up the Allure job this week. Time was running out, both on their close proximity to Amy and to whenever her heat was due to start.

I had to say something.

If I was going to leave the safety of my comfort zone, I may as well leap headfirst, I decided.

Kaito: *If you're free right now, would you be interested in going on another date with us? - Kaito Knight.*

Was that too formal? Maybe I shouldn't have used my surname. All this second-guessing caused pangs of insecurity in my chest, and it was not a sensation I enjoyed.

I glanced out the window, immediately cursing my stupidity. There had been fresh snowfall overnight, and while the roads were clear, Amy probably didn't want to leave her apartment when it was this cold out.

Where would we even go?

Amy: *Hi, Kaito Knight. Fancy seeing you in my inbox.*

I winced at the well-deserved barb. How was I meant to respond to that? Probably with an apology, not one of my strong points. I didn't like admitting when I was wrong.

Kaito: *I hope you had a good week. Sorry I haven't messaged you earlier.*

There. I said the dreaded S-word. It was like swallowing lead.

Amy: *Is this Cole? Did you steal Kaito's phone?*

Fuck. This wasn't going well at all. What could I say to show her that it was actually me? I supposed I could send a selfie, but my entire being cringed at the concept.

I'd just be myself. For better or worse, there was no one else like me in my pack.

Kaito: *I'd dismember Cole if he stole my phone.*

Amy: *Oh. So this really is Kaito? I was beginning to think you'd never message me.*

Why was it so hot in here? I set my phone down, yanking my sweater over my head and tossing it onto the island, though it didn't make me feel any better.

Amy: *It's okay, though. I'm sure you've been busy. What kind of date did you have in mind?*

Ah, fuck. I should have thought this through. I wasn't getting the impression that Amy was overly pleased to hear from me, so I really couldn't afford to blow this.

The closer Amy got to her heat, the less she'd want to be in a big crowd of people. Maybe outside was the best bet—I could bring a thermos of something to keep her warm. And an extra coat. Maybe a whole blanket.

That was romantic, wasn't it?

Kaito: *If you want to brave the cold, we could go for a walk along the Arboretum?*

There was a winter garden there, which I only knew from an awkward first date we'd been on with an omega a few years ago. I hit 'send' and stared at my phone, willing her to respond. Three little dots popped up before disappearing again. Think, Kaito, *think*.

Me: *Or if you don't want to go out in the cold, you could come here for dinner and board games? No pressure.*

Was that weird? Board games were a snow and rain day tradition we'd had since high school, back when our parents had to keep us entertained inside.

Amy: *I do love board games. Are you sure you want me to come over?*

I frowned at my phone. Was she asking just to

be polite, or was she asking specifically because of *me*? Because I'd made her feel unwelcome, and now she wasn't sure what to make of my invitation?

The notion sat uncomfortably with me, even if it made logical sense. My instincts were rusty—maybe nonexistent—when it came to omegas, but the urge to soothe rose up in me anyway.

Kaito: *I would like for you to come over.*

Was it reassuring? What was it that she wanted from me?

A text message, about a week ago, a voice in my head that sounded suspiciously like Arata supplied.

Amy: *All right then. What's your address?*

I responded in a daze. I'd *hoped* that Amy trusted my pack, but visiting our home was definitive proof of that. She assured me she'd take an omega car service and would be here around six, and I quickly reassured her that she was welcome to bring chaperones if she wanted to, though she said she'd be fine without them. I was so in shock that I'd almost tuned out Cole's voice in my ear completely.

"Helloooooo, is it the world's longest password or something?"

"What?"

"The password," Cole said slowly, enunciating each syllable. "For the app store. That you said you were finding for me."

"Right." As if I didn't have all the pack

passwords memorized. "Never mind that. Amy is coming here for dinner. She'll arrive at six."

Cole blinked at me.

"What?!" he yelled, throwing his phone down on the counter and scooping up the assortment of mail and random junk that always accumulated on the kitchen island, hastily shoving it into a cupboard. "Guys! Code Red! Amy is coming over in ... like ... seven hours—everyone clean something!"

"What the fuck, Cole?" Arata replied, sauntering into the kitchen, frowning as he pocketed his phone. "I'm excited to see her, but you couldn't have given us a heads up first? I know you're spontaneous—"

"Excuse you," Cole laughed, shoving his hair out of his eyes. "Blame Kaito. He's the Mr. Spontaneity who *organized* it." Cole grinned, grabbing a jacket draped over a chair in the breakfast nook and disappearing down the hall to the coat closet.

"You actually arranged a second date with Amy?" Arata repeated in disbelief, leaning against the door jamb. "You?"

I grabbed a cloth and some cleaning spray to wipe down the counters. "Yes, me. I said I would."

Arata hummed, the sound full of judgment.

I gave him a withering look, hoping it disguised the guilt I was feeling at my poor effort with Amy so far. "We could talk about it, or you could make yourself useful and vacuum."

Cole walked past with an armful of clothes, heading for the laundry room. "Kaito has the kitchen, Zach is on bathrooms. Arata, what are you doing?"

My twin rolled his eyes good-naturedly. "Vacuuming, apparently. Kai, this conversation is not over."

———————

By the time Amy's cab pulled up outside, the house was open house-ready, smelled faintly of the bleach Zach had used to clean the bathrooms, and all of us still had wet hair from the panic showers we'd had.

But both the house and the pack looked presentable, which was the most important thing.

Amy looked more than presentable. Amy looked ... *charming*. Which was a word I was pretty confident I'd never used before. Under the golden streetlights against the dark sky with bright snow on the ground, she seemed to glow in her bright red coat and matching red knit hat. The pom-pom on the top shook as she said goodbye to the driver, and she took a moment to smooth down her shiny brown hair and hitch her bag over her shoulder before approaching the door, probably not realizing that we were all staring at her like lunatics through the living room window.

Thank god for blinds.

"The door!" Cole yelled, skidding in his socks as he ran to the hallway.

"Act natural," I ordered, alpha command bleeding into my voice. Arata snorted.

"Amy!" Cole called, throwing open the door before she could knock and beckoning her out of the cold. "How are you? How was the ride over here? Are you hungry? Is it weird coming to our house?"

"Oh my god, let her get in the door," Arata laughed, coming to Amy's rescue in the hallway. "Hi, gorgeous, let me take your coat."

I watched through the archway from the living room as Arata helped her out of her jacket, revealing the fitted knit sweater and skintight black leggings she was wearing underneath as he moved away to hang her things in the coat closet.

Have mercy.

"I'm good. The ride was fine, not super hungry yet, and no...?" Amy replied to Cole, nudging him with her shoulder before bending over to remove her snow boots. Zach exhaled heavily from his spot further into the living room, slightly behind me, where he was hiding.

Despite her brilliant smiles, she couldn't hide the nerves tingeing her scent. Which made total sense, since she was visiting an unmated alpha pack house, unchaperoned. My rusty alpha instincts croaked to life, encouraging me to soothe.

"Welcome," I said, clearing my throat and aiming for a tone that was more ... relaxed. Aiming and missing. "I'm glad you could come over."

"Thank you for inviting me, Kaito." She shot me a wary smile that made my throat feel strangely tight. I wasn't sure I deserved a smile at all, but I'd take it.

"We're going to make pizzas. I hope that's okay," Arata told her with an apologetic look. I had no idea why—we were pros at homemade pizza, and it definitely couldn't be any worse than the restaurant disaster.

"Pizza sounds great," Amy replied absently, unashamedly taking in the features of our renovated craftsman. Pride swelled in my chest at the awe on her face, and I could see it reflected on my packmates' too.

"Want a tour?" Arata asked, grinning at her.

"Oh, yes, please," Amy breathed. "It's *beautiful*."

"It will be, when it's finished," Arata laughed, boldly placing a hand on the small of Amy's back and leading her into the living room.

"Is this paint *eggshell* white?" she asked, giving Arata a coy smile.

"It is actually." Arata chuckled. "That's Zach's room," he added, nodding at the only downstairs bedroom, just off the foyer. "He prefers the quiet of being down here."

Zach made a noise of agreement, waiting for Amy to acknowledge him, always worried that he was annoying people with his presence.

"Hi-lo, Zach," Amy said softly, leaning around me.

"Hi-lo, Amy," he replied with more confidence than I expected. He swallowed thickly. "You look really nice."

"Thank you! So do you."

Cole gave Zach the thumbs up over Amy's shoulder, and I didn't have to turn around to know that Zach was blushing beet red.

Arata pointed out the original details of the house as we walked through the living room, through to the formal dining room we almost never used, then into the kitchen. Zach and I moved to the counter and started pulling out pizza ingredients, while Cole dragged Amy to the window to show her the dimly lit snow-covered yard.

It was standard to show an omega through the pack house during courtship, but that wasn't what this was. Or was it?

Shit, we should have finished the nest. It now had drywall, trim, and after some debate over flooring aesthetic versus comfort, carpet. I'd installed the trim and carpet myself in the evenings over the past week.

"...there's a bathroom just through here, laundry in the basement, and the other bedrooms are upstairs," Cole finished. "So is the, uh, nest."

Amy flushed red, and Arata jumped in to save her from responding.

"There are still a few projects we have to finish, but we're getting there."

"Is this your forever home?" Amy asked, a slightly wistful look in her eye.

The four of us exchanged looks. Was it our *forever* home? I wasn't sure we'd ever given it that much thought. I liked it here, but I also liked the idea of starting a new project somewhere else too.

"I guess it's our ... forever-for-now home?" Cole replied eventually, tilting his head to the side. "Until our next forever-for-now-disaster-fixer-upper home comes along that we fall in love with?"

Amy grinned at him. "That sounds like an adventure waiting to happen."

"That's how we roll," Cole said, winking at her, all easy flirtations. To think, I'd been worried about *him* scaring Amy off. I should have worried about myself. "Come on, let's go set up the board games in the living room. What do you want to start with? Kaito and I prefer quick and easy games, Zach and Arata prefer strategic military planning shit. Guest's choice..."

His voice trailed off as he grabbed Amy's hand and tugged her toward the living room, Zach and Arata trailing happily behind, probably trying to figure out how to get Amy to choose Catan.

I hung back in the kitchen, checking that we had all the ingredients for pizza, making sure that we had enough "good" plates and glasses, and piling them unnecessarily on the kitchen island.

Napkins. Where were the napkins? We couldn't just use a roll of paper towels like heathens when we had a guest over.

There was a corridor between the kitchen and bathroom where we'd built a wall of storage cabinets into, and I headed through there to look for the napkins I was *sure* we had.

After looking through the entire row, I sighed heavily into the cabinet. We were going to have to use paper towels. Was that a deal breaker for omegas? Any decent alpha pack would have napkins.

The sweet scent of gingerbread hit me, and I slammed the cabinet door shut right as Amy appeared at the start of the corridor. Neither of us said anything as she made her way slowly toward me, occasionally pausing to look at the framed photos on the wall between the windows that showed the backyard.

"Were you looking for the bathroom?" I asked gruffly. "It's just through here—"

"I was looking for you."

I swallowed thickly. "Are you sure you don't mean Arata?"

Amy blinked. "I know the difference between your scents. I was looking for *you*, Kaito."

"Well, you found me."

Amy hummed, her delicious scent filling the confined space. She'd been subtly perfuming from the moment she stepped through our door, and my cock was already at half-mast in my jeans.

"You've been avoiding me," Amy said softly, crossing her arms over her chest and leaning her shoulder against the window frame, examining me a little too closely. "Not just now. The other three all took turns messaging me, but you never did. Look, I don't want to turn this into a huge thing—if you don't like me, that's fine—"

"I do like you," I blurted out. *For fuck's sake, man. Find your composure.* I cleared my throat. "I do like you. I don't know how to ... make small talk over text messages."

Amy blinked at me. "You didn't make small talk over dinner either. Or big talk. Or any kind of talk."

"I don't know how to make small talk in a crowded, terrible restaurant."

"What about the two times I saw you at Allure?"

My lips twitched. She really wasn't letting me off easily.

"I was having an off day?" I pursed my lips. "Two off days."

"Kaito," Amy sighed, giving me a slightly exasperated look. "I have a real case of omega insecurity right now. You say you're not good at small talk, and that's okay, but you also said you like me. Can you see how this is confusing the hell out of me? If you do like me, then I need you to at least try to talk to me. Not a lot, but at least give me something to work with."

"Okay," I agreed slowly. "That's reasonable. Very reasonable."

Fuck, she was looking at me like she wanted me to give her more. I'd told her I liked her. What else was I meant to say? To do?

My chest felt tight. There was something about Amy that took my breath away, and it was terrifying.

How was I supposed to keep my guard up when she broke it down with just a smile? How was I supposed to keep my pack safe from impossible expectations when she made it all feel within reach?

Amy turned her attention to a picture on the wall, giving me her back.

Shit. I needed to salvage this. How did I salvage this? There'd never been a negotiation I couldn't handle before.

"These pictures are so sweet, seeing you guys grow up together," Amy said softly, still not looking at me.

I glanced at the photo she was standing in front of—almost snorting at the baby-faced teenagers we were at our high school graduation. Arata, Zach, and I stood in a row, holding up Cole, who was lying on his side, one hand under his jaw, graduation cap in the other, absolutely hamming it up for his parents behind the camera.

She was giving me an out, and I was selfish enough to take it.

"We went out for dinner with all of our parents after that photo was taken," I offered gruffly. "Cole's older brother snuck us flasks of whisky as a graduation present, and we ended the night in the bushes outside Zach's parents' house, throwing up the fancy Italian meal we'd had while his mom raged at us for being … 'knot-addled morons?' I think that's the term she used."

Amy laughed, a proper throw-your-head-back, entirely unselfconscious laugh. "Sounds like quite a night. Has Zach's mom forgiven you?"

"She made us biscuits and gravy the next morning but still points out that particular section of the garden doesn't grow as well as the rest every time we go over there."

"Your families sound really great." Amy gave me a sad smile over her shoulder.

"What about your family?" I asked, my curiosity getting the better of me.

She raised an eyebrow at me. "You want me to spill my secrets, then you're going to have to spill yours, alpha."

I really *was* a knot-addled moron, because hearing "alpha" delivered in that sassy tone made me weak at the fucking knees.

"I *like* you," I reiterated, taking a step closer as

Amy turned toward me. Searching her face, I fought to find the words she needed for reassurance, to articulate the fear she inspired in me, but I wasn't even sure I *had* those words. If I even knew for myself what it was that terrified me.

"How much?" Amy asked softly, perfuming heavily as she closed the gap between us, reaching up to lightly brush her fingers against my stubbled jaw.

"A lot," I rasped, my cock growing stiff and painful as her exploring fingers trailed down my neck, dancing over my collarbone. I felt her touch everywhere, despite the thin knit sweater I was wearing. There was a slight look of wonder in her eyes, as though she hadn't expected me to allow this, and I hated that I'd given her the impression that she couldn't touch me whenever she wanted.

I'd gone drastically wrong somewhere for that to be the case.

"Your scent..." Amy murmured, stepping further into my space as my pheromones announced all the things I'd like to do to her.

"*Your* scent," I countered, inhaling her syrupy sweet perfume, tinged with need.

"We're in the middle of a very serious conversation," Amy pointed out breathily, leaning in and inhaling deeply.

"We can continue that very serious conversation after."

"After what?"

"After I make you come."

Amy gave me a coy smile, looking up at me through her lashes. "Is that why you invited me over here, Kaito Knight?"

I groaned, leaning in and dropping my forehead to her shoulder and lightly gripping her hips. "No. Unless that's what you want?"

"It's not a no. Why did you invite me over here?"

My fingers flexed against her hips, bunching the sides of her sweater. "So you could spend time with my pack. And with me."

Huh. The words came a lot easier when I had Amy's warm, soft body under my palms, her delicious scent filling my head, chasing away everything else.

The tightness in my chest eased, and the tension leached out of my posture. Suddenly the weight on my shoulders didn't feel quite so crushing.

A small purr escaped me, and at that moment, I felt like Amy could have asked me anything, and I'd have answered. Could have asked me to *do* anything, and I'd have agreed.

"Oh, alpha. This is why you need an omega," she murmured, running her hands through my hair before giving it a light tug, forcing me to lift my head and meet her gaze. I wasn't entirely sure I understood what she meant, but I hummed in agreement anyway. "How are you going to make me come, *alpha*?"

"With my tongue," I replied instantly, salivating at the thought of tasting the sweet pussy that haunted my dreams.

"Tempting," Amy said solemnly, pursing her lips as though she was giving the idea serious consideration. "There's just one problem."

"What is it?"

A problem? Not on my fucking watch. Whatever it was, I'd fix it. I'd burn down whatever obstacles stood in Amy's way, build bridges, walk on hot coals, whatever it took.

Amy used her grip on my hair to pull me close, her lips a hairsbreadth from mine, warm breath ghosting over my skin. "You haven't kissed me yet."

Fuck.

I'd beat myself up for the oversight later. For now, nothing was more important than closing the small gap between us, and pressing my mouth to Amy's. There was no coyness, no hesitation on her part. Amy met my movements with the same passion I had, parting her lips for me instantly, her tongue brushing against mine.

She tasted sweet and light, sultry and rich, something that was *all* Amy. Her back hit the wall with a light thud, my hips pinning hers in place, cock grinding shamelessly against her thigh.

Get yourself under control.

Except Amy hitched one leg over my hip,

opening her up to me, and suddenly losing control didn't seem like such a bad idea.

"I'm still not entirely sure where we stand, but this thing between us feels like... Well, it feels like you can make me come now," Amy breathed, tipping her head back against the wall. My fingers flexed against her hips again, grounding me, serving as a reminder that the unmarked throat on display wasn't mine to claim.

Needing to put some space between my teeth and that particular brand of temptation, I dropped to my knees with a dull thunk, running my hands up the back of Amy's thighs, plucking at the thin fabric of her leggings.

"Are you going to let me eat this needy pussy?"

Amy made a strangled noise, her perfume growing more potent. "Um, yes. Definitely. You can do whatever you want to me if you keep talking like that."

I hid my smile against her thigh, going to pull down her leggings.

"Wait!" Amy gasped, grabbing my hands and looking down at me in alarm, a fierce blush staining her cheeks.

"What is it? Do you want to stop? We can stop—"

"No! No, I don't want to stop. It's just..." She blew out a breath, and I sat back on my heels, giving her a second to gather her thoughts. "It's just that I, uh, I'm wearing a pre-heat pad."

I blinked at her. "Okay...?"

"It's not very sexy," Amy clarified, looking at me like she expected me to agree.

"I promise you, there's not a single thing about you that I find unsexy," I snorted, baffled that she could think otherwise. "I don't give a fuck about your pad, but I'll close my eyes if it'll make you more comfortable."

Amy gave me a soft, affectionate smile that I was pretty sure she'd never trained on me before. "Yes, please. And thank you, that was really sweet, Kaito."

I closed my eyes, frowning to myself. Sweet? No one had ever called me sweet.

There was a rustling of fabric, and I groaned quietly as I got a more potent dose of Amy's needy scent.

"You can open your eyes," she whispered. I didn't hesitate, finding her pressing her shoulders against the wall between two windows, long bare legs crossed at the ankles in front of me, her leggings discarded on the ground nearby.

I took my time running my gaze over every inch of her I could see before shuffling forward, drawn by the temptation that lay between her thighs.

There was truly nothing more natural than kneeling before the altar that was Amy and worshipping her the way she deserved.

I pressed a soft kiss to each thigh, running my hands up and down the backs of her legs, encouraging her to part them for me. *She needs me. My omega needs me. I need to make her feel good.*

She let me drape one long, toned leg over my shoulder, and I ran my tongue over her damp slit, groaning loudly at the first taste of her slick.

Mine. My omega.

My self-control snapped, and I all but devoured her, licking roughly at her dripping pussy before moving up to her needy clit.

"Kaito," Amy groaned, rocking her hips against my mouth. "What are you doing to me?"

No idea, sweetness, but you're doing all that to me and more.

"More," Amy demanded, sinking her fingers into my hair and gripping the strands hard enough to hurt in the best kind of way. "I want your *knot*," she whined, grinding against my face.

My knot swelled *very* enthusiastically at the idea, but I forced myself to stay focused, sliding one finger into Amy's warm, wet heat, her slick dripping down my palm. The sounds of me pumping one digit, then two, into her soaked cunt were obscene, but Amy was an omega. This was just one more way of her body letting us know that she was ready for a knot.

I didn't think I'd ever wanted anything more than to knot Amy, but that wouldn't be happening.

Not today. Not in the hallway, and not without making sure my pack was okay with it first, and it wasn't just her pre-heat talking.

"I'm so close," Amy whispered. I picked up the pace, sucking her clit with increased pressure until she came with a half moan, half whine, fingers digging relentlessly into my skull.

I slowed my ministrations, stroking her through her orgasm before reluctantly withdrawing and licking my fingers clean. Amy stared down at me, eyes glazed and sweater bunched at her waist. Her glistening pussy and slick-soaked thighs practically begged for a second round, but I was seconds away from coming in my pants, and Amy would never take us seriously if I did that.

I'd never take *myself* seriously if I did that.

"Oh!" Amy gasped, sliding her leg off my shoulder and pressing her thighs together with a start, the slick still making a mess of her. "Sorry! That was just so good, I think my soul left my body for a second."

"You don't need to apologize for that," I snorted, adjusting myself as I stood and doing my best to hide my wince of discomfort. My balls would never forgive me for this agony.

"Can I...?" Amy asked, a hungry glint in her eye as she stared down at the bulge in my trousers.

"As much as I'd like that, this was about you," I

assured her, because it sounded less humiliating than 'if you look at my dick, I'll come immediately.'

"Next time, then," Amy shot back, a challenge in her eye that dared me to deny her. If I didn't know better, I'd think there was a hint of *possessiveness* there.

"Anything you want," I agreed, scooping the bundle of clothes off the floor and handing them to her.

Amy accepted them, wrinkling her nose slightly. "I, uh, might need to change. There are extra supplies in my purse, but it's in the living room..."

"I'll get it for you," I assured her, noticing how red her cheeks had turned. "Be right back."

My packmates all grinned like idiots as I walked back into the living room, and I shot them my best "shut the fuck up" look as I grabbed Amy's brown leather bag off the window seat.

"Is it hard to walk with that third leg situation you've got going on there?" Cole asked, nodding at my crotch. The cushion Zach threw at his head stopped him from catching my death glare.

"Don't worry. He'll behave," Arata assured me quietly. "None of us want to embarrass Amy."

I grunted in acknowledgment, already making my way back to where Amy was waiting. I trusted that they'd never *intentionally* make her uncomfortable, but we'd also been on our own for a long time, and we'd never had an omega in our home. Cole, especially, could use the reminders to behave.

"Thanks," Amy said, blowing out a relieved breath as she took the bag from me. "I'll just go, um, clean up."

"I'll meet you out there." *After I rub out the world's most painful orgasm.*

I turned to leave her outside the bathroom before doubling back and pressing a firm kiss against Amy's temple. I felt her eyes on my back until I disappeared into the bedroom, out of her view.

None of what had taken place in the corridor had been my intention when I'd invited Amy over, but I hoped that, at the very least, she knew that I *liked* her. That I wanted Amy as my omega just as much as the rest of Pack Knight did.

CHAPTER 23

Eyes wide, I stared at myself in the bathroom mirror, unable to believe what had just happened.

My cheeks were flushed, my hair was a little wilder than it had been, and my lips were all swollen as if I'd just ... well. Like I'd been doing exactly what I'd just done, really.

I was also almost sure I was glowing. Not literally, just ... my eyes were brighter and sultrier. Even my smile seemed smug.

Out of all the things I'd worried about while getting ready for this date, having Kaito eat me out in the middle of the corridor while his packmates were in the next room had not been something to even cross my mind.

Kaito.

The same alpha I'd nicknamed Cinnamon Growl in my head and who hadn't contacted me or even exchanged more than a couple of words with me since we'd met. *Well, that had certainly changed now*, I thought with amusement.

And I had zero regrets.

In fact, if not for the fact pre-heat was riding me *hard*, I probably would've begged him to show me his room so we could continue with our *conversation* until I was impaled on his knot for hours.

That's not why you came here, Amy. Pizza and board games, remember?

I wondered if I could convince Pack Knight to play strip poker rather than whatever board game they'd picked for tonight.

Needing to cool the hell down, I splashed some water on my face. I felt feverish, and I was pretty sure that even with my new pre-heat pads, my perfume was way too strong. If I went back without at least calming down a little first, this date *would* end with all of us in the bedroom.

I'd known coming here when my hormones were so out of control was risky, but I still didn't regret doing it. Not when it meant I got to spend more time with Pack Knight, to get to know them better. Not when it had finally given me a chance to actually *talk* to Kaito, even if we'd only exchanged a handful of sentences before I'd had his tongue in my pussy.

And while I was all for the idea of having mind-blowing sex with Pack Knight, I couldn't shake my aunts' voices from my head, and all the ways they'd disapproved of them.

If I wanted to make sure we actually clicked, I needed to spend quality time with them *outside* of the bedroom. Part of me also wanted to be wooed by them. To let them make up for the disaster date.

I was omega enough to admit I liked the idea of having them work for it a bit.

Once I knew I was as in control of myself as I could be this close to my heat, I left the bathroom, following the voices to the kitchen.

Pack Knight was the picture of domesticity. All four alphas were working together in the kitchen, preparing our dinner. Kaito was at the stove, cooking some possible toppings, while Cole had his head bent over, a look of deep concentration on his face as he kneaded the pizza dough. Zach was shredding the cheese, and Arata was chopping away at something.

"Hey, how can I help?" I asked. They all looked at me at the same time. Cole grinned wildly, and Arata smirked. Zach quickly averted his gaze, but he was smiling down at the counter, his cheeks pink. Kaito, though, he looked at me like he was ready to devour me all over again.

I gulped, suddenly feeling very, very hot.

Arata was the first to break out of it. "Want to choose the toppings and put them on the pizzas?"

I smiled at him. "Sure! Anything you guys don't like?"

"Nah. We'll eat anything. Just go for it," Cole

replied, placing a plain pizza dough on a tray and grinning at me. "Surprise us."

"Well, all right," I laughed, situating myself between Cole and Zach, letting their scents of caramelized cashews and wine and spices envelop me as I worked.

We prepared the pizzas while the guys and I talked. They asked me about dancing and how I'd started it, and I'd asked them about their families in turn.

While we got to know each other better, Cole took every opportunity to brush against me and scent mark me, like he was trying to replace some of Kaito's scent with his own. Every time he did it, though, I brushed against Zach, which only made Cole try twice as hard.

Once there was no more dough to be kneaded, Cole went to the sink to wash off, and Arata took his place, helping me with my task while also making sure there wasn't an inch of space between us.

I loved it.

Kaito came up behind me, reaching up for one of the pizzas so he could put them in the oven. He pressed me against the counter in the process until I could feel the hard length of his dick against my ass and his breath against my bare neck. I let out a needy whine.

The twins growled in unison.

"Whoa, guys! As much as it pains me to be the

one to break the moment—and trust me, it does—Kaito, something is burning behind you."

Cole's words broke the spell.

Cursing, Kaito stepped back and rushed to turn off the heat while I took advantage of the opportunity to get my heart rate under control once again.

"You're home late."

I stopped in my tracks halfway to the elevator in my building and turned.

Roxy stood just by the entrance of the building, all bundled up in winter gear as if she'd been on her way out when I arrived. Her lips were tipped down, and she was frowning at me. Two of her alphas were behind her, right outside the door—even they weren't allowed inside. That was how strict the no-alphas rule here was. Lorne looked at me with clear disapproval while Justin was careful to keep his face blank.

"Oh. Hey." Feeling like a teenager who'd just been caught doing the walk of shame—by my boss, no less—I awkwardly waved at her. "Yeah."

I had no idea how to answer her comment since it wasn't exactly a question.

Roxy's frown deepened even more. "Are you sure you should be going out alone? Aren't you super close to—" As she spoke, she took a few steps closer to me, only to stop in her tracks.

Her eyes widened, and she gaped at me,

horrified. "*Amy*! You've been with *Pack Knight*? *Unchaperoned*? *Have you lost your mind*?"

My ears rang with how high her voice got at the end, but I held back my grimace and forced myself to smile brightly instead.

"Yeah, I went on another date with them. They wanted to make up for the first one, and since I already knew them, I figured there was no reason to worry about a chaperone." I shrugged, leaving out the fact there was no way I'd ask her to have chaperoned another date with Pack Knight when she'd already made her feelings towards them very clear. I may have been a bit naive the first time around, taking her up on her offer, but I wasn't that gullible.

Plus, any chaperone would have been strongly against allowing the second date to be at the courting pack's home. If Roxy was this horrified that I'd gone out with Pack Knight alone, she'd probably keel over if she knew I'd been at their house.

When she didn't immediately answer, just kept staring at me in disapproval, I cast Justin a "please help me" look.

Justin sighed. "Babe, Curtis just pulled the car up front. You know how he hates waiting," he offered.

Roxy's lips were pressed so close together that it almost looked like she didn't *have* any. Still, after one final glance at me, she turned her back and left without saying anything.

I refused to feel bad. I hadn't actually done anything wrong by going out a second time with Pack Knight, even if I had chosen not to take a chaperone with me. Over the past week, I'd gotten to know Pack Knight better, and I *trusted* them. Yes, I'd also been horny and lonely and jumped at the chance to get out of the house and see all of them when Kaito had invited me. However, Roxy was acting like I'd committed some sort of sin, and I hadn't.

Every omega had a different way of doing things, a different rhythm. Some mated right away, after their very first date. Others took months, even years. Some chose to go on multiple chaperoned dates before ever being alone with the packs courting them. Others chose to not be chaperoned at all. There were guidelines but no actual rules regarding the courting process.

It was all about trust, and all that mattered was that I trusted Pack Knight.

I felt safe with them.

And I wanted to keep seeing them.

CHAPTER 24

"Arata!"

I groaned into my pillow, despising my twin at that moment. Why was he knocking before my alarm had gone off? Did he *want* me to disown him?

"I made you coffee," he added in a cajoling voice.

"Ugh, fine, come in. But know that I am very unhappy about it," I called back, voice muffled by the pillow I'd buried my face in.

It had been a late night for all of us, assembling the giant bed we'd purchased for the nest after we'd finished work for the day, and heaving the vacuum-packed mattress up the spiral staircase.

Surprisingly, it was *Zach* who'd been on an online shopping spree after Amy had left our house a couple of days ago, ordering furniture and bedding for the nest "just in case."

Kaito strolled in, and I reluctantly sat up, leaning against the headboard and accepting the travel mug he passed me with a nod of gratitude. He was already dressed for the day in dark denim jeans and a Knight Construction pullover, his hair neatly styled back.

"Where are you going?" I asked, blinking groggily. "New client?"

"I'm riding with you, actually."

"To Allure? Why?"

It was our last day on site, mainly a few paint touch-ups to the new patch of ceiling and wall we'd added behind the bar, plus general cleanup. Nothing that required Kaito's help.

Kaito made a disgruntled noise. "Lorne Kennedy wants to go over everything with me, plus go over the budget for the roof replacement when the weather warms up... Probably a bunch of other things. He sent an email, and apparently, this morning is the only time he's available."

"I bet you love that," I teased before taking a sip of my coffee. Lorne Kennedy wasn't the first client we'd had who thought he was the only one in the world with a packed schedule, and he wouldn't be the last. "I can talk him through the progress. I could probably handle the budget stuff if you tell me what to say."

"It's fine. I don't want to disrupt *your* schedule," Kaito replied, flicking his hand dismissively.

Whatever, he totally wanted to come into Allure to see Amy. We hadn't seen her since our date. It had been almost *two* whole days.

I didn't blame him. We'd all been hoping that Amy would ask us once and for all to help her through her heat after she'd come over on Saturday. If not while she was at our house, then at least in a message afterwards. If anything, she'd been slightly quieter than usual.

It had made the others nervous, but I wasn't going to let myself panic about it. Trusting a pack they weren't bonded to during their most vulnerable time was a huge decision for any omega. If Amy wanted to take every available second until the point where her body chose for her, then I was happy to be patient.

At the end of the day, diamond necklace or not, I felt confident that Amy had a stronger connection with our pack than Roxy's brother's. There *had* to be more sexual chemistry. Her and Kaito had barely said ten words to each other in person since they'd met, and she was riding his face in the corridor within half an hour of arriving at our house. Surely, that was a sign.

"Come on," Kaito sighed, brow furrowed like it had been almost permanently for the past two days. "Get up. I'll meet you downstairs."

———

"You good?" I asked, nudging Kaito with my shoulder as we made our way through the side entrance to Allure, nodding a greeting to the alpha bouncers watching the door. Zach wandered along behind us, carrying his toolbox, lost in his thoughts as he was prone to do sometimes.

"Of course, I'm good," Kaito grunted, shooting me a sidelong look. "I do this all the time."

"I don't mean the check in with Pack Kennedy." I rolled my eyes at his deliberate obtuseness. "The last time you saw Amy, you had your tongue—"

"I know where my tongue was," Kaito interrupted, sighing as though nothing on earth vexed him more than my presence. He could pretend to be annoyed all he wanted, I caught that smug look he was trying to hide. "Are you worried I won't be able to control myself?"

"Of course not. I'm worried you won't *want* to. That it'll stress you out to be near her while maintaining some semblance of professionalism, especially with her heat so close."

"I'll be fine," Kaito said, though I suspected he was less confident than he was letting on. Being in a state of flux with Amy, not entirely confident that she was going to pursue things with us, that we'd be the ones to help her through her heat, was weighing on all of us. Instincts were no joke, and our instincts were telling us to do more, to provide, to *show* her that we were the strong, virile alphas she needed.

That Kaito had already *tasted* Amy, knew what she sounded like when she came... It would only weigh more heavily on him.

We headed straight to our usual corner to set

up, pulling off our thick winter jackets but leaving our beanies on. It wasn't quite as cold in here today, which I was grateful for. I'd been feeling like a terrible alpha, seeing the omega dancers bundled up in extra layers to rehearse.

"Morning, fellas," Jason, one of the bouncers we'd come to know, said, striding through the club to join us. "Boss man said to let you know he's running a little late for your meeting."

"Not a problem," Kaito replied with a tight smile, probably stressing about the rest of his day being disrupted.

"You could always help us clean while you wait," I teased, knowing he wouldn't risk a speck of dirt on his nice shirt.

"That's what I have you grunt workers for," he replied with a tiny smirk. Was that... a joke? Was Kaito joking? Kaito *never* joked.

"Arata! Zach!" Kevin, the bouncer on the door called, used to the two of us by now. "There's an alpha here by the name of Cole, says he's your packmate."

Well, there went Kaito's brief few seconds of happiness.

"What did you think was going to happen?" I laughed as Zach went to the door to collect him with an exasperated sigh. "You should have known that he'd never stay home now the Hayes project is wrapped up, Kaito."

"He's meant to be at home, working on the nest. He said he was going to build a window seat to enclose the HVAC duct today," Kaito grumbled.

I raised a disbelieving eyebrow at him. Did Kaito really expect Cole to stay home alone when all of us were at Allure? It was like he didn't know our packmate at all.

Sure enough, Cole was practically bouncing with each step, dressed in his nicer jeans and the branded company jacket we all wore when we weren't expecting to get our hands dirty.

The little shit. If he was going to show up here, I was going to put him to work.

"Cole—" Kaito began.

"Don't even start. You're *all* here. You know I can check your locations on my phone, right?" Cole pointed out, daring Kaito to argue. Apparently, our pack leader hadn't *told* Cole he was going to be here too. That tracked.

"Hey!"

We turned as one at the sound of Amy's voice, finding her waving at us from the stage, looking fucking *radiant* in colorful leggings and a matching workout... bra? Whatever it was, it was tiny, and did spectacular things to her breasts.

"Bubbles!" Roxy clipped, stalking across the stage in a pair of terrifying see-through heels. I couldn't hear whatever it was she said next, but Amy shot us a sheepish look while Roxy moved to the side of the stage to fiddle with the stereo.

"That omega does not like us," Zach murmured, and this time it wasn't his fear of *no one* liking him talking. Roxy had made it very clear she didn't think we were a good fit for Amy.

"Does it matter, do you think?" Cole asked quietly. "Does Roxy's opinion hold enough sway to matter?"

"It might," Kaito said grimly.

The sultry sounds of some music—nothing like what Amy had chosen for herself when I'd seen her dance—came through the speakers, and Roxy moved off the stage, miming movements from the club floor and loudly counting along.

Amy was totally off-beat, but I couldn't take my eyes off her, regardless.

Eventually, Roxy fell quiet, and just as Amy moved to the pole, the sound of voices coming down the stairs from the foyer drew everyone's attention.

Lorne emerged, followed by Justin, making Kaito straighten in anticipation for their meeting, but they weren't alone. They were with Pack Carmichael, who didn't even spare us a glance, too interested in Amy.

Fuck.

Fuck.

"What are they doing here?" Cole rumbled, a

low, steady growl building in his chest.

I slid in front of him, blocking his view of Pack Carmichael. "You need to relax. You're going to get us kicked out. Is that what you want? Breathe with me."

Cole pursed his lips, probably wondering whether it would be worth it to punch me in the face or not in order to get to Amy like his instincts were demanding.

I understood the urge, but I also knew it wouldn't achieve anything. At worst, it would frighten Amy.

Lorne joined his brother-in-law's pack near the stage with Roxy, while Justin crossed the space to meet us with a slightly sheepish look on his face. "Pack Knight, how are you? Stupid question?"

Oh no, even Kaito was fighting to maintain some semblance of professionalism.

"Justin, hey," I managed, my muscles coiling tight with the effort of not launching myself across the club. *Calm, be calm. Zen.* Everything was going to be fine.

"Sorry, guys. I know this looks bad, but Roxy really wanted her brother's pack to come and see Bubbles dance. I can tell there's something between you and Bubbles, and I'm sure Roxy will step back when she realizes your connection is stronger." He rubbed the back of his neck. "It's hard to say no to an omega."

That I could believe.

"Shall we go over the progress of the roof fix?" Kaito rasped, getting himself back under control. Mostly.

"Right, yeah. Let's do that," Justin agreed awkwardly. I almost felt bad for him, except he'd brought the enemy with him, so not *that* bad. "I'll grab Lorne. You, uh, going to be okay?"

Kaito nodded curtly, pulling out his phone, undoubtedly opening his project management app, but I tuned them out, too focused on the stage.

I had no doubt that whatever schemes and machinations Roxy was pulling, Amy had been entirely unaware of them. The smile on her face was completely forced, but she kept dancing anyway as Roxy loudly counted out the steps, encouraging her to continue.

No wonder the glass partition was down again. Roxy had wanted her brother's pack to have an up close and personal view.

I wanted to intervene. To march up there and tell Amy that she could stop if she wanted to, that it was wrong for Roxy to bring people here to watch her rehearse without giving her a heads up. Would Amy appreciate that, though? I didn't *want* to cause problems between her and her employers.

With another stiff smile, Amy pressed her butt back against the pole, folding forward and showcasing miles of long leg while she oh-so-slowly straightened. It didn't look quite right, though, and I didn't think it was just because she was off-tempo.

There was a stilted hesitancy to her movements I'd never seen before—Amy usually threw herself into each move with joyful abandon.

Was it discomfort at Pack Carmichael being here? Or something more?

"Something's wrong," Zach murmured, echoing my thoughts. "Is she hurt?"

"Maybe she's uncomfortable being displayed like a show pony," Cole grumbled, his voice only *just* low enough not to carry.

"Maybe, but I think Zach is right," I said quietly, inching toward the stage now that Kaito had Lorne occupied.

Amy stretched, reaching her arms up over her head to grab the pole behind her, and immediately bent double with a pained cry, wrapping her arms tightly around her middle.

"Shit. Amy!" I was running toward the stage before I even realized it, my pack members hot on my heels.

Not fast enough to beat Pack Carmichael, who were leaping up onto the stage. Toward *our* omega.

"Everyone calm down!" Roxy ordered, eyes wide as she climbed on the stage, pushing past her brother. "Give her some space!"

The moment Roxy got within a foot of Amy,

she retched violently, stumbling back.

"Bubbles, hun, your heat is starting," Roxy gasped, burying her nose in the crook of her elbow.

Cole got to the stage a moment before me, scrambling up despite Roxy's protests. Pack Carmichael took a step toward us, not entirely defensive, more like unsure.

"Stand down," Kaito bit out, hands flexing at his sides. "Amy doesn't need you standing in front of her like rabid guard dogs. She can make her own decisions."

"Amy," I called softly, careful not to move into her space without invitation. "Amy, look at me. I know it hurts, darling. Take a deep breath. Try to relax your muscles."

She whimpered in response, inhaling deeply before letting out a long breath, straightening as much as she could while keeping her arms wrapped around her middle.

"Hurts," she whispered, turning those big brown eyes on me, a sheen of tears ready to fall.

"I know. I know it hurts." I swallowed thickly, fighting the urge to ask her to come to me. It had to be Amy's decision, and Amy's alone. "One breath at a time, darling."

"Alpha," Amy whimpered, making all seven unmated alphas in the room puff up their chests. Roxy retched loudly in the corner again, safe in the embrace of one of her own alphas. I'd forgotten that omegas found the scent of *other* omegas' heats off-putting.

"Bubbles—*Amy*," Roxy croaked. "You have to choose. Pick a pack to help you through your heat, then get out of here before the pain gets worse."

Amy stumbled away from the pole, reaching for me with one hand, and that was all the invitation I needed. I wrapped an arm around her shoulders, pulling her into my neck so she could use my scent to soothe herself, my other hand rubbing her lower back.

"Do you choose us, Oatmeal? Do you want Pack Knight to see you through your heat?"

Say yes. Please say yes.

Amy groaned quietly, possibly in protest to the nickname, even as she clung to me.

"Yes," Amy mumbled into my collarbone before pulling away with a pained slowness, twisting to look at Pack Carmichael and her bosses over her shoulder. "I choose Pack Knight."

Roxy's brother stepped forward with a resigned smile on his face. "We wish you all the best, Amy."

"Let's get the *fuck* out of here," Cole announced, grabbing my arm and dragging me toward the stage front. "It's already going to be an uncomfortable drive for Amy. Let's not drag it out."

Right. An uncomfortable drive.

To our home.

To our *nest*.

THANK YOU

THANK YOU SO MUCH FOR READING
ALLURE PART ONE!
THANK YOU ALSO TO RACHEL AND
LYSANNE FOR BETA READING, AND
JENNIFER FROM BOOKENDS EDITING FOR
PROOFREADING.
ALLURE PART TWO IS OUT NOW.
T.S. & COLETTE

OUT NOW

KNOTTY BY NATURE

ALLURE
PART 2

T.S. SNOW
COLETTE RHODES

ABOUT THE AUTHOR

T.S. SNOW

A SCIENTIST AT HEART, T.S. SNOW LIVES IN A LAND FAR FAR AWAY, SECLUDED FROM MOST AUTHORS AND READERS (RUMOR HAS IT THAT IF YOU OPEN YOUR WARDROBE YOU CAN FIND HER HIDING IN THERE TRYING TO TAKE A NAP).

T.S. HAS A THIRST FOR LEARNING NEW LANGUAGES, EVEN IF SHE IS MOSTLY WORRIED ABOUT FINDING OUT NEW CURSE WORDS IN THEM. SHE HAS AN AMAZING SUPPORT SYSTEM THAT INCLUDE A LOVING PARTNER, HER FAMILY, FRIENDS, AND HER LOYAL—IF COMPLETELY LAZY—DOG.

WHEN SHE'S NOT WRITING, T.S. CAN OFTEN BE FOUND CAUSING COMPLETE CHAOS WITH HER FRIENDS ON SOCIAL MEDIA, INHALING UNHEALTHY AMOUNTS OF COFFEE, OR NAPPING. MOSTLY NAPPING.

AUTHORTSSNOW.COM

ALSO BY T.S. SNOW

ABOUT THE AUTHOR

COLETTE RHODES

COLETTE RHODES IS A HUGE FAN OF
PARANORMAL ROMANCE AND REVERSE
HAREM BOOKS. THEY'RE WHAT SHE
LOVES TO READ AND WHAT SHE LOVES
TO WRITE. #WHYCHOOSE, RIGHT?

COLETTE STUDIED BOTH HISTORY AND
ANCIENT HISTORY AT UNIVERSITY AND
LOVES INCLUDING BOTH HISTORICAL
FACTS AND ANCIENT MYTHOLOGY IN
HER WORK.

WHEN SHE'S NOT WRITING, YOU'LL FIND
HER SPENDING TIME WITH HER HUSBAND
AND DAUGHTER IN BEAUTIFUL OTAGO,
NEW ZEALAND.

COLETTERHODES.COM

ALSO BY COLETTE

19302954R00194